stealing the show

Polyam Fam

Book Three

phoebe alexander

MOUNTAINS WANTED
PUBLISHING & INDIE AUTHOR SERVICES

Mountains Wanted Publishing

P.O. Box 50

Harbeson, DE 19951

www.mountainswanted.com

Paperback ISBN: 978-1-949394-81-8

Cover design by the author

Editing and proofreading by Mountains Wanted Indie Author Services

❀ Created with Vellum

I'm dedicating this book to any reader who has experienced infertility, miscarriage, or infant loss. I know not every story has a happy ending, and my heart goes out to all who have struggled to have a baby. I had a series of miscarriages between the births of my first two sons, but I am beyond blessed to have three healthy adult sons now. Not everyone is so lucky.

one

. . .

raine

I DIDN'T REALIZE a surprise was on the menu when I planned to have lunch with my former roommate, Danielle. I hadn't seen much of her since she moved in with her boyfriends, Aris and Noah. Yes, boyfriends. Plural.

They were a polyamorous throuple, and I was here for it. They were adorable together, and I was so thrilled to see them all admit they were meant for each other.

Our favorite café was practically dead. Summer in Bloomington was always a little slower—there weren't nearly as many students on campus for summer classes, and a lot of families took vacations while school was out. I watched Danielle walk through the restaurant, her face absolutely radiating love and happiness.

"Raine!" She threw her arms around me so exuberantly, she nearly knocked me on my ass. Danielle was a beautiful statuesque woman, and, though I was equally curvy, I was barely five feet tall on a good day. She'd been blessed with height.

"Sorry, didn't mean to bowl you over. I'm just so excited to see you. Tell me everything!" She plopped down on one side of the booth, and I took the other.

The server came by, and Danielle grinned. "We're catching up. It might take us a few minutes to get to the menu."

The server, a waify, androgynous human with purple and green hair, smiled knowingly. "I'll be back in a few."

"Well, tell me!" she gushed, lacing her fingers together on top of the menu. "What's happened since my party? Are you ready for graduation? Have you found a job?"

I sighed. "There's not much to tell. My last class ends only a couple of weeks from now, and I still haven't found *The Job.* yet. However, I did get *a* job working at the Brown County theater this summer as the costume director, but it's only a seasonal position. I hope to get my thesis turned in by the end of August."

"Right…" Danielle's beautiful features twisted into a frown. "Well, I'm sure you have tons of applications out."

I clasped my hands together to simmer down my excitement. "Yes, I'm starting to send them out—Chicago, New York, LA. Maybe I'll end up in Hollywood!"

"That would be a lot different than stage work, wouldn't it?" She reached out and grasped my hand. "I'm so glad you're gonna be able to graduate on time and not have to stay another semester like me. I'm supposed to have my sinus surgery later this summer, but—"

Sinus issues and a broken leg had sidelined Danielle from completing her master of fine arts with a performance concentration in musical theater. "But what?" It didn't look like her statement was going to turn into a true "but" by the glow on her face.

"Well, I have some news." She sucked in a breath, looking nervous and excited all at once.

"Don't hold me in suspense!" Naturally, the server came back right then to ask if we'd made any decisions. The menus remained untouched in front of us.

"Let's just order really quick, and then I'll fill you in," she suggested, opening her menu. "Besides, I'm famished."

We both placed orders, and the server skedaddled away. "Now, spill it, girl."

She giggled and toyed with her napkin. "So…the big news is…"

I leaned forward. Leave it to an actress to draw this out and have me on the edge of my seat.

"I'm pregnant!" she nearly shouted.

"Whoa, what?!" I was sure I looked like one of those cartoon characters whose eyes comically bug out from their faces as their jaws hit the floor in shock. "Oh my god, Dani, that's great! Not at all what I was expecting to hear, but wow! So what does this mean for…"

I trailed off because I didn't even know how to verbalize all the changes she'd already been through in only a few short months' time.

"I guess we weren't as careful as we should have been," she admitted with a sheepish smile. "No, I don't know if it's Aris's or Noah's. I don't want to know. I'm still going to teach the theater camp this summer, but we're going to put my surgery off. And after that? I don't know. I'm due in December. I guess I'll figure things out after that."

Now her glow made perfect sense. "You seem really happy."

She grinned. "I am. Raine, I—I never knew this was what I wanted in life, to be with two amazing men, to be expecting their child. I would have never imagined in a million years this was the right path for me, but here I am."

"And Aris and Noah are happy?" I imagined Aris was— he was a happy-go-lucky guy and a true optimist, like me. But I didn't know Noah as well. They both worked in the medical field. Aris was an orthopedic nurse, and Noah was an ear-nose-throat specialist.

"They are thrilled! The whole polycule is thrilled, to be honest. This baby is going to be so loved. I'm only eight weeks along, but everyone's so excited and making plans and buying stuff already. It's so crazy. Noah is talking about buying a house."

"Wow. That's awesome, Dani. I'm going to be an aunt!"

She squeezed my hand. "That's right! Aunt Raine has a nice ring to it, doesn't it?

My friend Bonnie, one of my fellow MFA students at Indiana University, moved in with me after Danielle moved out to live with Aris and Noah. She was belting out a Broadway tune in the shower when I got home from my lunch date. By the time I put the tea kettle on, she was walking down the hall, still singing "Don't Cry for Me, Argentina" from *Evita*.

"Hey, you!" I greeted her. She was wearing a blue terrycloth robe and had her long hair twisted into a thin pink and green striped towel. "Want some tea?"

"That would be lovely!" Her face was shiny, like it had just been scrubbed. "I'm going out tonight. You wanna come?"

I groaned. "I peopled today for lunch. I don't know about two social events in a day." As an introvert, it had taken me a while to learn how to deal with bigger crowds and meeting new people. I was usually convinced no one liked me or enjoyed my company, but I was getting better. Being around Danielle, Bonnie, and their friends had helped, but I still had a ways to go.

"C'mon," she exerted maximum peer pressure, "I know you need to blow off some steam. You've been working on your thesis project too hard, girl."

She was right. My thesis was on the evolution of costume design from early twentieth-century to the twenty-first century, and I had to also design three costumes from period-appropriate shows for each era. It had been consuming nearly every waking moment—but it was in the final stages now. It was due by the end of the summer.

"Where are you going?" One night out wouldn't put me that far behind, right?

She grinned and rocked back and forth on her bare feet. Her toes were painted with sparkly lavender polish. "Aris and his crew are meeting me at The Barn tonight for a drag show and karaoke."

"Oh!" My nose wrinkled in confusion. "I had lunch with Danielle today, and she didn't mention it."

"I'm not sure if she's coming, but Noah and Aris definitely are. A couple other people you met at my last party will be there too."

Bonnie was a social butterfly and was great at connecting people. I met her in one of my first grad school classes, and she was responsible for hooking me up with almost all the great people in my life, except for Danielle, whom I'd known since we were undergrads. Danielle and I met Aris through her, which obviously worked out well for Dani.

"Don't you ever get FOMO, girl?" she pleaded. "I think this will be good for you. Besides, watching a drag show should give you plenty of inspiration for your costume designs."

I rolled my eyes. Well, she did have a point. "Fine, fine. Peopling at a gay bar is easier than peopling with the general public."

She snapped her fingers. "Facts!"

maggie

I stared at the doctor, blinking. Leo put his hand on my knee, but I couldn't look at him. Not now.

This was not the news I was expecting. It was not the news I had prepared myself for.

The doctor went over some options with us, but I didn't hear any of them. I slung my purse over my shoulder and rose from the plastic chair like a zombie, my husband's arm feeling like a chain as it wrapped around my waist and guided me out of the room. He handled the checkout and then ushered me to the car.

"Do you want to talk about it?" his voice was stiff, like he was trying to be strong for me, but he was barely holding on.

I shook my head.

"Let's go out tonight. Let's do something to get your mind off things," he offered.

"It's a Wednesday," I shot him down.

He drove home silently, pulling our car into the garage and hurrying around to my side to open the door for me. Always a gentleman. Always watching out for me. Always putting my needs above his.

Is it any wonder I want to give him a baby?

As we made our way inside the house, my phone buzzed. Leo bent down to pet our hyper Cavapoo, Blue, who thought the sun rose and set with his daddy. Maybe Blue was the only baby we were meant to have. Just fur babies for us.

> Noah: Aris and I are heading to The Barn
> tonight for the drag show and karaoke. Is
> Leo working? If you're bored, maybe you'd
> want to come hang out with us?

The Barn was the local LGBTQ bar, and ever since I admitted to Noah and Aris that I was bisexual, they'd been inviting me. When Aris and Noah started dating Danielle, I'd also let it slip that my husband and I are also polyamorous. It was clear they thought I needed a girlfriend.

"Leo works such weird hours," Aris had said. "You're alone so much. That has to get old sometimes, doesn't it?"

It was true. Leo was a police officer, and he did have a crazy schedule. Sometimes he was on day shift. Sometimes he was on night shift. He was always on call for the crisis management team. He sometimes got called out again as soon as he got home.

Noah had started as my client, but we had become friends. He dealt with a PR nightmare and a bogus malpractice suit a few months ago, and I'd counseled him through it. I was pretty sure he thought he still owed me because he was pretty adamant about buying me drinks every time he convinced me to get out of the house.

"Can I get you anything?" Leo asked as he stood in front of the refrigerator like he was willing the perfect snack to just magically appear.

"I don't really feel much like eating." I looked down at my phone, fingers hovering over the keyboard so I could gently decline Noah's invitation.

Before I could type anything, Leo shut the fridge doors

and slid behind me, using his strong hands to massage my tense shoulders. He was also clearly looking at my phone.

"Oh, Noah invited you out tonight?"

"Nosy much?" I looked over my shoulder at him.

"They're still trying to hook you up, I guess?" His tone dripped with hope.

He wanted me to have a girlfriend as badly as they did.

I rolled my eyes. "I don't know if I'm in the mood tonight, you know?"

He took my hand and guided me over to the table. "Sit," he commanded in his cop voice that always garnered compliance from me, whether I liked it or not. It was like my body obeyed even if my mind wanted to come back with some bratty, snarky response.

After pulling out the chair next to me, he sat and took my hands into his. "Maggie, I know what we heard today sucked. It was bad news for sure. You're upset by it. I'm upset."

I nodded. Every word he said was painfully true.

"We're both still processing our options, and we won't be able to change the situation right now, tonight. So, I think a distraction is in order. I know I'd feel better if I got out and had a few drinks and some laughs with friends. What could be more distracting than a drag show and terrible karaoke?"

I tried not to crack a smile, but it was difficult when he was being so adorable.

My husband was a tall, beefy guy with impossibly broad shoulders, weathered olive skin, short dark hair with a hint of silver at his temples, and deep brown eyes. They could be as sharp and piercing as a German shepherd's or as gentle and playful as a puppy's. Right now, they were the latter.

I set my phone on the table and texted Noah back. Then I turned to Leo and cocked my head. "Fine, you win. We'll go to The Barn, and I'll flirt with all the pretty girls. You're right. That will take my mind off things."

"You don't have to flirt with the pretty girls," he said with a wink, "unless you really want to." He wrapped his arms around me and pulled me into his strong embrace. "No matter what happens, just know I love you."

I bit back the sob that was trying to well up in my throat. "I love you too."

two

. . .

leo

MY WIFE LOOKED ABSOLUTELY MOUTHWATERING in a stretchy black dress that accentuated every delicious curve of her body. She surprised me by going all out with her hair and makeup—her eyes were so sultry and smoky, I just knew she'd turn heads.

I held the door to the club for her after the bouncer nodded us in. She pouted momentarily at not getting carded, but I brought her hand to my lips and pressed a soft kiss to her silky skin. "It's my fault—me with all this gray hair. You're absolutely gorgeous, baby."

"You don't think I look forty, right?" Her eyes briefly landed on me before bouncing around the club.

"You won't be forty until Christmastime, and no one would ever guess you have a big birthday coming up," I assured her.

Her approaching birthday was one of the reasons she was so upset about the news we got at the doctor's office this afternoon. We learned that she has two different issues keeping her from becoming a mother. One involved a genetic issue with her eggs, and the other involved her uterus. That combination of problems meant she was unlikely to conceive or carry a baby, and her eggs probably couldn't be used for a surrogate either. We were looking at the options of adoption or a surrogate using her own egg fertilized with my sperm.

But I wanted to get her mind off that tonight. Maggie had worked so hard, trying to do everything right. She had wanted to be a doctor originally, but after getting her undergraduate degrees in biology and chemistry, she decided to go to law school instead and focus on medical malpractice law. We'd waited to start a family because she wanted to be established in her career, and by the time we started trying a couple of years ago, we didn't have a lot of time for unexpected obstacles.

Her job was how she met Noah, an ear-nose-throat specialist who had some legal problems earlier this year. He was the one who invited her out tonight.

"Do you want a drink?" I asked as she surveyed a group of ladies dancing near the DJ's booth. The drag show wouldn't start for another hour.

"Yeah, a glass of white wine please. You know what I like." She brought her lovely grayish-green eyes to me and flashed a sexy smile. "I saw some ladies I recognize from Danielle's party. I thought I might go say hi."

"You do that," I encouraged her before leaning down to press a kiss to her cheek. She flitted off to join the dancers, and I ambled up to the bar.

"Hey, you're not working tonight!" Noah's deep voice came from one of the barstools. His boyfriend, Aris, sat next to him, his brown hair bunched up in a bun on top of his head.

"Nope, not tonight. Where's your better third?" I grinned at my little joke about their throuple.

"Danielle stayed home," Aris pouted. He glanced at Noah and said, "We're telling people now, right?"

Noah nodded.

"Telling people what?" I wondered as I picked up the little laminated card with The Barn's drink specials on it.

"Well, our happy family is growing." Aris beamed. He held his beer bottle up in the air and clinked it with Noah's wine glass.

"Adding to the throuple? Does that make it a quadrouple?" I joked.

Aris's brows wrinkled in confusion as Noah shook his head. "No, no, not that kind of addition." He mimed rocking a baby. "This kind."

My eyes widened. "Oh! Wow, congratulations! That's incredible news." As soon as it sank in, a stabbing pain pierced my heart. I didn't want to rain on their parade, but… protecting my wife's mental state was at the top of my priority list at the moment. "Hey, can you hold off on mentioning it to Maggie?"

Noah's brows drew together this time. "Everything okay?"

I let out a sigh as I tried to figure out how to explain. "We got some disappointing news in that department today."

Aris patted me on the back. "Say no more. But I hope Raine and Bonnie don't let the cat out of the bag." His man-bun pointed in their direction as he cocked his head. "Looks like they're all dancing."

After dipping my chin in acknowledgment, I grabbed the wine and the beer bottle the bartender set in front of me and headed over to the dancing ladies. The song was changing over to a new one, and the fast dance beat mellowed into a slow, swaying ballad.

Maggie gratefully took the wine from me. "Leo, you remember Raine and Bonnie?"

The two women smiled at me as I shook each of their hands. "How could I forget?" They were both Danielle's friends. Raine was a petite curvy lady with jet-black hair, and Bonnie was tall and willowy with strawberry blonde hair and fair skin.

My wife rose up on her tiptoes, gesturing for me to bend down. "I was going to ask Raine to dance with me," she said in my ear.

A thrill raced through me at the thought. "Oh, yeah, of course. Have fun!" I gave her a wink and stepped aside.

I watched her ask Raine for the slow dance as I sipped my beer, and the two headed for a dark, empty corner of the dance floor several yards away. Bonnie flashed me a hopeful smile, which prompted me to query, "Well, shall we?"

"Thought you'd never ask." She batted her eyelashes at me as I set my bottle down on a nearby table next to my wife's wine glass. I'd keep an eye on both of them while I danced to make sure no one got any nefarious ideas. Fuckery like that was always the first thing to pop into my mind. I'd been a cop for so long now, I couldn't help but prepare for the worst after nearly two decades of dealing with shitty humans.

"It's nice to dance with a tall man for a change," Bonnie said as she swayed to the slow rhythm of the song.

"Yeah? I'm glad you approve." She smelled like a mixture of vanilla and cinnamon, almost like a snickerdoodle. Or maybe I was just hungry.

"So you and your wife are poly?" she inquired as I spun her in a circle.

"Word gets around, huh?" I grinned as she gave an embarrassed giggle.

"Danielle mentioned it. I think it's really cool. I don't have much experience with it personally, but I can see how it would have its advantages. So, do you and your wife have lots of rules?"

I glanced over to check on Maggie, who had her arms wrapped around Raine's body. She was actually a couple of inches taller than the younger woman. I was sure she was enjoying that dynamic for a change.

"We don't have a lot of rules," I answered Bonnie's question. "We've been doing this a long time. We work off vibes. If we get bad vibes about a metamour, we simply discuss it. No veto power, just frank discussions about concerns."

"Veto power?" Bonnie's fair eyebrows arched.

"Yeah, some poly couples have veto power. It's a really hierarchical thing, and we don't believe in it. It gives the couple too much power and the paramours practically none. So, in a veto scenario, if Maggie was dating Raine, and I didn't like her, or I was jealous, I could simply veto her, and Maggie would have to break up with her."

"Ouch," Bonnie sighed. "That sounds rough." Then her face brightened. "So Maggie is bi, then?"

I laughed. "Well, yeah."

"And you?"

"Not really. I've done some stuff… Guess you might call me heteroflexible."

"Nice, haven't heard that one before." She looked duly impressed. "So, you can date other women too? Can Maggie date other men?"

"Why all the questions?" I was starting to feel like I was the subject of an interrogation. I liked it better when I was the one asking the questions.

"I'm just curious," she admitted. "You know, about how it works. Raine and I were talking about it after Danielle moved in with Aris and Noah. She didn't know much about how it worked either, to be honest."

"We don't have a one penis policy, if that's what you're asking."

"A what now?" Her features had morphed past curiosity into pure shock.

"Some couples have a policy where the man or the woman can date another woman, but the woman can't date another man. There's only one penis allowed in those relationships," I explained.

Her expression screamed "outrage." "Well, that doesn't seem fair!"

"No, it doesn't." I grinned. "Maggie's free to date whoever she'd like. But so far, she's mostly dated women."

"Oh really?" Bonnie's eyes trailed over to where her roommate was swaying in rhythm with my wife, their bodies so close together, there was no visible space between them. "Do you think she likes Raine?"

I shrugged. "I mean, just looking at them, I'd say all signs point to yes."

Bonnie giggled, and the song we were dancing to slowly faded like a music box that ran out of turns. "Thanks for the dance." She didn't have to lift up very high on her tiptoes to press a kiss to my cheek. Her lips were warm and moist against my stubbly skin.

"You're welcome. Anytime." I watched her head for the bar, then I claimed our drinks, which I'd been keeping an eye on. My beer was still nice and cold.

The next song started up, and Maggie and Raine had moved apart, but they were still dancing. As I chugged my beer and contemplated a second round, I noticed Maggie's head falling back, her mouth open wide. It was so refreshing to see her laugh.

She'd been so nervous the past week waiting for these test results. Then they confirmed our worst fears. I didn't think she'd be laughing for some time…but I'd been proven wrong.

And I had Raine to thank for that.

raine

I didn't expect to see Maggie and Leo at the club tonight. They were a couple I met at Aris and Noah's polycule's house when we were celebrating Danielle getting her cast off after she broke her leg. Maggie was Noah's lawyer, and Leo was a cop. Danielle told me later that they're polyamorous. Maggie and Leo were law and order, but make it hot and spicy.

I also wasn't expecting Maggie to make a beeline over to me and Bonnie as soon as we made eye contact. She threw her arms around me for a hug—didn't have that on my bingo card either.

Or how she smelled so damn good, like exotic flowers and a rainstorm all at once. When she stepped away, I noticed her eyes for the first time. I couldn't quite tell their color in the vibrant flashing lights of the club, but they were round and sparkling. She wore her honey-colored hair pulled back in a tortoiseshell clip, and her black dress hugged her wide hips and accentuated her plump ass.

I hadn't found myself noticing women since getting my heart stomped on by one of my classmates in my graduate program. Her name was Sarai, and she was a massive tease. But I didn't want to talk about her, not when Maggie asked me to dance with her when the DJ played a slow song.

You guessed it—I wasn't expecting that either!

She was a little taller than me (who wasn't?) but was wearing sexy, strappy wedge heels that made it seem like she was towering over me. Her narrow shoulders contrasted with her wide hips, which rocked perfectly in time with the slow, sultry beat. She pressed her body to mine and swayed, her eyes closed as her breath fell on my cheek.

My hands gravitated lower until the voluptuous curves of her ass were right under my fingertips. It was too tempting not to give them a squeeze, and I was surprised by how firm they were. She pulled back a little to flash me a wicked smile, then her tongue darted out to lick her lips.

It was pierced!

I definitely was not expecting that!

And I didn't notice her piercing when I met her at Danielle's party, or tonight before she asked me to dance. Before I could stop it, a little fantasy played in my head about her tongue swirling around my clit. My nipples tightened, and my core clenched in response.

"You can squeeze my ass anytime you like," she whispered in my ear, sending a chill dancing down my spine and straight into my nether regions.

"You like that?" I squeezed again, and she brushed her lips against the shell of my ear, letting out a moan that made me go weak in the knees.

I glanced over and caught her husband staring at us. I wondered if they were a package deal. I wasn't sure how polyamory worked for them—if they only dated the same women. He was a tall drink of water with a bulky dad bod. It appeared as though he'd once been an athlete in his prime, but over the years, being a cop had toughened his mind and softened his body. I liked that look on a man—snuggling with him would be like cuddling a bear.

I'd always had a thing for older men, but I'd never dated an older woman. Most of the women I'd dated were younger than me and so immature. It would be refreshing to date a woman in her thirties who knew what she wanted and wasn't afraid to ask for it.

Was Maggie like that?

The way she moaned in my ear and commanded, "Do it again," made me think she was.

The way she moved her hips and ground them into me made me think she was.

And when our dance was over, the way she boldly asked for my number definitely made me think she was.

A giddy rush of excitement raced through me when I handed her back her phone after entering my number, and she texted me right away.

> Maggie: You're <fire emoji> and smell good enough to eat.

My face flushed as I struggled for a response, but she just stared at me, that piercing gaze looking as though she was imagining feasting upon me—just like my earlier fantasy.

And I was pretty sure I would let her.

three

. . .

maggie

THE TRIP to The Barn had sufficiently distracted me. From the tantalizing slow dance with Raine, to the hilariously entertaining drag show, to the cringey but still amusing karaoke session, I enjoyed myself. And after two beers, Leo announced he was driving, so I should drink up.

I indulged in a few glasses of wine, and I was a light-weight anyway... Alcohol made me super horny and handsy, so I was groping my sexy husband all the way home.

"We're almost there, Mags. Can't you wait two more minutes?" he groaned as I stroked his cock through his khaki pants.

"Let me suck it right here?" I leaned across him, letting my hot breath soak through the fabric.

"Wait until we at least pull in the driveway." He sighed, his head leaning back against the seat as he negotiated the curves of our neighborhood. He'd be negotiating some different curves later if I had my way.

I deftly unbuttoned his pants and slid the zipper down, tracing the bulge in his boxer briefs with my tongue I tried not to impale myself on the gearshift. He braked hard as he almost missed the driveway, making me giggle.

"Let me put it in park, geez, babe!" he growled as the garage door lifted and he slid into the parking space next to his police cruiser.

As soon as our SUV was in park, I pulled back the elastic waistband and freed his cock, giving it a firm stroke up his shaft, back down and then squeezing a few drops of precum from the tip. "Mmm, well, would you look at that? A tasty treat." My tongue darted out to sample his essence.

He yanked the clip out of my hair and gathered up a fistful as I wrapped my lips around the head. Then he guided my mouth up and down his shaft, tightening his hold around the ponytail he'd made. "That's it, baby. Did you need some cock?"

I gurgled in the affirmative as I continued to take him deep into my throat.

"Really? It looked like you were craving some pussy when you were dancing with Raine." He got the words out just as I swirled my tongue around the ridge under his crown, making him gasp as I then plunged back down, swallowing him clear to his balls. "Fuck, baby…if you keep that up, you're gonna get a mouthful of cum."

I popped off and sat up straight in the passenger seat. "Let's go inside. I need that cock inside me."

"I'm gonna have to take you out and get you liquored up more often." He chuckled as he climbed out of the SUV before coming around to my side to guide me out. "That and have you dance with more pretty girls."

We didn't make it into the bedroom.

Instead, he ripped the black bodycon dress up over my

head and flung it across the room. Meanwhile, I slipped my panties off and reached around to unhook my bra. After he tossed his clothes aside, he turned his ravenous gaze to my now naked body.

"Fucking beautiful," he declared, his eyes raking up and down my generous curves. His hands went to my face, tilting me toward him so he could claim my lips. His tongue dueling with mine, he pressed his cock, still wet from my saliva, against my soft belly. "I wanna bend you over this couch and take you."

"Don't let me stop you," I egged him on.

That was all the permission he needed. His fingers dug into my curvy hips, whipping me around to face the other direction. Then his firm hand on my back pressed me forward, raising my ass in the air. He leaned over me, his breath hot on my ear. "Are you ready for this cock?"

"Touch me and find out," I dared him.

He didn't hesitate before wrapping an arm around me and swiping a thick finger through my folds. "Holy fuck, you're soaked… Is that from me or her?"

"A little of both," I confessed.

Turning my head to look over my shoulder, I witnessed him fist his cock and smack it against my ass before nestling it in the crack between each globe. His eyes fluttered closed as he rubbed it up and down in the crevice.

I bit my bottom lip and begged, "Don't tease me!"

"You mean like you teased me dancing so seductively with Raine?"

"Who…me?" I fluttered my eyelashes innocently.

He pressed me back down, forcing my head into the sofa cushion. "I'm gonna imagine your face buried in her cunt, baby, while I drive my cock deep inside you."

My core tightened at the thought. Raine's beautiful cat-like eyes rimmed in coal-black liner, and her full red lips popped into my mind. Her smell, like cherries and vanilla, wafted in my memories. I wondered if her pussy tasted like cherries and vanilla too—I could practically taste her on my tongue as my husband's cock breached my entrance.

He pushed inside, growling as my walls clenched around him. "Fuck, baby…you feel so wet, so tight…"

"Fuck me!" I pushed back against him, eager to feel him move inside me as I imagined bringing Raine to orgasm with my lips, tongue and fingers.

"You would make her come so hard while I fucked you, baby, wouldn't you?" He thrust deep and held himself there as though he might explode if he moved another inch.

"You wanna watch me lick her pussy?" I rasped as I moved my hips, dislodging him slightly before ramming back into his pelvis to take him deep again.

"I'm in control here." His grip on my hips tightened, reminding me who was in charge.

I loved it when he got all growly and commanding.

"Then fuck me, bury your cock deep inside me and empty your balls. Fill me with your cum."

"Fuuuuuck…I'm not gonna last if you keep talking like that."

"Do you wanna fuck Raine after I make her come?"

We had shared a woman before, a long time ago. We'd mostly dated separately after we gave up that cringey unicorn hunting thing that a lot of couples new to nonmonogamy try. It was still a fantasy we revisited in the bedroom, but neither of us had any expectation of it actually happening.

But apparently that fantasy was alive and well—and perfectly capable of getting my husband off, because, as soon as the words were out of my mouth, his hips moved like pistons against mine, driving his cock in and out of me so fast, it stole my breath and made my pussy throb with the need for release.

"Come with me," he commanded, and that was all it took.

We fell together over the edge, ecstasy crashing over our bodies as our fantasies about Raine ebbed, and our ever-lasting love for each other wrapped us both in its blissful embrace.

raine

"Did you hear from Maggie?" Bonnie dumped an absolutely ridiculous amount of creamer into her morning joe.

"Not yet," I sighed, not even looking up from my phone. Scrolling through my emails before heading to campus was supposed to wake me up, but I found myself yawning again.

"You will." Bonnie sounded confident, and when I finally glanced up at her, she was beaming a knowing smile at me. "You two looked so cute together."

"I'm not sure what to think about dating a married woman," I confessed, setting my phone on the kitchen table. "That's definitely way out of my comfort zone."

"He seemed to be eyeing you too." Bonnie took the seat next to me and set her still-steaming coffee mug on the table. "I liked dancing with him. He's fucking hot. Love the burly cop vibe. Maybe they're a two-for-one special? Did she mention that at all?"

"No, we didn't talk about him. We didn't talk about much of anything. We mostly groped each other." I chuckled at the thought, but when the memory creeped up on me, my cheeks flushed.

"You're blushing!" Bonnie accused, still grinning at me. "Adorable!"

I rolled my eyes. "Well, I'm gonna let her contact me. The ball is in her court."

"Summer flings are so fun. Wish I had time for one." She sighed and took a sip of her coffee, which was so pale, it almost matched her skin.

"Well, we can't all be earning the big bucks this summer," I teased her. She was working as a research assistant for a professor writing a book about Tennessee Williams. So far her assistantship was mostly running errands.

"On that note, I better get going." She stood up and downed the rest of her coffee in just one swallow. Then she sputtered, "Oh my god, that was a lot hotter than I thought. Even with all that cream!"

"That's what she said," I joked as she cracked a smile and headed to grab her purse off the sofa.

I picked my phone back up as I heard the door click shut, forcing my eyeballs to digest the emails on my screen. Then one caught my eye. It was from the dreadful woman I called the Costume Czar. She was in charge of the costuming department at the Indiana University Theatre, and she was my nemesis.

Well, not literally. She probably had no clue that she was universally hated by MFA students with costuming specialties. But she was rigid, stern, and absolutely pedantic about every piece she was responsible for, from the rarest gown to the most insignificant hat.

Ms. Rivera:

On April 17th, you checked out Costume Lot 223, parts A, B, C and D. All parts of the costume lot were returned to storage in adequate condition except for Part D. Part D

was a jewelry set consisting of an art deco-style gold and pearl necklace, earring and bracelet set valued at $12,475 at its most recent appraisal. I am including an invoice in this amount, plus the $250 lost item fee, in accordance with the contract you signed upon checkout. Please remit this amount within thirty days or return the missing set. Your degree cannot be finalized until this matter is resolved.

If you should have any questions, please contact my administrative assistant at 812-555-2510.

Sincerely,

Dr. Monica Wharton, Head of Costuming – Indiana University Theatres

Oh, fuck. I take it back. She is literally my nemesis!

What the fuck was a $12,000 jewelry set doing in the costume warehouse? I was told all the jewelry was costume jewelry.

After walking around my house contemplating bashing my head against the walls or seeing how sharp the knives in the kitchen were, I figured the safer bet was to call a trusted friend. So, I dialed Danielle and gave her an earful.

"Oh my god, Raine, I don't even know what to say," she rushed out. "I only answered the phone because I knew you wouldn't call if it wasn't important. I'm about to head into the building for camp. Going to teach music from *Les Mis* today."

"I'm sorry—I know you're busy. But what the fuck am I gonna do?" I lamented, my voice nothing more than a pitiful whine.

"Let me think about it." She paused for a moment, then her voice grew breathy as she must have started walking. "You're sure you don't have the piece?"

"I'm sure the jewelry was with the other accessories—there were gloves, a fascinator, and a fur stole that went along with the gown. Everything but the stole was in a little black case." I envisioned the costume in question. I needed to study it and photograph it for research purposes. It was for my thesis. I only used it for a week and then returned it. All of it.

"Oh, sweetie, try not to stress about it. I can help you look for it if you want. You don't think it got mixed up with my things when I moved out, do you?"

"I don't see how it could have." I sighed. "I didn't bring it home. I kept it in the lab the whole time."

"Could someone have stolen it?" she questioned.

I sighed again. I hadn't thought of that, but now that it was in my mind… "I guess that's possible."

"Ugh! I will think about it and text you later. Do you mind if I ask Noah and Aris if they have any ideas?"

"Yeah, whatever. Maybe ask them how much I could get for a kidney." What? They worked in the medical field. Surely they knew the going rate for organs.

"Raine!" my friend chided me. "I'm sure we can figure it out, and you won't have to pay the twelve grand."

"I better not because there is no way in hell I can come up with that kind of cash. I'm a poor grad student, for fuck's sake. And I am thinking about asking the Dean why an expensive set of jewelry was with a costume in the first place. Seems like a huge liability since graduate students are in and out of that storage facility all the damn time!"

"You tell 'em, girl!" Dani cheered me on. "I better get in there before the kids stage a coup instead of a musical number."

That earned a snicker from me, even in my stressed state.

"I better get to campus." I huffed out another long, belabored sigh. "Are you feeling okay?"

"Some lingering morning sickness, but otherwise I'm A-OK. I have an OB appointment this afternoon!"

"Wow, that's awesome. Are you guys going to find out the baby's gender?" That was what people did, right? And those gender reveal parties? They always seemed stupid to me, but to each their own.

"I don't know yet. We'll see." She muffled the phone and said something I couldn't hear. "Hey, love, I'm right outside my classroom door. I gotta run. I'll talk to you soon, okay? Keep me posted on all this."

"Let me know how your doctor's appointment goes." I felt bad for keeping her on the phone so long. She probably needed that time to prepare for her class.

I did feel a little bit better, though, for having shared my plight with her. But that didn't stop the raging headache that began to pound at my temples. It was going to be a long fucking day.

Then my phone buzzed again. I figured it was Dani, texting me something she forgot to tell me.

But nope.

> Maggie: Had so much fun last night. Want to grab dinner some night this week? Let me know.

four

. . .

leo

BEING ON NIGHTSHIFT SUCKED, but when Maggie
didn't have any clients until noon, it could make for a nice
morning. We leisurely lounged in bed after making love,
both of us scrolling our phones.

I put my phone down on the nightstand and rolled over,
slinging my arm around her waist and pulling her flush with
my pelvis. Mmm, she was so fucking warm and soft. "You
came first, so you have to go make coffee."

"Is that how it works?" She set her phone down too.

"I think it's fair, don't you?"

"I just got an email back from the surrogate place I
contacted for info," she said.

Oh. So we were being serious now.

I might need coffee for this conversation.

But it was still progress. I had been trying to get her to
discuss our options since our appointment with Dr. Levin
earlier this week, and all she would commit to was filling

out the information request form on this pregnancy surrogate website. She didn't seem too thrilled about that option.

"What did they say?" I nuzzled her neck, hoping I could keep her relaxed and get the conversation flowing.

She seemed to have an easier time facing away from me. "They suggested making an appointment to come and go over the details and costs. They also have a database of potential surrogates we can search. They are all over the Midwest."

"Oh, they're not local?"

"We could try to find someone local," she clarified. "Possibly in Indy."

I imagined what partnering with a surrogate might look like. "I just thought we'd be involved in the process, you know? Going to doctor appointments, being there at the ultrasounds and the delivery. Holding our baby when it's still fresh from the womb."

"Eww," she shuddered against me, "that sounds gross."

"That is mild on the grossness scale compared to some of the shit I deal with at work," I reminded her, and she let out a soft chuckle. Then there was a beat of silence until she sighed loudly. "I'm glad we're talking about it, baby."

Her voice was so small, but she eked out, "It's just not the way I envisioned any of this, you know?"

I pressed a kiss right behind her ear. "I know, but it's okay. If we have a baby in the end, it doesn't matter how he or she got here, you know?"

"I just envisioned us...you know...making love. You putting a baby in me. Planting a seed. The old-fashioned way. Missing a period, taking a test. Getting all excited to see those two lines come up."

"Tell me more about this planting a seed thing...?" My cock twitched at her description of the process.

It was true, every time we had tried for a baby, I was raring to go. There was something so primal, so animalistic about trying to impregnate my wife. To fill her with a baby. My baby. Why did it make me feel so feral…so…

Oh yeah, I was hard again. I couldn't help grinding my stiff cock into her fleshy ass cheeks.

"Leo…"

"What?" I tried to sound innocent.

"Are you actually turned on by this conversation?" Her tone was incredulous.

"Um…" My cock pulsed. *Kinda hard to deny it now, buddy,* I thought in a southerly direction.

She flipped over in my arms and pierced me with her stare. Her lawyer stare. It meant her lie detectors were on. She was mentally recording every word that came out of my mouth, and anything I said could and would be used against me in the future.

She reached down and fisted my cock, eliciting a groan from deep in my throat. "What about this conversation is making you hard?"

"Uh…"

"Don't lie to me. Tell me the truth."

I cleared my throat just before she squeezed me again from base to trip. I was pretty sure a little pre-cum oozed out onto her hand because she gasped.

"I think the idea of knocking you up is hot," I confessed.

Then I felt bad.

Because I *couldn't* knock her up. According to the doctor.

She was quiet, considering what I'd said. Too quiet.

"I'm sorry. You asked for the truth, and I… Look, it's just very manly to think about making a baby with you. About planting my seed, as you so eloquently described." *When in doubt, go for flattery, right?*

"I guess we can still pretend to try… Even if it's not going to work," she said.

She took that better than I thought.

"You mean right now?"

"I thought you wanted me to get up and make you coffee…but if you need my pussy again, well, then, who am I to deny you?" She looked at me with those lovely gray-green eyes.

"Damn, baby…" I climbed on top of her, settled between her legs and pressed the tip of my cock to her pussy lips. "You sure?"

Her sultry voice oozed out, "Pretend you're trying to breed me, you stud muffin."

Fuck. I know she's joking but…something about it does things to me.

I never came so fast in my life.

maggie

"You look gorgeous tonight," I said as she slipped into the booth across from me. Raine and I were dining at a quaint little Mexican place near my house, and I hoped our dinner would go well enough that I could invite her back for…you know, whatever came to mind.

"Thanks, so do you." She folded her hands on the table and smiled. She looked a little nervous.

Raine was petite, probably not even five feet tall, and she had curves for days. She wore her jet-black hair in a bob with bangs. Her skin tone was a lovely shade of taupe and looked silky to the touch, and her eyes were the most curious shade of hazel-brown, upturned on the ends like a cat's. She made them look even more striking by outlining them with thick black eyeliner.

"Is my face okay?" Her hands visibly trembled as she stared at me.

"Your face is beautiful. Sorry for staring—you're just so exquisite. I was wondering about your skincare routine. Or maybe you were just blessed with flawless skin, I don't know." I matched her mood with my own nervous giggle.

My eyes trailed down her chest, taking in the silver chain with an R charm hanging around her neck. She wore a feminine floral peasant-style blouse that emphasized her beautiful decolletage. I couldn't see now, since only her upper half appeared above the tabletop, but I thought she'd paired it with high-waisted khaki shorts.

She was so young and stylish. I hoped I didn't seem hopelessly out of fashion in my navy pencil skirt, silk camisole and beige cardigan. I didn't get a chance to change clothes after work.

I hadn't had a first date for a while. The last six months, Leo and I had been focusing on getting pregnant, and we'd both taken a bit of a break from dating others. Each failed cycle brought more heartbreak, and now, after that doctor's appointment…well, it didn't seem like we had any hope of making a baby the old-fashioned way.

Now that I was back into the dating scene, I was seeing women a little differently, but I couldn't quite figure out how to articulate the difference. I just knew Raine was gorgeous and highly intriguing, and though I had a lot on my emotional plate right now, I wanted to see where this went.

"You're too kind," she blushed ever so faintly, "but it's probably just because I'm twenty-six. I don't take care of my skin as well as I should, but I do try to wash my face at night instead of wearing makeup to bed. And sunscreen, of course."

"Well, that's more than I did in my twenties," I admitted. "Now I'm turning forty in December, and I—"

Her eyes widened.

"What?" I called her out on it. *I'm a lawyer—that's what we do.*

"Sorry, I just...didn't think you were that much older than me." She raised a hand apologetically.

"I'll take that as a compliment," I assured her.

The server stopped by, and we both ordered margaritas—peach for me and raspberry for her—and some chips and queso. I lifted the menu, meeting her eyes over it. "Sorry, I don't want this to be awkward, but...I have a million questions, so maybe we should figure out what we want to eat first."

"Good plan," she agreed with a lovely smile.

She seemed happy to let me lead the conversation. "Are you from Indiana originally, or did you move here for college?"

"I grew up all over the place. My dad was in the military. But we ended up in Texas." She kept her upper body so stiff. I almost felt like she was giving off interview vibes. Hopefully she would relax when tequila hit her brain.

As if on cue, the server returned with our margaritas. They were huge!

"Wow! I hope I can drive home after drinking this." I swirled my straw around the frothy mixture, then took a sip. "So good!"

When she tested hers, her face lit up. "Mmm! I approve." She seemed to relax a little already and swiped one of the chips from the basket the server left through the cheese and brought it to her mouth.

"Oh—" I pointed to her chin. "You dripped just a tiny bit there."

She laughed and dabbed at her chin with her napkin. "Did I get it?"

I smiled. "Yes. So what else should I know about you? You're gorgeous, a good dancer, and you like cheese and margaritas. I mean, that's enough for me, but there's probably more, right?"

She had the most adorable giggle. "I mean, yeah, there's a little more… I'm getting my MFA in design, costume design specifically. I've been designing fashions since I was a kid—just ask my mom. And I became a huge theater nerd in high school, so it only seemed natural to put the two together."

"That's amazing. Sounds a lot more exciting than being a lawyer!"

"Well, I'm sure being a lawyer is hard work. I bet just getting through law school was way harder than my MFA program." She crunched on another chip and then carefully dabbed at her face again.

"If I had to sew something, I would probably break out in hives because I would be so nervous," I admitted. "I'd much rather sweat it out while my client is cross-examined."

We both had a laugh over that.

"Well, it sounds like we both followed career paths that suit us," she said diplomatically. "My parents weren't thrilled about me going into the arts, but I'm a thousand miles away, so who cares what they think?"

"You're not close with your family?" It always made me sad to hear that, but I could relate. "I lost my dad a few years back, and I was a daddy's girl, so I miss him a lot. I'm not as close with my mom or sister, but they both live in Indianapolis. I just never see them."

"My parents are divorced," she admitted. "I don't really get along with my stepmom, so I don't see my dad much. He moved to San Antonio, and my older brother went with him, back when I was in high school. My mom and I stayed in Austin."

"I see. Well, they clearly passed along good genes," I complimented her as my eyes raked up and down her face and chest again.

"Thank you, but I was adopted," she admitted. "I don't know much about my birth mom except she was Japanese."

"Oh, wow, well, that's interesting. Adoption is—" I had just taken a sip of my margarita and realized I was in danger of saying something that was, at best, trite and, at worst, offensive. So I chose not to pursue the completion of that thought.

"I never had a burning desire to meet my birth parents," she explained. "I only know my mom was Japanese because I have a half-brother who contacted me a few years ago after we both did one of those DNA tests. I haven't really pursued getting to know him or the rest of that side of the family. I did find out from the test that my dad gave me a wild mix of genes, from Irish to Indigenous American to a few countries in Africa."

"I see…" This discussion had gone from flirty to serious, and I didn't know how to get it back on the flirty track. Or if I even should. *Serious doesn't mean bad, right?*

"So, do you and Leo have kids?" she asked.

And then I knew there was no coming back. A tear tried to sting at my eye, but I stubbornly willed it away. "Well, we were trying, but it turns out we're not able to."

"Oh…" She set down the chip she had just picked up. "I'm sorry, I didn't mean to—"

"Well, I didn't mean to—" I still felt bad about the adoption thing.

The server came back to check on us. *Saved by the server… is that a thing?*

"So…" She laced her fingers together and gave me a hard stare. "How long have you and Leo been poly? How'd you get into it?"

I smiled. She probably thought she was asking a truly probing question, but this was one we answered all the time. We were pretty open about it too. Both of our families knew —they thought we were nuts and always suspected we were on the verge of divorce—but they'd known for a long time.

"We started off as swingers," I admitted, and that usually drew a shocked gasp from our audience. But she didn't even flinch. "Then we realized we weren't really into the fucking people without knowing them thing. We liked to get to know our partners. We had a couple friends we had…feelings for, you know? Stronger feelings than just friendship. I guess you'd call them romantic feelings. We didn't even know polyamory was a thing."

"And then what?" She was leaning forward, absorbing every word like oxygen. She was very interested in this, and I wanted to be completely honest with her about every aspect of my marriage.

"Well, I did some reading on the subject, like any lawyer would. Leo has done some reading too. He's a cop—he has to be completely strait-laced at work, all buttoned up. We found there are a ton of cops in the swinging lifestyle—and nurses, teachers, all the public-servant-type jobs. They really like blowing off some steam on the weekends and just cutting loose. That was initially what attracted us to it, but we both have a geeky, intellectual side, I guess you'd call it. Yep, that's right, Leo's not just a dumb cop. He's a bit of a nerd too. We started asking around and probing a bit deeper in our circle of friends, and it turned out a few of us had more polyam tendencies.

"We really liked how open and accepting they were. How we could freely discuss things with each other. And, well, Leo ended up dating one of our swinger friends a bit more seriously for a few years. Until she and her husband divorced, and she remarried someone who wanted to be monogamous."

"Wow, wasn't that hard? The breakup, I mean?"

"Yeah, it was," I shared openly. "But, if you think about it, most relationships aren't going to last forever. Whether they're monogamous or polyamorous, you know? People grow and change. They move. Their needs fluctuate."

"So what about you? Have you had many poly relationships?" she asked.

I smiled. "A few. I was involved with a couple for a while, but he was in the military, and they got transferred somewhere else. Then I had a girlfriend for a little bit. I always thought maybe Leo and I would fall in love with the same woman…you know, the stereotypical unicorn. But that has never happened."

"No?" Her thin dark eyebrows arched with curiosity.

"Well, we're still open to it…if it happens organically."

"Organically," she repeated.

"Yep. You just never know who's going to come into your life and vibe with you, you know?"

She grinned. "Yeah, I think I do."

five

. . .

raine

I DIDN'T KNOW if I wanted Maggie to be my big sister or my lover at this point. I was crushing on her for sure, but part of it was this big sis vibe she had going on. She was so unafraid to be herself, giving zero fucks what anyone thought of her. Was it her age or her profession? Or the fact that she was unapologetically bi and poly?

She was beautiful inside and out, with her wispy honey-colored hair that framed her heart-shaped face, and her wide, expressive eyes that were the color of a misty mountain lake. She had a lovely pear shape, so curvy and womanly, and I couldn't help but remember what her voluptuous ass felt like when I grabbed it on the dance floor.

She was completely different than any woman I'd dated before, and I couldn't help but wonder what that might translate to in the bedroom. So, naturally, when she invited me back to her house after our meal, I enthusiastically accepted.

I followed her down a tree-lined boulevard in one of the

nicest neighborhoods in Bloomington and parked behind her sleek silver SUV. I was having such a delightful evening, I'd almost forgotten about the threatening email I received from the Costume Czar yesterday.

I'd scoured my entire apartment, plus my office I shared with another graduate student, and the costume lab in the basement of the theater. No gold and pearl art deco jewelry set anywhere, and no one I asked about it had a single clue where it might be.

Did I really have to come up with twelve grand? And if so…how the fuck would I do that?

"You okay?" Maggie stood in the garage, beckoning me toward her. She opened the door to the house and gestured me inside.

"Oh, yeah, I'm fine." I smiled, but as soon as I took another step, an assault of high-pitched barking hit my ears, and a furry little demon made a beeline to my knees.

"Bark! Bark! Bark! Bark!" the fluffy dog protested my being in his space. He had curly caramel-colored fur with white patches on his chin and chest.

"Blue!" Maggie shrieked, the first time I'd ever heard her voice rise to such a loud volume. "Get down! C'mon, leave Raine alone. Sit!"

The fluffy terror expertly ignored her, bounding on its hind legs as though he could generate enough momentum to spring up into my face. I'd never seen such a tenacious beast.

"You're not a dog person?" she inquired as she reached down and snatched him away from me after her commands failed.

I held my hands out in front of me to protect myself as he tried to squirm out of her arms to get to me. "Uh…just haven't been around one for a while," I admitted.

My dad was the dog person in our family. He had two

chunky bulldogs who were too lazy to jump up to greet guests, but he took them with him when he and Mom divorced. I had no idea if those dogs were still alive or not.

"I'm so sorry about Blue. He is so fucking much. He failed out of obedience school. You'd think a cop would have a better trained dog, but nope!"

I laughed. "I'm sure he'll get used to me."

She smiled. "I like the sound of that."

Oh. Right. That did make it sound like I planned to be around. Well…if the rest of the night went as well as the first part, there was a good chance I would be.

Maybe Maggie could take my mind off this bullshit I was dealing with at school right now.

"How about some wine?" She set Blue in front of his food dishes, which were there in the mudroom where we entered. Then she swept into the kitchen, apparently expecting me to follow her.

Their kitchen was a dream. Sleek, modern stainless-steel appliances and gorgeous black granite countertops. The cabinets were a light gray, and the light fixtures were so cool. I wanted a kitchen like this someday when I grew up.

"Wine is fine." I giggled as I took a seat at a barstool at the counter while she pulled a bottle of wine out of the fridge.

"Chardonnay okay?" She winked at me before pulling down two stemless wine glasses from a cabinet near the sink.

"Sure, sounds good."

She handed me one glass and then called over her shoulder as she left the room, "Follow me."

We entered her living room, which was almost open to the kitchen save for two thick support columns holding up the second floor above us. A gray leather sectional centered the room with an enormous custom-built bookcase and entertainment center against the opposite wall, and the other wall was made up of windows. The outdoor lights illuminated what looked like an amazing deck…and was that a hot tub I spied?

"Make yourself comfortable." She took a seat in the middle of the sectional and patted the space next to her. "Unless you don't want to be so close…"

"Oh, I do," I assured her, lowering myself onto the buttery soft leather cushion. "Wow, these are so comfortable."

"Thanks, Leo has great taste." She grinned and took a sip of her wine before placing it on the glass-topped coffee table in front of her.

"So he's working tonight?" I confirmed.

"Yes, he usually gets off around midnight when he's on second shift."

"Gotcha. It must be hard to keep track of his schedule."

"It is." She sighed and put her arm around the back of the sofa, not far from my shoulders. "Some weeks, we're both so busy, I hardly see him. That's another reason it helps to have other partners. Otherwise, I might feel like a single dog mama, you know?"

I smiled. I wondered about our earlier conversation—she mentioned something about trying to have kids, but they couldn't. Did that mean they intended to stay childless? Or they were looking into other options? Just glancing around their house…it didn't look particularly child-friendly.

How did children work with polyamorous couples, anyway? I'd been meaning to ask Danielle about that… Like, who was going to be listed as the father on the birth certificate? Even though we were close friends, it felt too nosy to ask.

After the long pause, Maggie reached down and grabbed her wine glass again, draining it in one gulp. Then she turned her whole body to me, leaning toward me with a playful smile on her face. "I'm a little out of practice, so please forgive me, but I really want to kiss you, Raine."

I gulped. Her forwardness was unexpected, but very much welcomed. "O-okay," I stammered. "I'd like that."

We locked eyes then, and her hand reached out to brush her fingertips across my cheek as she leaned closer to me. My senses were filled with her exotic floral perfume as she inched toward me, the slightest flutter of her lips against mine sending a shockwave through my system. When I moaned, she grasped my face in her hands, angling her mouth to cover mine as she gently nibbled on my lips.

It was so delicate, so sensuous… I'd never been kissed so tenderly before. This was a woman who was accomplished at everything she did in life, from her house to her marriage to her job to the way she kissed. It was overwhelming to be in her presence, to soak up her easy sophistication, her gracious but classy style and her generous touch.

"Your lips are so soft," she murmured against my neck as she made a trail from my ear to the top of my chest, which was heaving under her roving fingertips. "Can I take your shirt off?"

This lady was not messing around. But I was down…so down. I groaned my approval, and she undid the tie at the back, loosing the lacings of the corset-style peasant blouse. She pulled back long enough to lift it over my head, leaving my rock-hard nipples pressing against the soft peach lace of my bra.

"Exquisite," she declared as she ran her fingers over the tops of my mounds, eliciting goose bumps down my arms.

"So creamy…so perfect… I want to see those beautiful nipples."

"Uh…okay…" I started to reach behind to unfasten my bra, but she gently stopped me.

"I'll do it." A wicked smile curled her lips as she used one hand to deftly release the hooks in the back. The lace fell away, and she carefully set the bra aside with my blouse.

Male partners were often rushed, in such a frenzy to get to the point of Insert Tab A in Slot B, they glossed over the breasts. They might give my nipples a tug or a lick, but there was no urgency right now in Maggie's touch. She tenderly cupped one breast and lowered her mouth to it, teasing my nipple into an even tighter point than I realized was possible.

I closed my eyes, arousal rocketing through me as her mouth closed around the tight bud, sucking it between her teeth and swirling her tongue around it again and again. I was going to lose my mind if she kept this up. She cupped the other breast with her right hand and squeezed them both together, moaning at my beautiful cleavage.

"Your breasts are absolute masterpieces." She gave the other nipple its due with her mouth while she continued to tease and torment the one she had already suckled with her fingers. I couldn't believe how turned on I was, and I was still wearing my shorts. If she kept playing with my nipples, I might explode right here on the sofa before she even got to my pussy.

I'd never done that before. I'd never come without my clit being touched.

"I want to touch you too," I blurted out.

"You will…" she promised, but instead of allowing me the chance, she slid off the sofa and between my thighs. "I'm going to take off your shorts now."

"Oh…okay…" My voice was more breath than sound as she reached for the button and zipper, then slowly slid them down my legs. They got folded neatly into the pile with my other clothes.

"Panties too." She tugged them down my thighs. "Lift that sexy ass, babe."

I complied, and soon my panties were joining the rest of the clothes. "I don't want to get anything on your sofa…"

"Are you a squirter?" Her face was filled with hope.

"Uh…well, no, not that I know of, but…"

"Lots of cream?" She licked her lips. "Just a sec. I'll run and get a towel."

She stood up and headed down a hallway, and I just sat there for a moment, feeling the soft leather against my bum. My thighs were trembling, and I was tempted to see how wet she'd already made me, but before I could, a door opened somewhere on the other side of the house, and the dog started to bark. Then a door closed.

I sat there listening, my heart racing. What was Maggie doing?

"Oh!" I jumped up, naked as the day I was born, just as heavy footsteps sounded on the hardwood floors.

I whipped around and froze.

Leo was standing there in his police officer uniform, a thick gun belt around his waist and heavy boots on his feet. And when his eyes met mine, they trailed down my body and back up again like he had no intention of averting his gaze.

"Looks like I interrupted something." The smirk on his face was priceless, and I was so caught off-guard, my limbs refused to move.

Then Maggie reappeared with a stack of towels.

As my limbs finally unlocked, I reached for my clothes,

but in my clumsy discombobulation, I knocked the neatly folded pile to the floor.

"Don't get dressed on my account," Leo's voice boomed along with a hearty chuckle. "This is the best thing I've seen all day."

Maggie tossed the towels in a heap on the sofa. "Well, I doubt you saw anything good at work. Why are you home so early?"

"I forgot my handcuffs." He was grinning ear to ear. Why did I get the impression he didn't actually forget anything, he just wanted to stop by and check up on Maggie and me?

"I was about to have dessert," Maggie complained, smacking Leo on the arm.

"Well, don't change your plans on my account..." He stepped further into the living room, making it clear he intended to watch.

I had already grabbed one of the towels and wrapped it around myself.

"Oh, now that's a pity," Leo said, "covering up that beautiful body. Seriously, I didn't mean to interrupt you guys. I didn't think you'd be here."

"Hey, I got game," Maggie defended herself. "Raine, I'm so sorry. I can take a raincheck on playtime if you'd like..."

The way Leo's face fell intrigued me. He really wanted to watch, didn't he?

I wasn't an actress, and though I did some stage work in my teens, I hadn't performed in a long time. However, in this moment, the thought of putting on a show for Leo was rather...tantalizing.

leo

"You can stay," Raine said, spreading out a towel on the middle cushion of the sofa.

"Oh. I…uh… Maggie?" My eyes rocketed over to where my wife was standing with a shocked expression on her face.

"Raine, are you sure?" she took over the conversation. "I'm sure Leo needs to get back to work."

"Well, I have a few minutes. No one will miss me." I looked from one woman to the other. "But I will definitely go if either of you feels uncomfortable with me being here. I know this is your first time, and I—"

"I want you to watch," Raine declared. "It'll be hot. I'm down. Maggie, you okay with that?"

Maggie and I had both watched each other with other partners, and it definitely was hot. A thrill raced through me as I took a seat in the armchair across from the sofa. "Pretend I'm just a fly on the wall." I settled back, excited to see where this went.

"As you wish." Maggie moved into position between Raine's thighs. "Let's take it back a few steps, okay?"

I couldn't see Maggie's face, but I did see Raine's lips curl into a smile as she nodded in agreement. I wondered if the twenty-something-year-old had ever done anything like this before.

As my wife tenderly took her face into her hands and claimed her lips, my cock sprang to life in my uniform pants. They were already tight, but with my erection pressing against the zipper, it was uncomfortable. As quietly as I could, I undid the fastener at the top and slid the zipper down to relieve some of the pressure.

Raine let out a sultry moan as Maggie worked her way down her neck and chest, kissing, sucking and biting along the way. God, watching two beautiful women make love was one of my favorite things in life. It just didn't get any better—unless those two beautiful women were also making love to me.

I might be getting ahead of myself…

I spread my legs, giving my manhood a bit more room as Maggie played with Raine's breasts. The younger woman's back was arched in pleasure, her mouth gaping open as soft gasps and winces escaped from her throat. If Maggie's oral talents were as effective on women as they were on me—and I had every confidence they were—Raine was in for quite a treat.

"That's it, good girl," Maggie softly praised as she slid down Raine's body, spreading her thick thighs further.

My cock began to ache and drip with need as Maggie pressed gentle kisses and licks to Raine's mound and inner thighs. Raine's knuckles whitened as she gripped the edges of the towel spread under her to collect any mess she might make. I wondered if she was a squirter. We were in for a treat if that were the case!

Maggie used her fingertips to spread Raine's pussy lips and reveal her swollen bud. "Can I nibble on your clit, or are you too sensitive?"

"You can…gently at first please," came out in a rasp.

"And penetration? With my tongue? With my fingers?" she checked.

Raine sighed as my wife's finger circled her clit. "Both are fine."

Oh, god, I was really starting to get uncomfortable now. The ache had spread to my balls, and every cell in my body was begging me to take my cock into my hand. I lifted it out of my boxer briefs and winced when the air hit it. I needed more, so much more. I hoped Maggie would let me fuck her when she was done with Raine. How was I supposed to go back to work like this?

"Mmmm…" Maggie moaned as her tongue swiped through Raine's folds. "You taste so sweet, so fucking delicious, I could eat this cunt all night."

Raine groaned in response, then gasped as one of Maggie's fingers slipped inside her.

Maggie lifted her head from Raine's mound. "Can I touch your ass?"

"I guess so." Raine's thighs looked like they were trembling now as Maggie added another finger to her hole and then lowered to tease her back entrance.

Raine's eyes popped open when Maggie made contact with her asshole. Those lovely cat eyes snapped to mine. My hand was wrapped around my cock, slowly stroking it from base to tip, and when she noticed, her eyes hooded with lust.

"He's touching himself," she told Maggie, but her eyes never left mine.

"He can't help it," my wife defended me. "You look so fucking hot all splayed open like this, your beautiful breasts bouncing and your hands fisting the towel as you writhe against my mouth and fingers. Now, I need to get back to work. I wanna make you come on my face, Raine. I want to taste all your juices, lick up every last drop. Let Leo stroke his cock while he watches me make you come, okay?"

"Okay…" She bit her bottom lip as Maggie's tongue darted out to collect a taste of her nectar.

Then my wife went to work, moving her mouth, tongue, and fingers in perfect rhythm as she brought Raine closer and closer to the edge. I got to witness the younger woman falling apart, her body clenching and hips rocking against Maggie's face as she expertly drew her climax from deep within her core.

"Fuuuuuck!" Raine shouted, bucking wildly as my wife fucked her with two fingers and licked up the fluids flying out of her pussy. "Oh my god, what the fuck?"

I watched the torment on her face cross over into surprise and then bliss as she coated my wife's entire face with a gush of juices, which Maggie happily lapped up. It was too much for me to endure. My orgasm shot through me before I could stop it, cum erupting from the crown of my cock and flying everywhere.

Maggie rocked back on her knees. "I should get credit for both of those," she proclaimed with a proud smirk on her lips.

six

. . .

raine

DANIELLE PULLED into a parking space on campus near the theater department's office building. "I love that there's actually parking here in the summertime."

"I appreciate you coming with me to face the dean," I said. "I honestly didn't think we'd get an appointment with her so quickly. I thought I'd have to take off from my summer job."

"See, it all worked out. I had today off anyway, and my doctor's appointment is right after! Since Noah is in surgery and can't come, I appreciate you stepping in to fill his shoes."

"I'm sure you would have been fine going with just Aris." I slung my purse over my shoulder and climbed out of the car.

"I'm sure too, but might as well get my new OB used to having a crowded exam room." She laughed as she bounded up the steps to the building where the theater department offices were.

She seemed to be so much happier and have so much more energy than before. I didn't know if it was because she was getting fucked by two gorgeous men or due to pregnancy hormones. Either way, the glow looked great on her, and I was a tad bit jealous since my life was not quite as peachy at the moment.

"Hopefully this will all be a silly misunderstanding," she said as we tackled the stairs to the second floor. "You'll get this off your record, and when you finish up your thesis, they can grant your degree, and then you can get a kick-ass job!"

I thought about that as we turned the corner and headed down the long hallway to Dean Chow's office. If I got a kick-ass job, that would mean moving away from Bloomington. Leaving Danielle, Bonnie, and all my friends. Leaving Leo and Maggie, whom I'd just met but liked very much.

I'll cross that bridge when I come to it, I reassured myself. *You're not gonna be going anywhere if you can't come up with this jewelry or twelve grand!*

The administrative assistant ushered us into the dean's office, and we settled in chairs across from her desk as we waited for her to return from another meeting. Danielle scanned the office, looking at the framed playbills decorating the walls. "You think she did all these shows?"

I shrugged. "Probably. Why else would she have them on her office walls? I'm pretty sure she did Broadway when she was our age."

"That's amazing. I wish I could do that." A wistful sigh floated out of my friend's mouth. Right before she got pregnant, a broken leg and some throat issues had derailed her own thesis project. She was supposed to have surgery to correct a deviated septum, but now she was holding off until after the baby arrived. Would she ever make it to Broadway if she was a mom…and if she was still with Aris and Noah? They were pretty deeply rooted right here in Bloomington with their jobs.

Okay, so maybe she wasn't quite walking on easy street. Her future was uncertain too.

Dean Chow hustled into the office, tossing apologies out as she got situated behind her desk. She flexed her fingers, then bent them, and all her knuckles cracked. "So what can I do for you?"

I liked that she was very straightforward and down-to-earth. Hopefully that would make this easier.

"I got an email from Dr. Wharton about a costume I checked out earlier in the year for my research project. Something about some missing jewelry that was part of the accessory kit?" I handed her the printout of the email I'd received.

When she bent over the paper, Dean Chow's long, straight fifty-shades-of-gray hair fell over her cheek like a silver waterfall. Then her head popped up, and her narrow dark eyes met mine. "Why didn't you take this up with Dr. Wharton?"

"I did. She insists the jewelry was with the dress, and that I am responsible for it. But I don't understand why very valuable jewelry was being used for a costume. I was under the impression that the costume department only used, well, *costume* jewelry," I explained.

Dean Chow huffed. "That particular costume was worn by the actress who played Velma Kelly in our last production of *Chicago*," she enlightened us. "The jewelry was lent by a local antiques dealer who is a patron of our program. I believe he's been pressuring Dr. Wharton to return it."

"But I didn't even open the accessories bag," I argued. "I was studying the design of the gown, trying to replicate it for one of the designs for my thesis. I was trying to use it to create a pattern. I have to actually sew one costume for the project, and it's going to be a gown like that one. I returned the bag and accessories kit with the dress. I am sure the jewelry must not have been in there when I checked it out."

"Costumes and accessories, all components of a lot, are checked in fastidiously upon return to the costume ware-house," she reminded me. "You know Dr. Wharton is a stickler for policy and procedure. I can't imagine that anyone would defy her by cutting corners."

I wanted to retort, *Oh, really? Well, we all hate her, so…*

"So you're saying I have no recourse?" My stomach twisted in knots as I thought about what I would do if I really was on the hook for this jewelry set.

"It was a rare antique set. I have photos of it from our run of *Chicago* if that's helpful." She made a few clicks on her computer and then angled the screen so I could see it. Sure enough, there were Velma Kelly and Roxy Hart, sporting their elegant sequined dresses, white fur stoles, white gloves and, in the next photo, a close-up, I saw the beautiful gold and pearl necklace around the actress's neck.

I sighed. "I don't know what I'm going to do."

"I'm sorry you're in this situation." Dean Chow settled back in her chair and folded her hands in her lap. "I wish there was some way for me to help you, but the antiques store owner donates a lot of money to our program. We certainly don't want to disappoint him. I fear that even if we pay him back the money the set cost him, he will not forgive our transgression. It was a one-of-a kind set. He's not likely to be able to replace it—at any cost. And I know he won't be loaning any more pieces to the department, not even costume jewelry. And that's a shame because he has access to a wide selection of period-appropriate pieces."

I buried my face in my palms, biting my cheek to keep

the tears at bay. Danielle put her hand on my back and rubbed circles, trying to soothe me.

"So there's really nothing else to be done?" she asked the dean. "How do you know another student didn't steal it before Raine even checked out the piece?"

"We don't know that for sure," the dean agreed. "But we have no way of knowing. We have to go by the paperwork, which says Raine is responsible."

I thanked the dean for her time and hurried down the hallway with Danielle trying hard to keep up. "I'm so sorry, sweetie," she called after me as I took the stairs as fast as I could.

"Well, at least your appointment should go better than that one did." I didn't mean to slam the door after I climbed into her car, but I just couldn't seem to help myself.

"Hey, Aris," I greeted Danielle's partner when we arrived in the parking lot of the obstetrician's office.

"Hey, Raine." He wrapped his arms around me and squeezed me tight in a bear hug.

I pulled back and took in his happy face. He looked absolutely ecstatic. I was still worried about my own situation, but I was going to shove that aside so I could be happy for my friends who were embarking on a journey to parenthood.

We all walked inside, took the elevator to the third floor and stood a few feet back while Danielle checked in with the receptionist.

"How've you been?" Aris patted me on the back while Dani filled out paperwork.

"Oh, not too bad." I rocked forward on my heels a bit as if to distract from my obvious lie.

"Great!" He rubbed his hands together. "Ready to be an aunt to the most kick-ass baby who's ever lived?"

I couldn't help but laugh at his exuberance. "Yep, I'm pretty stoked."

"Me too!" We both sat down, and Danielle joined us a few minutes later.

"My hand is cramped from signing so much shit!" She shook her hand dramatically as she plopped down next to Aris.

"I'll rub it later, baby," he promised, "and anything else you have that needs rubbing."

Dani rolled her eyes but giggled. We were all laughing and chatting so loudly that we almost didn't hear the nurse call Dani's name.

She leapt up. "We're coming!" She led her entourage through the doorway and into the hallway where all the exam rooms are.

The nurse took her blood pressure, heart rate, pulse ox, and temperature, then she promised she'd send the doctor right in. She didn't even bat an eye at the fact Danielle had brought two people with her.

Dr. Cameron waltzed in a few minutes later. She was a short, squat, no-frills woman wearing a white lab coat, stretchy black leggings, and brightly colored Hoka sneakers. *Hey, good for her, staying comfortable racing from patient to patient all day.*

"Well, howdy, y'all! Which one of y'all are fixin' to have a baby?" I was not expecting a deep southern-fried accent to come out of her mouth, but that was what we got.

Aris and I both pointed to Danielle, who was perched on the end of the exam table. The nurse came back in and handed the chart to Dr. Cameron, who perused it for a moment. "Well, we're at about twelve weeks today, so we're gonna do a quick scan and see what we can see. Make sure our dates are good."

"Oh, an ultrasound today!" Danielle squealed. "Right now?"

"Yes, ma'am. We're gonna have ya strip down and put on this gown. It'll be a transvaginal ultrasound, so there'll be a wand stuck up your hoo-ha. Do you have any objections to that? We can ask your entourage to leave if you'd like?"

"Oh, they can stay. I don't care about that." She grinned.

"Excellent, we'll be back in a few. Catch ya on the flip side!"

She waltzed right back out the door.

"Wow, I've never met a doctor like her before," I commented as Danielle stripped down to her bra and panties, then tucked herself inside the gown.

"Pretty sure you need to take those off too," Aris said. "I'll help!"

"She's awesome, right? Noah's partner recommended her. Said they don't come any better than Dr. Cameron." Dani allowed Aris to unhook her bra and slide her panties down. She kissed him on the forehead as she stepped out of the panties. "What would I do without you, love?"

"You'd probably get to wear panties a whole helluva lot more often!" He chuckled and helped her climb back up on the exam table.

Dr. Cameron, the nurse, and another woman came back in wheeling a cart with equipment. They got Danielle all set up while Aris and I watched from across the room. I locked eyes with my friends as the ultrasound tech inserted the probe and the screen began to flash in black and white as she moved it.

"I'm nervous," Danielle mouthed.

"No need to be," the doctor assured us. "Look—stop it right there, Carrie." She pointed to the screen. "There's your baby, looking just fine and dandy! Its little heart is beating away."

"Oh my god!" Danielle cried. "It's got little arms and legs!"

"Well, of course it's got arms and legs." Dr. Cameron chuckled. "You're not growing a football in there!"

We all laughed. The ultrasound tech moved, took some screenshots and measurements, then moved again. We were all quiet while she finished, then Dr. Cameron pointed out a few things to us. "The embryo is measuring twelve weeks, two days. That's right in line with the gestational age we calculated by your last period. The heart rate is 155 and looks nice and strong. And I'm only seeing one baby, right, Carrie?"

Carrie smiled. "Just one healthy baby!"

A tear trickled down my friend's cheek as Aris stepped over and took her hand into his, bringing it to his mouth for a tender kiss. "I'm one of the dads," he said proudly.

Dr. Cameron and her staff didn't even bat an eye at that comment. I felt like a fifth wheel sitting over to the side, but the overwhelming emotion was sinking into me, filling me with my own sense of joy for Aris and Danielle—and Noah too, of course. I wished he could have been there instead of me, but I was so honored to share this moment with them.

I had never thought much about being a mother. I was adopted right when I was born, and my adoptive mother wasn't the most nurturing soul. I'd never been close to her, and I always sort of assumed I wouldn't have kids of my own.

But right now, I wondered what it might be like to be in

Danielle's shoes, lying up there on the exam table, seeing a tiny human I was growing for the very first time. The relief that everything seemed to be progressing normally. The anticipation of meeting the little one face to face. The worry that something might go wrong in the interim. The excitement of finding out if it was a boy or a girl and whose genes had won out.

It was hard to imagine the swirl of emotions Danielle must have been feeling, but it also was hard not to wonder if it was a swirl of emotions I might ever experience myself.

maggie

I'd received an email reply from the surrogate agency on my drive home from work, but I knew better than to try to read it before I got home. I wanted Leo there too, and since he was on days this week, we'd be able to discuss it together, in person, right away.

"Hey, baby, you're finally home!" He swept me into his arms, pressing his lips against mine as I breathed in his manly, musky scent. "How was work?"

"It was fine, but I'm tired and glad to be home." I hugged him back. "What do you want to do for dinner?"

"I've got baked ziti in the oven," he said. "Not home-made. It's one of the frozen dinners we picked up at the store, but it's starting to smell good. Can you smell the garlic?"

I took a huge whiff, and I could still only smell his scent. I wasn't complaining. "Hey, I got an email back from the surrogate agency. They were supposed to send me an appointment date and time."

"Oh!" His face lit up. "When is it? I will make sure to schedule that day off."

I pulled out a barstool and took a seat, and he joined me as I worked my way into my email. "Oh…"

"What? What is it?"

"They can't get us in for six months?" My nose wrinkled up in frustration. "Six months? For fuck's sake. Just for an appointment? Then we still have to go through the process of finding a surrogate and then a nine-month pregnancy!" I slammed my phone down and raked my hands through my hair.

He wrapped a strong arm around me and pulled me to his side. "It's okay, sweetheart. We've waited this long. We're just going to have to be patient."

"We're not getting any younger," I reminded him. "We're going to be ancient by the time this kid goes to college." I sighed. "The appointment is in November! That feels like a million years from now."

"It's almost June," he reminded me. "It's going to go fast. Forward me the email, and I'll get it on my calendar at work right away."

"Okay." I was quiet as I contemplated whether or not there was anything we could do in the meantime. I couldn't think of anything else. There were other surrogate agencies in Indiana, but this one had the highest rankings and best outcomes. And I'd done my research.

If there was one thing I could do, it was research.

"Let's take our mind off all this tonight." Leo grabbed my hand and kissed up my arm, all the way to my neck, sending chills up my spine. "We haven't had a night in by ourselves in forever, you know?"

I turned toward him. "What do you want to do?"

"I want to feed you a hearty dinner, watch something on Netflix, give you a nice massage, and then make sweet love to you."

"Only if we can be in bed by ten," I challenged him. I was exhausted.

"Well, we better get a move on." He stood up. "Go put your feet up. I'll make a salad, and dinner should be ready in twenty minutes."

How did I manage to marry the best man in the universe? Seriously. I was beyond blessed.

He was going to make such a great dad.

seven

. . .

leo

A DAY off in the middle of the week might sound luxurious, but I was often too tired from the three or four days on shift prior that I couldn't make myself do much more than lounge around watching reruns of *NYPD Blue*. Maggie nearly always had to work, so it was just me and Blue hanging until the lady of the house returned. And, yes, Blue's name did come from that show.

Not from *Blue's Clues*, which my niece used to enjoy teasing me about.

I sat in the living room drinking coffee and thinking about how different our lives would be when we had a little one. I'd be on dad duty when I was off-shift and Maggie was at work. Arranging daycare coverage was going to be challenging since my schedule was so erratic. I was leaning toward trying to take a year off work with parental leave.

Did I know anything about newborns?

Not a chance. But I'd learn. Maggie and I would learn together.

The thought thrilled me. I wanted to see a baby in my wife's arms so badly, I...

I would do almost anything.

And then an idea struck me. An idea so wild, so crazy...

It would never work, right?

Well, there was no way to know without asking. I picked up my phone, pressed a few keys and waited.

raine

My first day at the theater in Brown County was short. They had me fill out some paperwork, gave me a tour of the facilities and the costume loft, and handed me a stack of plays they'd be producing. They asked for some sketches by the end of the following week.

I didn't realize I would get to work from home most of the time, but it made sense. They didn't exactly have an office for me. Their staff didn't have offices either. There was one small, cramped office for the house manager, and that was it. She was my boss, and she seemed thrilled to have me on board.

I was thrilled, too, because I needed something like this on my resume when I applied for full-time jobs. Which I would need as soon as I got my diploma.

If I got my diploma...

As I was driving the curving, hilly roads between Nashville and Bloomington, my phone buzzed with a text. I couldn't see who it was from, and all sorts of ideas fired off in my imagination. I couldn't help hoping it was from Maggie, though. I hadn't talked to her since our makeout session the previous week.

I hoped she wasn't upset that I allowed Leo to join in on

our date. He mostly just watched. I wondered what happened after I left.

As soon as I pulled into the parking lot at my apartment, I grabbed my phone and hurried to my text messages. I did not expect what I saw. It wasn't from Maggie, but close…

> Unknown Number: Hey, it's Leo Katz. I wondered if you had a moment to chat, just the two of us. I'm happy to buy you coffee. I'm free today, but we can work around your schedule. Let me know.

Suspicion rocked through me. Why would Leo want to talk to me alone? Was something wrong?

> Me: Uh, okay. I am home from work early. What did you have in mind?

> Leo: Meet you at Hounds & Grounds in an hour? I think I'm gonna bring Blue with me. He seems bored.

> Me: Oh, okay. See you there.

I hadn't been there before, but I knew of the small coffee shop located downtown on the square. The owners were huge dog lovers, and part of the shop's proceeds went to support local dog rescues. Blue and I might have gotten off on the wrong paw, so to speak, but he settled down later and wasn't completely obnoxious.

I left my dressy clothes on, a billowing, tiered Bohemian-style skirt, a chambray shirt open and tied at my waist over a white tank top, and accessorized with silver and turquoise jewelry. I changed out of my ankle-high moccasins and into silver sandals.

Bonnie came in while I was looking through the plays I'd be working on this summer. "You're back already?"

"And so are you?" I teased her. She was working as a research assistant for an eccentric professor, so it always seemed like she was coming and going at odd hours.

"How was it?" She ignored my jab.

I filled her in on my orientation at the theater and showed her the plays I'd be reading in the next week.

"So are you going somewhere else? You're all dressed up."

She was a regular detective, huh?

"Yeah, I'm meeting Leo Katz for coffee at Hounds & Grounds in about forty minutes," I shared.

Her eyes widened. "Maggie's husband?"

"Yeah." I scanned her face, and it was clear she was surprised by this turn of events, almost as surprised as I was when I received his text. "So, that's weird, right? That he would want to have coffee with me?"

She cocked her head as she thought about it for a moment. "He watched his wife lick your pussy the other night during your date, right?"

"Uh, yeah, so?" I bit my lip to stifle an embarrassed laugh.

"Well, he probably wants in on the action." She made pelvic thrusting motions and threw her head back like she was in ecstasy.

"Oh my god, stop that!" I begged her. "You think that's what's going on? He wants to date me too?"

"Couples love a unicorn," she said with a smirk.

Was I a unicorn? Did I want to be a unicorn?

I'd never dated more than one person at a time, and I'd never identified as polyamorous. Did Maggie and Leo want to change that?

I wasn't sure of the answers to my questions, but just the idea of it sent electric sparks racing up and down my spine. Then Bonnie killed the buzz.

"Any luck finding that missing jewelry?"

That was it. My spirits plummeted, making my whole body sag.

"No, and I told you about my meeting with the dean. She seemed pretty adamant that I was responsible. They are getting a lot of pushback from the jewelry's owner, like I said. So I don't know what to do. I won't even earn that much the entire summer working for the Brown County theater, and I still have to pay for rent, groceries and gas anyway."

"Have you considered other ways to make money?" Bonnie tilted her head as her gaze roamed over my face. "You could sell plasma. Or a kidney. Or eggs!"

"Eggs?" My nose wrinkled up. "From chickens?"

"No, dumbass, *your* eggs." She gestured to where her ovaries were.

I rolled my eyes. "Any suggestions that don't involve selling body parts."

"Only Fans?" Her eyebrows waggled.

"Again, something that doesn't involve selling myself?

"There are a lot of guys out there into feet, you know… I wouldn't dismiss the idea. I could take pictures for you. We could make those tootsies look so sexy, baby!" She was trying to restrain her giggle but failed miserably.

"I'm going to meet with Leo," I announced, even though I was early. I knew Bonnie meant well, but I didn't find any of her suggestions even remotely funny. This was a serious situation, and I died a little inside every time I tried to figure out the puzzle of how to raise twelve grand.

"Have fun!" Still laughing, she waved as I huffed in frustration, grabbed my purse and keys, and headed out the door.

Hounds & Grounds looked adorably charming with its checkered curtains and tablecloths with tiny paw prints in the white squares. I was early, so I ordered a latte and made my way to a table in the back that had a tiny bit more privacy, but still not a lot because the place was pretty small. I only sat there for a few minutes before Leo's burly form came through the door, making the bells ring.

Blue pulled tenaciously on his leash, trying to drag his master toward me, but he was no match for Leo's tall frame and bulky muscles. Leo looked a bit more relaxed in khaki shorts and a navy polo shirt than when I saw him last. That uniform, though, it did things to me. I had no clue I had a thing for uniforms until he appeared in his living room wearing his.

He waved and gestured to the counter, and I held up my porcelain mug to show I already had my drink. *Oh, yeah, he offered to buy. Oops. Well, no matter.*

Did Maggie know he was here? Did she send him? I had so many questions, and seeing him meant I was that much closer to the answers, if only he would hurry up and get his order so he could join me. Blue was definitely anxious to say hi. He stared at me the whole time his master was ordering and waiting for his coffee to be made.

A few minutes later, there they were, sitting across from me. After Blue excitedly greeted me, he occupied himself with a brand-new bone, looking as thrilled with it as we were with our coffees. After giving the furry demon some attention, I concentrated on his master, whose face was covered in dark scruff, and his eyes looked like two glittering gems as he made himself comfortable and took a sip of his coffee.

"So, how's it going?" Leo asked smoothly, like we did this every day.

"It's going," I assured him.

"Thanks for meeting me here. I know you were probably surprised to get my text, and, no, Maggie doesn't know yet," he revealed.

My brows furrowed as my eyes bounced between his. "She doesn't? Well, I don't know if that's a good idea. I thought you polyam folks believed in transparency and communication—everything on the up and up."

He looked as though he was about to choke on his coffee, his eyes widening. He set down his mug and wiped his lips with a napkin, clearly scrambling for an answer to my accusation.

"No, no—this isn't about our poly relationship." He shook his head, coughing to dispel a smirk that tried to creep across his face. "Sorry, I should have been more forthcoming in my text, but, to be honest, I had no idea how to broach the subject with you."

"What subject?" My heart kicked up into a faster beat. He was a cop. What he just said sounded...suspicious. His voice lowered at the end of his sentence. It made me think the subject in question might be...dangerous? Illegal?

Surely not. He's a cop.

And though he seemed to enjoy "dirty" activities, I didn't think he was a dirty cop.

He sighed, took a deep breath and then reached down to pet Blue. Whatever this was about seemed to make him nervous. I didn't think men like him got nervous. He looked like he ate nerves for breakfast. He carried a gun and dealt with hardened criminals, after all.

"I'm not sure how much Maggie told you, but we're dealing with…um…infertility," he enunciated the word like it had more syllables than it actually did.

"Well, she did say something about not being able to have kids," I remembered from our dinner at the Mexican place.

"Right. So we've been looking into surrogacy," he explained.

"Wait…what?"

"Surrogacy," he repeated, "you know, like someone to have our baby. All expenses paid, of course," he threw out right away. "There'd be a sizeable payment up front, and then monthly payments, and…"

He scrubbed his hands down his face. "I'm sorry, this is a stupid idea. I don't know why I even thought of it. I just… I want Maggie to have a baby so bad, and I mean, she wants to, you know? I just hate thinking her dreams of motherhood have been crushed. And we have to wait six months to even get an appointment with the surrogate agency, and—"

I sat there trying to absorb his words. My roommate's earlier jokes about selling body parts and products, including eggs, leaped to my mind. My fucking god, did these two chat about this beforehand? Was he asking to rent out my uterus? Buy my eggs? What. The. Actual. Fuck.

He scooted his chair away from the table, making an absolutely excruciating screech that made Blue stop chewing his bone. Leo stood up and gathered the dog's leash in his hand. "I'm sorry. It was wrong for me to ask you here today, especially without Maggie's knowledge. I probably fucking blew it for you guys, relationship-wise, and all because I just had this crazy idea that—"

"Wait," I repeated from earlier. "Can you sit back down a sec?"

He plopped down, looking completely dejected.

"Are you asking me to carry your baby?" I tried to keep my volume down, as there were a few other patrons at a nearby table.

"I was, but I don't know what I was thinking." He looked down at the table and shook his head again. "Forgive me? Please don't let this interfere with your relationship with my wife, okay? She had nothing to do with this. I was just off work today, and my imagination got a little carried away, and I—"

"Will you please just stop?" I was tired of his rambling apology. Trying to wrap my head around this completely unexpected proposition was making it hurt, but I kept going back to something he said about a payment? Downpayment and monthly payments?

"Sorry," he said again.

"Backing up a moment…I just want to make sure I understand what you're talking about. Because maybe I *could* help. But I've never had a baby before. Don't they like women who have already given birth once as surrogates?"

"Probably," he admitted, "I already said I didn't think this through very well. We just found out that we can't even get an appointment at the agency that matches you with surrogates until November. We're just getting impatient, that's all. She turns forty at the end of the year, and—"

"Well, assuming I could do it, how much would it pay?" *Please be more than twelve grand*, I added in my head.

"I don't really know, but I think the going rate is like fifty thousand," he shared.

I nearly fell out of my chair.

"Are you okay?" He reached out to steady me when I nearly had a rude meeting with the floor. And Blue, who seemed rather concerned about me and started licking my hand.

"You're serious about this," I confirmed, "not bullshitting me?"

He had the tiniest glimmer of hope in his dark eyes. "You would consider it?"

I straightened my back and sat tall in my chair. Well, as tall as I could with my five-foot frame. "I'd want to talk to Maggie about it and, of course, know the logistics, but I'm not saying no."

A smile curled his lips ever so slightly upward. "Okay, yeah, of course. We'd have to get all our cards lined up, our ducks in a row, all of that. Don't tell Maggie yet, please? I want to mention the idea to her first and see if she thinks it's absolutely crazy, and then... I don't know... We'd probably have to talk to a doctor or something. I have no idea, but, my god, I'm so glad you're willing to consider it."

He reached across the table and squeezed my hand. "I want a baby too, of course, don't get me wrong. But it's been Maggie's lifelong dream to be a mother, and...I want to give that to her so bad, I... Well, I'm willing to do almost anything."

I smiled. He was so sincere—it was beautiful to see how much he loved his wife. Relationship goals for me someday, huh?

But, wow, if this worked out...I wouldn't have to worry about the money I owed the theater department. I could graduate and get on with my life as soon as I had the baby...

My god! Was I actually considering this? It was crazy, right?

But I really couldn't afford not to. And Maggie and Leo were some of the best people I'd ever met. If I could help make their dreams come true while also solving my own problems? It sounded like a win-win to me.

eight

. . .

maggie

THE WEEKEND COULDN'T GET HERE FAST enough. I was getting ready for a date with Raine when my phone buzzed with a text from her. My heart immediately leaped, hoping she wasn't canceling.

> Raine: Hey…just curious what Leo is up to today?

> Me: Nothing, really. He's off work. Why?

> Raine: Do you think he'd like to join us? It's okay if he doesn't…just thought it might be fun.

I left the message on read for a bit while I finished applying makeup. We were going for a hike at McCormick's Creek State Park, which was about a half hour away from Bloomington. Leo had already expressed disappointment when we made the plans because he loves hiking, and he was off work on a rare Saturday.

I sighed. Leo was attracted to her—especially after the scene that played out in our living room during our last date, but I didn't know if Raine felt the same about him. Judging by her text, she did. Maybe we had found our unicorn—without even looking?

> Raine: I hope I didn't upset you by asking. I just haven't been able to get the other night out of my mind…

I didn't want her to think I was upset. I wasn't. This was what we wanted all along, right?

> Me: That was pretty hot, wasn't it? Hold on —I'll ask him if he'd like to join us.

"Honey?" I called out into the hallway.

Leo came lumbering up the stairs, holding a mug of coffee. "What do you need?"

"Hey, Raine asked if you'd like to join us today on our hike?"

His entire face lit up. "Really?" And then, "But I don't want to be a third wheel. If you'd rather I stay here…"

"You like her, don't you?" I asked—not in an accusatory way. I tried to keep my tone playful. She was young and hot. Why wouldn't he like her? And she seemed to be kind, smart, funny. Truly, I couldn't think of any negatives where Raine was involved.

"Well, of course I do." He walked down the hall, stopping right in front of where I stood in the doorway. My phone remained on my vanity, waiting for an answer.

"Then come. It'll be fun." I reached out and stroked my fingers across his stubbly jaw. Being off work today meant he didn't shave, and his scruff was so fucking sexy.

In seconds, his arms were around me, pulling me into his thick, muscular chest. "You're the best, you know that? So generous...so beautiful... If you didn't just finish getting ready, I'd throw you down on that bed and fuck your brains out," he teased me.

"Well, damn, why didn't I ask you ten minutes ago before I got dressed?" I bit my lip and fluttered my eyelashes at him.

"Don't tempt me," he practically growled. "When do you need to leave?"

"When do we need to leave," I corrected him. "Fifteen minutes. If we want to get to the park by ten, which is when we're supposed to meet."

"I can be ready by then." His smile was electric. "Should I shave?"

"No. Leave it. It's sexy." His Italian heritage meant he could grow a beard in just a few days, so every time he had more than two days off work in a row, I got to see that sexy scruff outline his jaw. Damn, it did things to me.

"Okay, but be warned that I'm going to claim that fucking your brains out appointment when we get home."

"Promise?"

He grinned. "Promise."

I texted Raine back.

Me: He's in. See you at 10!

McCormick's Creek was busier than I thought it would be, even on a Saturday in June. I was hoping we'd have a little more privacy on our hike, but it was not meant to be.

Hopefully we'd at least be able to find a quiet spot for our picnic.

"This is so gorgeous!" Raine carefully traversed the creek via the flat stones rising out of the water. "Look at that waterfall! This is my first time visiting here."

"I'm glad you were free." I stepped on the rock behind her but started to lose my balance.

"Oh no!" she shrieked as we both toppled over into the shin-deep water.

"Great, now we're wet! I'm so sorry!" my apology gushed out of me.

Leo, who had already crossed the creek, turned around and spotted us splashing around. "What happened, ladies? Wait, don't move! I want to get a picture!" He pulled out his phone and aimed it toward us.

"We should at least make this worth his while." Raine gave me a suggestive wink.

"What did you have in mind?" There was a family on the other side of the creek where we'd come from, but they seemed to be busy navigating their own crossing and trying to avoid ending up in the creek like we did.

"Kiss me?" Raine's dark eyebrows quirked.

I drew her into my arms and pressed my lips against hers as Leo let out a whoop. I was afraid the family would make a comment, but they didn't.

"Got a great pic!" Leo beamed when we finished crossing the creek, and he pulled both of us up on the bank. "Let's hike down closer to the waterfall."

We made our way down the narrow trail, enamored by the way the sunlight filtered through the bright green leaves. There was a gentle breeze that took the edge off the climbing heat, and though soggy shoes and socks were no fun, at least my feet weren't hot.

Once we made it down closer to the waterfall, there was no one around. "You know, I should get a shot of you two." I gestured toward Raine and Leo.

"Oh?" My husband's brow shot upward. "The same kind of shot?"

I studied Raine's face to see if she seemed interested or repulsed by the idea, and it was definitely the former. She looked adorable in her cut-off overalls with a tiny floral tank top underneath. Her hair was pinned back with a pink paisley bandana, and she was wearing tiny watermelon earrings to complete the look.

"Let's do it!" Raine quickly agreed and posed herself on one of the rocks that jutted out into the creek. Leo stepped in next to her and draped his arm around her shoulder.

I snapped a pic. "Got it. Now—a kiss?"

They turned toward each other, and there was not as much awkwardness as I expected. Leo said something to her that I couldn't hear over the rushing water, and Raine smiled and nodded. He tenderly stroked a finger down her cheek before bending to capture her lips with his. It was a long, sweet kiss, and I got the whole thing on video for posterity's sake.

So…we were really doing this…

I wasn't sure how, but we managed to find a picnic spot that was shady, comfortable and not people-y. Go Leo for scouting it out!

Raine and I spread out the blanket while Leo got the picnic basket and cooler from our SUV. We both made whoops and cat-calls while he flexed his muscles carrying it back to the blanket.

"Look at those sexy arms!" Raine praised as he sat down between us.

He did have damn fine arms—thick, muscular, and perfect to wrap around you. I didn't mind sharing with a beautiful lady like Raine. Especially not when I got to touch her too.

Raine and Leo exchanged a little look as I dug into the picnic basket. I couldn't quite tell what it was all about, but it was something private.

"More hiking after this, or are you ready to call it a day?" Leo asked.

"Whatever you guys would like," Raine said. "I don't have any plans today."

"What do you want to do, hon?"

Leo smiled at both of us. "I was kind of thinking we could go back to our house after this. Maybe I could grill out some steaks tonight. Might be a nice night for the hot tub?"

"I'd have to go home to shower and change clothes first," Raine said, "but that sounds like fun."

This was moving fast. Leo was more aggressive than I was—and maybe that was a good thing. Raine didn't seem fazed by it at all. I popped the tab on the soda I pulled out of the cooler and swallowed down a big gulp. I hoped I could keep up with these two.

"I've never done a hiking date," I admitted before I stuffed a grape in my mouth, "but it's kind of nice."

"I didn't expect to get so wet on this type of date," Raine joked, flashing me a grin.

"Yeah, sorry about that. I was staring at your ass and lost my balance!" I apologized.

"You two looked so sexy in that water," Leo said. "Good

thing that family was there, or I would have wanted to fuck you both under the waterfall."

"Damn, honey, tell us how you really feel!" I teased him, and Raine bubbled up with laughter.

There was an easy vibe between us as we enjoyed the sandwiches and fruit I'd packed. Leo reclined with his head on my lap while Raine told us about her summer job at the theater.

"So, you read the plays, and you come up with costume designs?" Leo asked. "How do you decide what kind of costumes?"

Raine smiled and explained, "I look at a lot of things, like the type of character it is, the historical period, their socioeconomic status. Colors and fabrics can be used to convey a lot of character attributes too, like their disposition or motives, you know? And there's tons of research you can do online about what kind of costumes have been used in other productions. Naturally, you want to come up a unique take on it, but some characters have really classic costumes—think Dorothy from *The Wizard of Oz* or Annie's red dress from Daddy Warbucks, you know?"

"That's really cool," I ran my fingers through Leo's hair to catch a blade of grass that was stuck there, "and makes my job seem so boring."

"My job's not boring, but it definitely isn't that much fun," Leo added.

"I know it seems like it's all fun and games," she said, "but it's actually hard work. You have to take a lot of things into consideration, and then sometimes you can't find what you're looking for in the costume lofts or any rental agencies, so you have to sew it yourself or find a seamstress. And it's not like you just need a few costumes. Depending on the show, you may need hundreds of costumes. And you have to keep track of them all."

"Oh, I didn't mean to imply your job was easy," I defended, "just that mine seems boring by comparison."

Raine shrugged. "Well, we all have different talents."

"I'd like to show you some of my talents," Leo interjected.

I smacked him on the shoulder. "Leave it to you to turn an innocent conversation into something sexual!"

But Raine was laughing, obviously amused by his joke. "I hope to experience these talents you speak of…maybe later tonight?"

Well, he'd certainly succeeded in bringing her out of her shell. She had been slightly reserved with me, but she seemed more open, more adventurous with him. I hoped I'd be the beneficiary of that openness…

nine

. . .

leo

I HAD both of these beautiful ladies just where I wanted them. And I'd had all day to bring up the idea I'd mentioned to Raine but had failed to do it. I couldn't bring it up during sex…but that was what remained on the table as far as opportunities were concerned.

We'd eaten a hearty dinner of grilled steaks, baked potatoes, asparagus, flaky croissants, and wine, and, after a stimulating conversation, we climbed into the hot tub to continue our time together. Surrogacy didn't seem like a hot tub topic to me. Especially not when my wife and Raine started fondling each other under the surface of the bubbling water.

"That feels good," floated out of Raine's mouth, more breath than voice, as my wife stroked her back.

"Sore from the hike?" she asked, massaging the tension out of the younger woman's shoulders.

"No," she shook her head, "not from the hike, but maybe from poring over those plays the last few days."

My wife's voice oozed with concern and sensuality, "Oh,

well, we don't want that. We want to get you nice and relaxed. Do you want more wine?"

"More wine might be nice." She opened her eyes briefly, and they landed on me before drifting closed again.

"I'll pour you some." I scooted the tray with the glasses and half-full wine bottle closer to the edge of the hot tub and filled all three glasses to the halfway mark. Then I crossed the bubbly cauldron to deliver their glasses.

"Thank you, handsome." Maggie smiled and took a sip while Raine did the same.

I watched while they both placed their glasses on the edge of the tub and Maggie maneuvered herself so she was straddling our guest. "I need those lips," she sighed as she tilted Raine's chin up to meet her mouth. As she hungrily devoured her lips, my cock swelled under the water.

God, I wanted to sink this cock deep inside my wife while she licked Raine's pussy. I wanted one of them to ride my cock while the other rode my face. Just thinking about all the different combinations and positions we could get into tonight made my balls tight with need.

The other night when Raine was here, I just watched. But after she left, Maggie let me fuck her over the couch like I had the night after she danced with Raine at The Barn. I came so fucking hard imagining this scene unfolding right now in reality.

Could the reality live up to the fantasy? That was always the question, wasn't it?

"Hey, what about me?" I captured their attention. "I like watching and all, but I sure would like some attention too." I stood from the water, gripping my thick, hard cock in one hand, steam rising off my body as two pairs of hooded eyes zeroed in on my hand stroking up and then back down again.

Raine stood and walked toward me, pressing her body against me as she pulled me down into a kiss. My cock throbbed against her thighs as her tongue tangled with mine. Then Maggie came behind her, reaching her hands between us to cup and fondle Raine's breasts as we continued to kiss.

"Come here," Maggie directed us both, tugging Raine down onto the seat next to her and jerking me forward to stand in front of them. My cock was at the perfect height for their mouths.

Oh, damn…

"What do you think of my husband's cock?" Maggie took Raine's hand and wrapped her fingers around my thickness.

"It looks absolutely perfect. Nice length, so thick." She stroked me from base to tip, making my eyes roll back in my head.

"I think you should see how it feels in your mouth," Maggie suggested, and I whimpered as Raine lowered her head, her tongue darting out to tentatively lick a stripe around my head.

"Mmm…" She moaned as she licked up my shaft, teasing me as Maggie cupped my balls and gently kneaded them.

"He likes to have them played with," she shared with our guest.

"Duly noted." She swiped up my cock again with her tongue before putting the tip in her mouth and sucking lightly while Maggie squeezed my balls a little harder.

Fuck…these two…they were gonna make me come so fucking hard. I hoped I could last long enough to give them both plenty of orgasms.

"See if you can take him all the way down your throat," Maggie challenged Raine as she looked up at me with a devilish glint in her eyes.

Raine accepted the challenge, sliding her mouth down my shaft until she sputtered and choked. She made it about three-quarters of the way, sending a shock of pleasure right through me.

"That's pretty good," Maggie praised. "Here, watch me." She positioned herself closer to me as Raine moved aside. My wife sank her mouth down on my cock, taking me in my entirety to the back of her throat, almost as though she unhinged her jaw. She managed to use the back of her throat to suck at my head, making me weak in the knees.

"Fuck, you better stop that, or I'm gonna come down your throat," I warned her.

"Oops, better back off—wanna save some cum for Raine." She popped off, licking her lips. "What's wrong, big guy? Can't handle two hungry ladies?"

"We'll see if you can handle this cock buried deep inside your pussies, how about that?" I backed up and climbed out of the tub, handing both of them a towel. "Dry off, then get on the bed. I'll be right there."

I needed to cool down for a second, or I'd never last. My two beautiful lovers followed my instructions, drying each other off with their towels, stopping to fondle and kiss as they went.

Fuck me. These two were gonna be hard to handle. And I was gonna love every minute of it.

I put the hot tub cover on as they made their way inside. I hoped moving around in the brisk night air would soften my erection, at least a little, but I was hard as ever as I returned to our bedroom to find my two little cumsluts lying dutifully side by side on the bed. They were giggling and touching each other, but they had obeyed my command.

"Good girls," I praised them as I climbed onto the mattress, my knees sinking into the softness as I crawled toward them. They were both naked, their lovely curves displayed for my viewing pleasure.

Their bodies were both beautiful but in different ways. Maggie was a little taller, with smaller breasts but bigger nipples. Her stomach was rounded with a soft curve that slightly draped over her mound. Her shoulders were narrower, and her hips were wider than Raine's.

Raine was a bit more compact but with larger breasts and smaller nipples. The curve between her waist and hips wasn't as defined as Maggie's, but her thighs were nice and thick, and I knew that ass was begging to be played with.

"Like what you see?" Maggie's voice broke the silence as I studied the masterpieces of their nude forms.

"Well, what do you think?" I rocked back on my heels, presenting my thick cock for their perusal. "I'm just trying to decide what I want to do first and to whom."

"I think Raine's pussy needs some attention," Maggie suggested with a soft smile.

Memories of kissing her by the waterfall flooded my mind. Her lips were so soft, all I could think about was tasting them again. I grinned and nodded at my wife before swinging a leg over Raine's hips to straddle her. "May I kiss you?"

She nodded, her lips parted in anticipation. I cradled her head in one hand as I lowered my mouth to hers, tentatively brushing my lips against hers before swiping at the seam between them with my tongue. She opened to me, allowing me to sweep my tongue inside, swallowing her moan as it escaped her throat. I nibbled on her lips as she arched into me, pressing her bare pussy into my engorged cock.

Oh god, I was going to enjoy fucking her for the first time. But I needed to make her come on my tongue first.

I broke the kiss and moved down her body, kissing every

inch along the way. As soon as I made it to her breasts, Maggie rolled toward her, guiding Raine's head to turn her way so she could kiss her while I teased her nipples into hard points. Her little mewls of need spurred me on as I continued in a southerly direction to her adorable softly dimpled stomach and her mound, decorated with springy black curls.

Maggie usually preferred herself clean-shaven, but there was something about natural pubic hair I found so earthy and enticing. I breathed in her cherries and vanilla scent as she thrust her hips up to me, begging for more contact. I held her thighs down with my hands as I pressed kisses to her curls and continued lower until I could part her labia with the tip of my tongue.

She jolted underneath me as I found her clit, teasing it until it swelled more and more with each stroke. Her sweet flavor burst on my taste buds as I dove in, fucking her slick pink flesh with my tongue until she was writhing beneath me. I stilled for a moment, lifting my chin to witness my wife suckling Raine's nipples as Raine's fingers twisted in her hair and expletives fell from her lips.

Her thighs tensed as I slid a finger inside her, curling to hit her G-spot, and she bowed off the bed in response. "Fuck, don't stop," she gasped as Maggie moved to her other nipple, eliciting a squeal that was somewhere on the edge of pain and pleasure.

She was close, and I couldn't wait for her to come on my face like she did Maggie's the other night. But I wanted to draw out her orgasm, edge her a bit to make it more intense. She was leaking juices onto my tongue as I continued to lash her clit and fuck her with two fingers, but I held back a little. She grunted in frustration as she thrust up into my face, grinding her mound into me.

"More…oh my god…I'm so fucking close…"

I had her right where I wanted her. I considered sheathing myself in a condom and sliding deep inside her to feel her quaking from the inside out, but, no, I wanted to give this to her. I suddenly remembered our conversation over coffee—how she said she would think about my proposition—but we hadn't had a chance to discuss it.

A wild fantasy of fucking her raw and spurting my seed deep inside her, breeding her, rocked through me. I damn near thought I was going to come right there, my cock pressed against the mattress as my fingers rocked into Raine and my tongue circled her clit.

But Maggie had moved again and was now straddling Raine's face, letting Raine lick her cunt while she held on to the headboard for balance. Fuck, that was hot. My wife's ass was visible, moving up and down, and then my fantasy shifted to fucking her tight back hole while she buried her face in Raine's cunt.

Damn it, there were too many things…and I was making a huge wet spot on the sheets.

"Please, more, faster, harder," Raine managed to groan, the sound muffled as Maggie fucked her face.

I sped up the tempo, sucking her clit into my mouth, then I held on for dear life as her whole body convulsed beneath me, her orgasm rocking through us both as she screamed in pleasure. Maggie was coming at the same time, her own mouth expertly spewing obscenities as any silver-tongued lawyer would in the throes of ecstasy.

When the aftermath was over, and both ladies lay recovering side by side, I rocked back on my heels and observed them, licking my lips to savor the fading flavor of Raine's pussy.

It was Raine's head that popped up first. "Leo…will you fuck me now?"

I looked at Maggie, who nodded. I went to grab a condom, but Raine put her arm on me.

"We talked about it," she said. "You don't need one."

maggie

While my handsome and very-much-aroused husband cooled off and took care of the hot tub cover, I slipped inside the house with Raine. We had a quick chat about limits and STIs.

"We were tested last month," I told her. "I have it here on my app if you want to see." I gestured to my phone on the bedside table.

"No, no, I don't need to see." Raine waved me off. "I believe you."

"When were you last tested?" I gave her an expectant look.

"Oh…well…it's been like a year, but…I haven't been with anyone since I last got tested." She smiled. "Sorry, grad students don't get out much." She shrugged sheepishly.

"No need to apologize about that. What about birth control?" I ran down the checklist in my head.

"I'm covered there," she said. "You guys don't use condoms with other partners?"

"Not if everyone has a recent negative test…"

Her eyes grew wide, so I definitely needed to explain.

"We don't really do this very often, Raine. It's been a long time since either of us have had another partner, and, to be honest, we were trying to get pregnant. After we found out I can't conceive or carry a baby, that's when we decided to start dating other people again. A lot of the women Leo and I have dated have been older—they've had hysterectomies or their tubes are tied. Pregnancy wasn't a possibility. And…we don't make a habit of fucking strangers. At least not like we did in our late twenties—whew, that was a—" Seeing her eyes widen again, I opted not to finish that statement. "Anyway, we've had committed relationships in the past few years. Fluid-bonded, if you will."

"Fluid-bonded?" Her curiosity appeared to be piqued if her eyebrow arch was anything to go by.

"Yeah, meaning that we only share bodily fluids amongst our committed partners. It doesn't mean *you* can't have any other partners, it just means you agree to use condoms with them if you aren't with us," I explained.

"Oh…"

"Is that something you'd be interested in?" I smiled. I could tell this was all a bit overwhelming for her—a lot to throw at her all at once. And we'd been drinking. We should have discussed this before dinner. I was out of practice.

I shook my head. "You know what? Let's not decide that now. Let's wait until next time when we're all sober and clear-headed. We'll use condoms tonight, okay? I really do hope this will become a regular thing. I really like you, Raine, and I know Leo does too."

She blushed, the color extending onto her bare chest. "I'm pretty sober right now, actually. And I like you guys too…"

"We better get up on the bed before he comes back. We wouldn't want to be disobedient girls, would we?" I winked at her.

"No, ma'am!" She climbed onto the bed and gave me a devilish grin.

That was how we left it when Leo came back in the room from the deck.

And then, when it came time for him to put on a condom and fuck her… she said, "We talked about it. You don't need one."

The look that flickered across my husband's face was one of pure primal passion. "I can't wait to feel that pussy squeezing me tight." He tapped the tip of his cock against her clit.

She whimpered and arched her back. "Please?"

"Be a good girl now and take this cock inch by inch," he groaned as he pushed very slowly inside her until he was balls-deep. A mixture of bliss and need crossed his face as her gasp filled the space between us.

"Fuck her, Leo," I encouraged him, getting behind him on my knees and wrapping my hands around his chest to play with his nipples. He loved that.

He leaned forward and thrust inside her, pumping a few times as he grabbed her legs and pushed them back for deeper access. "Oh, fuck…you feel so damn good, Raine. I can feel you throbbing."

I moved from my position, crawling to her until my face was in line with hers. "Are you gonna come on my husband's cock?"

She gritted out "yes" as I twisted her nipple hard between my fingers, then soothed it with my tongue.

"You're such a good girl taking his cock like that. How does it feel inside you?"

"So good," she gasped as he hit a particularly sensitive spot.

I kissed her then, tonguing her mouth in rhythm with Leo's thrusts as he began to make the noises I knew meant he was getting close to climax. I really wanted Raine to come before he did, so I reached down between their bodies and played with her clit.

Leo rocked back, holding her legs up as he drilled into her, giving me room to work. I lowered my head to her clit, and her hands immediately went into my hair, pushing me closer as she ground her face against me. His cock brushed against my cheek as I sucked on her swollen bud, and it wasn't long before they were both coming, screaming out into the stillness as they both coated me with their cum.

How fucking beautiful is this moment? Sharing something like this with my man and a beautiful woman I could easily see myself falling in love with.

How fucking beautiful indeed.

ten

. . .

raine

"I CAN'T BELIEVE I'm telling you this," I confessed to Danielle, "but it was literally the hottest sex I've ever had in my life."

My friend's eyes grew as she licked her ice cream cone, but she didn't dare interrupt.

"Seriously, it's so intense having two people's hands and mouths on you!" I closed my eyes to enjoy a flash of vivid memory as it painted a picture in my mind.

She paused her licking and grinned at me. "Well, duh. I coulda told you that!"

"Maggie drove me absolutely wild with her tongue, and Leo…fuck…he is an amazing kisser. And sucking his cock with his wife in the hot tub was—"

Danielle made a loud throat-clearing noise and then put her hand parallel to the table. "Shh, there are kids nearby."

"Oops!" The memories and feelings were coming back so strongly, I had to clench my thighs together. I swallowed hard to get myself under control, then glanced around to see who had filled the small area in the ice cream parlor. Uh, yeah, there were three or four kiddos here now.

"So, you guys are like a throuple or what?" Dani asked as she reached her cone and took a big crunchy bite.

"I mean, I don't know. We haven't really given it a label yet." I sighed. "But I do have an issue…"

"What's that?" She took another crunchy bite of the cone. I'd talked so much that my ice cream was starting to melt. I stirred it with my spoon and took a small bite of the creamy raspberry goodness.

"Well…I had coffee with Leo a few days before our date to the park and the whole hot tub night," I began. "And Maggie doesn't know."

"What? That's not cool, Rainey; that's not how poly works. I can't believe Leo would do that!" she protested, her voice rising in volume.

I made my own "keep it down" gesture as she rolled her eyes. "Well, it wasn't a date. It was a proposition."

"What do you mean?" Dani stuffed the rest of the cone in her mouth and chewed as she awaited my answer.

"Okay, this is going to sound weird, but…" Ugh, I didn't know how to say this without it sounding super weird. Because it was weird, or, at the very least, unconventional. Especially when I thought about Maggie telling me their preference for being fluid-bonded.

"Just spit it out, girl! You're making me anxious, and that can't be good for the bébé, you know?" She patted her tummy.

"Fine. So, speaking of babies…" *That seems like a natural segue way, right?* "They want one."

"Oh yeah?"

"Yes. And Leo wanted to know if I would carry it." I dropped that bomb right there and waited for the aftermath.

Danielle crumped up her napkin in her hand. "Holy shit. What, like a surrogate?"

"I guess so. He told me they were pursuing surrogacy because Maggie can't conceive or carry a baby, and she told me the same thing. Well, not the surrogacy part, but the part about not being able to have a baby. And, well, he said it was going to take six months to get an appointment with the surrogate agency, and that the going rate for surrogates is like fifty grand!"

"Whoa!" Danielle's eyes were as wide as our two scoops of ice cream had been. "So they want to pay you? Do you mean like go through a doctor's office or like…um…you know, the old-fashioned way?"

"I don't know. He was just testing the waters, trying to see if I would even consider it before he discussed it with Maggie. But, damn, Dani, I have to say that I'm considering it either way… Like, I could really fucking use that money. It would take care of my bill at the university, and it would really help me make ends meet until I get a full-time job."

"But then you'd…you'd be a mom, Raine." Danielle suddenly wore a sober expression. "You'd be bringing a child into the world, but it wouldn't be yours. Do you think you could do that? Like carry a baby for nine months and then give it to them?"

I hadn't thought much about how things would be after the birth, to be honest. But…yeah, that was what it amounted to, right? "I don't know. I mean…they are such an amazing couple, and Leo almost brought me to tears talking about how much he wants to see his wife as a mom, how it's all she's ever wanted."

Danielle looked worried now as her eyes roved over my face. "They're not just using you, are they?" came out barely louder than a whisper.

"Oh, god, Dani, I don't think they would do that. Hasn't Noah known them for a while? He trusts Maggie, right? And, like, Maggie is the one who first approached me. Leo didn't come into it until later, but then he's the one who mentioned…" I huffed out a long sigh and closed my eyes as I collected my thoughts. "I don't know what to do. It just seemed like such a win-win, you know? Like I would be able to pay my debt and graduate, and they'd get a baby."

"Well, there's a lot that would have to happen first. You'd have to get pregnant. You'd have to carry the baby. You'd have to deliver said baby. You're making it sound like an easy transaction, and as someone who is going through pregnancy right now, well…I think that might be a little short-sighted on your part."

"You're right." I leaned back, nodding. "And I'm putting the cart before the horse anyway because he hasn't even talked to Maggie about it." I sighed again. "But the money… damn it, I really need that money."

She reached over and covered my palm with hers, which was warm and a little sticky. "I know you do, but try not to let that decide for you. Besides, you're on the Pill, right?"

I nodded. "Yeah, have been for years…just to regulate my cycles."

"Well, you'd have to go off that before you did anything. It might be a while before you could even conceive."

"True." She'd given me a lot of realistic shit to think about. I was a dreamer, an idealist, an artist. Having to plod through all the logistics and contingencies was not my thing. "Sorry for bringing all this up, Dani—"

She waved her hand, brushing aside my apology. "Don't be silly. You're one of my closest friends, Raine. You and Cynda, really, are my best friends. And I've gotten to know Molly and Poe, and I think the world of them too. They would be good to talk to about poly stuff, you know. Cynda, especially. She has tons of experience."

"Thanks…I'm just kind of reeling right now, you know? This all came out of nowhere, so I'm scrambling to figure things out." I took another bite of my now soupy ice cream.

"That's perfectly understandable, my friend. Perfectly understandable. I'm here for you, whatever you need," Dani assured me.

"I know you have your own stuff to worry about." I set my spoon down. Why did leaning on friends have to be so hard for me? I always felt guilty. Like I had to earn friendship and love. "Everything going well with the pregnancy?"

She sighed. "Things would be great if I could go more than a day without puking. I'm in the second trimester now. It should be over. Aris and Noah have been arguing over which one of their spawn would be more likely to give me morning sickness," she joked with an eye roll. "Those two. It's never a dull moment with them."

I grabbed her hand and squeezed it. "Well, I'm over-the-moon excited for you. Who knows? Maybe we'll end up being pregnant at the same time?"

"That would be fun," she agreed, running her fingers through her long chestnut-brown hair. "You know what? If you'd told me last year at this time we'd be having this conversation a year later, I'd have called you crazy."

"I know, right?" I shook my head. "Things change fast."

"Like lightning speed," she said. "Except for pregnancy —which happens at approximately a snail's pace."

We both laughed at that. She was still glowing, even if she was spending an inordinate amount of time throwing up. My friend was gonna make a great mom. Like me, she had a strained relationship with her own mother, but she excelled at everything she did. I had no doubt motherhood would be among her best starring roles.

leo

I wasn't expecting to get a text from Raine this afternoon asking me if I was available. I told her I was on nights, and I only had two hours before I had to get ready for work. She asked if she could drop by to chat about my proposition, so I said yes.

She arrived only twenty minutes later, wearing a summery dress with white flowers on a black background. "Hey, thanks for letting me stop by. I won't take up too much of your time."

The way she said that made my heart sink, like she was preparing me for bad news. I swallowed hard and forced a smile. "No problem. Do you want some coffee?"

"Sure, that sounds nice, thanks." She followed me into the kitchen, where I set out two coffee mugs and coffee pods.

While we waited for the coffee to brew, I asked, "Hope you're not too weirded out by what happened last week."

She laughed and waved her hand. "Oh, no, 'weird' is definitely not the word I would use. I really enjoyed myself. Hope you and Maggie did too."

"I was worried Maggie would be upset that I was butting into her girl time," I admitted. "But she said she enjoyed herself. She told me she would text you the next day. Hope she did." I had purposely not contacted Raine because I didn't want to seem pushy about the idea I'd mentioned. I'd been waiting for her to bring it up.

"Yes, yes, we've been texting. I'm going to see her tomorrow for lunch, actually. I'm still working at home this week, reading plays and working on my designs. I won't have to go back down to Brown County for two weeks, when they're ready for fittings."

"Oh, okay, great. It's nice you can do that work from home." I handed her the first mug of coffee and started the second one for me.

"Yeah, well, I don't have an office at the theater, so no choice, really. It's just a summer job. It doesn't pay much, but I'm hoping it will help me when it comes time to apply for real jobs."

"So…" I had to admit I was curious about her future plans, not only because I liked her and was interested in her, but also because her plans determined whether or not she was able to help out with our issue. "When will you be 'applying for real jobs,'" I used air quotes, "and where do you anticipate these jobs being?"

"You want to know if I'm leaving the area," she picked up right away.

"Well, yeah." I grabbed my coffee mug and stirred a little creamer into it—half and half, not the frou-frou oat milk caramel macchiato shit my wife liked. "Not just because of the logistics of…the proposition. But because Maggie and I both like you and…well, we're poly. We tend to get attached to people."

"Right. That's understandable." She looked like she was trying to figure out a way to let me down easily. "The truth is…I don't really know what the future holds. Planning is kind of difficult right now."

"Okay…" I let the syllable resonate for a couple beats.

I ushered her over to the little breakfast nook at the back of the house. The big windows looked out over the back-yard, including the hot tub. Just seeing it caused a little thrill to race through me when memories of our time out there bombarded me.

She took a seat and sipped her coffee before setting the mug down on the table. "I have a problem, and right now it's looking like it might keep me from graduating."

"Oh?"

"So…this is going to sound so weird and convoluted, but bear with me." When I nodded, she continued, "I checked a costume out of our wardrobe department a few months ago. I needed to study it for a design I'm creating for my thesis. It was the dress I was interested in, but it came with some accessories, which I never opened. One of the things in the accessories case was a rather expensive gold and pearl jewelry set, and now the department is expecting me to pay them back for it. They're going to withhold my diploma until I do."

"My god, Raine…that sounds terrible." Now it made sense why she was being elusive about her future plans. Her future was up in the air. "And there's no way to prove you're not responsible for the set?"

"Nope," she popped the P on the end of the word. "I signed out the piece and signed it back in, and supposedly it was checked both times."

I couldn't help but go into cop mode. "How much time passed before they let you know the set was missing?"

She cocked her head. "I've known for a few weeks now. Why would that matter?"

"But there was a lag between when you borrowed it and when they let you know?" I pressed.

"Yes. A little over a month." She took another sip of coffee, her eyes nervously darting between the mug and me.

"Hmmm… sounds like there could be some legal ramifications here. Where was the piece stored while you had it checked out?" I had already crossed over into detective mode. There was no stopping me now. Leo Katz was on the case.

"I bet you're good at your job," she said, smirking. "But, to answer your question, it was checked out to me, but it was stored in the costuming lab the whole time, which lots of other people have access to."

"Well, then. It seems pretty unfair to assume you're the one who lost or stole the jewelry," I said.

"That's what I said!" she agreed, nodding vehemently. "But I have zero power, and the dean and the Costume Czar are in cahoots. What else can I do?"

"Go to campus police?" I suggested. "See if they will investigate? Are there cameras in the lab?"

She rolled her eyes. "I don't have any contacts there, and I really doubt they're going to go out of their way to help me."

"I have some contacts in the IUPD," I offered. "I can put out some feelers for you if you'd like."

I didn't mean for "feelers" to come out loaded with innuendo, but it did. And it made her giggle. That beautiful sound made my cock hard…and there was nothing I could do about it when I had work in another hour or so, and Maggie and I hadn't established any parameters about playing with Raine alone.

I hoped that was something we could agree to, but…

"So," she folded her hands together, "I appreciate you doing that for me, but, in the meantime, I wanted to talk about your…other offer."

"Oh, right." I grabbed the mug again to take another sip of coffee, which had finally cooled to a comfortable temperature.

"Well, I'm considering it…strongly," she shared, her tone wavering between guarded and pragmatic. "I need the money if I have to pay for that jewelry, but, truth be told, I need it anyway. I'm a poor grad student, after all. And having a cushion as I try to get my adult life rolling would be super helpful. My car isn't going to last forever, and—"

"It sounds like you're trying to rationalize doing it," I cut her off. "You don't have to justify it to me. If you have to justify it to yourself, maybe it's not the right decision."

She looked down at her mug and bit her lip. When she looked up, her eyes looked sad. "Did you change your mind? Did Maggie say no?"

I shook my head. "It's not that. I haven't spoken with Maggie about it yet because I wanted to hear back from you first on whether or not it's even something you'd be interested in pursuing. I don't know…from a medical point of view…what all we'd need to do."

"Well, I'm on the Pill," she shared, "so the first thing would be to go off it."

"I don't want you to do anything you're not comfortable with, one hundred percent. And I know some might think talking to you first before mentioning it to my wife is wrong, but, honestly, I couldn't bear to get her hopes up that this crazy idea of mine might work out unless we both really thought it could."

"I don't think you're wrong for asking me first," she assured me. "The way you talk about Maggie, about your marriage, and how much you want to have a kid… I have nothing but respect, Leo. The amount of love and care you have for her," her eyes got a little misty as she finished her thought, "well, I hope to have that someday for myself."

I smiled and patted her hand. "You will. I have no doubt."

"Well, put my hat in the ring," she said. "I know it's time-sensitive, and I don't know how long it will take for these pills to get out of my system, so I'm stopping them now."

I swallowed hard. Could this really be happening? "Are you sure about that?"

She nodded. "I've been on them for several years. My body needs a break. I don't even know if I still have the issues I was taking them for, and I don't have any other partners besides you guys. Nor do I plan on having any. Maggie talked about us being fluid-bonded…"

"And?"

"I'm down." She grinned. "You just need to be sure she's okay with accidental pregnancy in case the scientific path doesn't open up fast enough."

I closed my eyes as the thought of filling her with my seed and making a baby bounced around in my mind. Holy fuck…I was getting so damn hard thinking about draining my balls deep inside her.

I cleared my throat, trying to distract myself from the way my cock painfully pressed against the seam of my shorts. If I had the okay from Maggie, I would be bending Raine over and fucking her brains out right now. But I was going to be good and restrain myself—no matter how hard it was. And it was pretty fucking hard.

"Okay, I'll talk to Maggie. Then we probably all need to have a big discussion together."

She smiled. "Yep, that's what I was going to say."

Before she left, I held myself to giving her a soft, sweet kiss on the cheek.

"I'll be in touch soon," I promised as she walked out the door.

eleven

. . .

maggie

IT HAD BEEN a day at work. The kind of day that made me wonder if I could actually be a successful lawyer, let alone a devoted mother and half-decent lawyer at the same time. And…I was coming home to an empty house. Leo was on night shift this week.

Blue greeted me in the mud room, eager to see me, but even more eager for dinner. While he was chomping away at his tasty vittles, I had enough time to make myself something for dinner. But my first stop was the bottle of wine I'd opened up over the weekend and put into the fridge for later.

Later was now.

I poured myself a glass and contemplated my dinner options. Then I sent Raine a text:

> Me: Hey, sexy lady, how is your week going? Design any good costumes lately?

Maybe I could see her one night this week while Leo was working. It would be nice to have some female company, and I hadn't been able to get the sounds she made when she was coming out of my head since we all played the other night.

Just as I decided on a lame frozen dinner, Blue started to bark his head off. I heard the garage door opening. What?!

Seconds later, a sexy cop was walking into my kitchen, looking so damn tall and broad-shouldered in his uniform. He had left his hat in the car, so his dark hair with salt-and-pepper highlights at the temples glowed silver under the kitchen lights. He flashed me an arresting smile. *Pardon the pun.*

"Good evenin', ma'am, we got a report of a disturbance at this address. Is everything okay?"

He still made me swoon, and we'd been together for fifteen years.

"No disturbance, but I can give you something to investigate if you'd like." I shot him a wink and stood up, letting him pull me into his arms. He squeezed me to his chest, which was rock-hard with his Kevlar vest. And his badge was a little sharp too.

"Oops, sorry, don't want to hurt you." He backed away, leaving me breathless.

"Did you forget something?" I checked as the microwave dinged to let me know my food was ready. Couldn't wait for this frozen vegetables and chicken concoction. *Sigh.*

"No, I just wanted to talk to you about something real quick, and I knew it was going to be hard for us to chat while we're working opposite each other this week." He leaned against the counter, his right hand resting on the handle of his gun.

"Is there something wrong?" I was a lawyer; I couldn't

help it. My brain was immediately running through a list of potential issues, in order from most disastrous to least.

"No, no, not something wrong, but I wanted to let you know I chatted with Raine today. She came over for a little bit—just to talk, nothing sexual, so please don't think I violated any agreement." He held up a hand as though he expected me to protest.

"You can date her by yourself, Leo. You know I'm not territorial like that!" I was a little miffed he thought I would be upset.

"You and I hadn't discussed specific parameters where she's concerned, but she and I wanted to talk about something." He blew out a breath like whatever he said next was important.

"Such as?" I opened the lid to my microwaved meal and let the steam billow out. I stabbed a piece of broccoli with my fork, but it looked rather unappetizing.

"What if..." his dark eyes zeroed in on mine, "...we asked Raine to be our surrogate?"

I dropped my fork with a clatter to the bar top. It was so quiet in the house that the echo seemed to go on forever. I just stared at him, blinking.

"She said she would do it," he continued, "provided you're on board."

"What? You already asked her?" *What the fuck is going on here?*

I didn't know whether to feel betrayed...or turned on.

"Wait, is this about the breeding kink you just figured out you have?" I studied him through narrowed eyes.

"No, Maggie, it's about us having a baby together and not having to wait six months for an appointment, then six months to find the right candidate, and then nine months to have a baby! We could conceivably have a baby like a whole year earlier—see what I did there? Conceivably?" He chuckled.

I stood up. My thighs felt like jelly, and my knees felt like rubber, but I needed to walk for a moment. It was like when I delivered my opening and closing arguments in the courtroom—pacing helped my brain work. It unlocked some sort of logical argument part of my brain that sitting still in a chair couldn't access.

"And she said yes? She'd do it?" I stopped just long enough to search his face for the truth like I would a defendant on the stand.

"She said she was going off the Pill," he declared as if that was answer enough.

I swallowed hard. My head was spinning. This was crazy, wasn't it?

When I saw Raine at The Barn and remembered meeting her at Cynda and Jason's when we were there for Danielle's cast-off party, there was no way I was thinking about her as our potential surrogate. I was thinking, *wow, she is a very beautiful young woman. She has a lovely, curvy shape. That jet-black hair. Those striking eyes.* I mean... I was thinking about kissing her or touching her breasts. No way was I thinking about putting our baby in her uterus.

I made a lap around the kitchen while my analytical brain attempted to make heads or tails out of this situation. "Did you offer her money? What's she getting out of it? What if she doesn't want to give up the baby?"

"I told her what the going rate is for surrogacy," he shared. "And she needs money—she's a poor grad student, so, yes, that is part of her motivation for agreeing. But, also, she thinks we'd be awesome parents, and she wants to help us achieve our dreams. I don't know about the other question... I mean we'd have to have some sort of contract, right? You're the lawyer. I defer to you on that part."

I closed my eyes and sucked on my lip, just breathing and letting the blood flow to my brain. "Did you talk about going the artificial insemination route? Does she know my eggs are bad too? That she'd be donating her egg as well? Biologically, it would be her child."

"We didn't get that far, baby." He plopped down at the kitchen table and laced his fingers together, suddenly looking remorseful. "I'm sorry to spring all this on you. I just…I was really excited when I first had the idea, but I didn't want to even bring it up to you unless it was some-thing she could get on board with. I figured, why get your hopes up? We have the appointment with the surrogacy clinic, and that can be our back-up if this falls through but… What if it doesn't? What if it's meant to be?"

"You know I don't believe in shit like that," I reminded him. I was an atheist through and through. Leo was brought up in a half Jewish, half Catholic family, and his ideas on the spiritual world were…some weird mishmash of the two faiths.

Yeah, we'd have to address how we were going to handle that with our kids…but that discussion was a long way off. We had plenty of ground to cover before we got to that.

I had wanted a baby my entire life. I couldn't remember a time when I didn't think, *oh, yeah, I'm definitely going to be a mom when I grow up.* I had baby dolls galore when I was a kid, and unlike a lot of kiddos, I didn't abandon them or get tired of taking care of them after a few days. I was consistent with that shit. Feeding, burping, diapering, bathing, dressing them in cute outfits and taking them for a stroll down the sidewalk in our cute little cliché suburban neighborhood.

If there had been a category for "most likely to be a mom

when she grows up" in our high school yearbook, I would have been the clear favorite.

I was the mom among my peers, the one everyone trusted with their secrets or would come to for a hug or for support or advice. That was true in junior high, high school, college—hell, even in law school, I had to give some tough love to group project members who weren't pulling their weight.

I had never had a baby, but I was a mom through and through.

I looked up at my husband through the unshed tears glittering in my eyes. "Do you really think this could work out?"

He pulled me down onto his lap and wrapped his arms around me, pulling me into that hard-as-fuck vest. "Yes, I think it's possible. It might not pan out, of course, and we need to prepare ourselves for that, but there's no harm trying. We have several months before our appointment…"

One tear dripped down, turning his light blue uniform dark blue in one tiny circular spot. "Okay, then. I want to try."

raine

After a long week contemplating my decision to stop taking the Pill, Leo and Maggie invited me over for dinner. Maggie was the one to text me, saying she discussed the situation with Leo, and they wanted us to talk about it in person. I assumed that meant she was on board. I had done as much reading as I could about surrogacy, so I felt prepared.

Leo made an amazing chicken cordon bleu for dinner, which I'd heard of but never had before, and I definitely ate too much. In some ways that was good because, being overstuffed, I was less afraid of feeling frisky in their presence. They were both so hot and seemed so sophisticated and worldly, I really wanted to drag them back to their bedroom and see what kind of trouble we could get into together. But they were the adults, and they were going to force us to have an adult discussion first.

So, maybe I'd at least get a chance to digest first, right?

"It's hard to know where to start," Maggie said from the sofa beside me. They had arranged themselves strategically with Maggie next to me on the sofa, well, one cushion between us. And Leo had taken the loveseat.

I had done a little reading on polyamory and specifically about couples looking for their unicorn. Couple's privilege showed a basic disrespect for the new partner's time, energy and feelings. They seemed to be trying to mitigate that, but, in a way, this whole conversation was steeped in couple's privilege.

"Before we talk about the surrogacy thing," she continued, "I just want to make sure you're comfortable. And I want to make sure you know this was not at all on our radar when I first approached you at The Barn a few weeks ago. We had just found out that night that we needed to consider other options besides conceiving and carrying our own child, and, after getting that news, we went out to distract ourselves. I really had put it out of my mind that night. I was so overwhelmed by the emotions that I wasn't in the headspace to actually think about our options. I just don't want you to feel like you're being used. We both genuinely like you and enjoy your company, and we'd want to date you whether this was on the table or not."

"I appreciate your honesty, both of you. You've both been totally honest and transparent with me from the beginning, and I really do appreciate that." I looked down at my fingers for a second, noticing I had an ugly hangnail on my index finger. Oops. Probably from looking through so many fabric swatches this week.

I continued, "I know I'm in a slightly younger generation than you guys, and I'll just say that honesty and transparency are certainly not the usual for me when it comes to dating or relationships. And it's been a real breath of fresh air to see it working differently for us." I gestured around the room.

Leo smiled and took over. "Great, well, those are two basic tenets of polyamory. If you don't have honesty and transparency, your relationships are going to fail. I mean, it's really that simple."

Maggie picked up from there. "And I don't want you to feel like we're interviewing you tonight. I want to ask you a million questions—but it's not a job interview. As far as I'm concerned, we're all on board to at least try this and see where it goes. If it doesn't work out, no problem. We have our appointment with the agency in November. We will go that route. This is just an alternative—a better alternative, I think."

"Right." I straightened my spine and smoothed out my sundress over my knees as I crossed my feet at the ankles. Despite their reassuring words, I was still nervous I was going to say the wrong thing or mess this up somehow. I had to remember that, no matter how altruistic I thought I was being by agreeing to help them realize their dream of having a baby, I was also doing it for the money. I really needed to settle up with the school so I could get my degree and find a job after I graduated.

This was just going to buy me some time.

"Well, probably the first question…" Maggie looked at Leo until he nodded, then her gaze returned to me. She looked so beautiful and classy tonight in an elegant strapless black maxi-dress with chunky gold jewelry. "I'm not sure how much Leo told you, but my eggs are…not viable…" I could tell that word was difficult for her, and I certainly wasn't going to pry into what the exact issue was. "So, a lot of surrogates are impregnated with embryos that were conceived through IVF with the partners' eggs and sperm. But in our case, we would need donor eggs as well."

"I see. Well, that's not an issue for me." I smiled. "As far as I know, mine are in good working order. Not sure if Leo told you, but I was on the Pill. I stopped taking it last week, but I don't know how long it takes to get out of your system…"

"We'll have to check on that," Maggie answered. "Do you know if you have anything that runs in your family we should be aware of, any medical conditions? Any genetic issues?"

"Well…" I sighed. "This might be a dealbreaker, to be honest."

They looked at each other, and I could tell Maggie was struggling to keep her face from falling. "What is it, sweetheart?" she asked.

"Well, nothing that I know of is wrong with me. It's just that, as we discussed before, I was adopted. So I don't really know much about my biological parents. My birth mom had Japanese heritage. My dad had a much more diverse background. But I don't know anything about their medical histories."

"Hmmm…" Maggie flashed Leo a look that I tried to interpret but came up blank. She smiled and gave me a very lawyer-esque answer. "We'll take that under advisement, but let's press on as if that's not an issue."

"Okay…"

"How old are you?" Leo asked. "If you don't mind telling us."

"Well, if we end up doing this, I'm sure you'll need to ask me a lot more personal questions than that," I teased him. "I'm twenty-six."

"And have you ever been pregnant before? Or had a baby?" Leo continued going down what appeared to be a mental checklist.

"Nope and nope." I sighed. "Had a pregnancy scare in college, but I turned out to just be late. Went on the Pill after that, and I've been on it ever since. Haven't had any issues. All of my gyno appointments have been routine, pap smears, all the tests and stuff. Everything's always come out fine. I'm up to date on my vaccinations. I don't have any medical conditions I'm aware of except I did have an irregular cycle—that was another reason I went on the Pill."

"That could be an issue," Maggie noted, looking at her husband.

We went over some more details, and then I asked a question of my own. "So, how would this work? I'd have to see a doctor to get knocked up, or we'd do it the old-fashioned way?"

When it became obvious Leo was straining to keep his chuckle inside, we all ended up laughing. "Sorry," I giggled, "I didn't know how else to phrase it!"

They looked at each other, and Leo cleared his throat. "Well, I'd love to do it the old-fashioned way, or at least give it the old college try, ya know?"

Maggie rolled her eyes. "My husband is very turned on by the idea of getting someone pregnant. You could say it's a kink for him. I hope you don't think that's weird."

I shrugged. "Actually, I think it's kinda hot."

Maggie was still the most serious of the three of us. "If

we went through a doctor, it would certainly cost more time and money, and we'd certainly rather put that money in the pot toward your compensation. Of course, we wouldn't be asking you to do this for free. All of your medical and living expenses would be covered, as well as your food, gas, clothing. Really, everything. You'd have a monthly allowance."

"We did have some questions about how this would fit in with your career goals," Leo added. "We don't want you to sacrifice any career opportunities. We weren't sure how long it typically takes to find a job in your field after you finish graduate school."

I chuckled softly and played with the R pendant that hung on a chain at my throat. "Well, that is the million-dollar question, right? I don't really know how long it will take, though I suspect most of the jobs will be in bigger theater markets like Chicago or New York. I could delay actually moving until the baby was born, though, if I had a monthly allowance. In a way, this would give me an opportunity to do a thorough and relaxed search, relieve some of the pressure, so I wouldn't have to take the first offer that came my way."

Leo and Maggie looked at each other and smiled.

"There'd be a contract of course," Maggie advised.

"I assumed there would be, considering!"

They both laughed.

The three of us sat there for a moment in silence, just looking around the room. Then Leo said, "And part of that contract would be that we are the legal parents of the baby. Just so there's no misunderstanding."

"Of course," I agreed with a nod, "what is a poor grad student gonna do with a baby?"

Another beat of silence. I drained the rest of my wine from dinner. "Anything else?"

"I can't think of anything at the moment," Maggie said, "though I'm sure I'll have more questions when I draw up the contract."

"That's no problem." I uncrossed my legs and laced my fingers together in my lap.

Leo stood up with a wide grin on his face. "Well, I've been saving some champagne for a special moment. And I think this might be it."

Maggie scooted over and pulled me into her arms. Tears were streaming down her face. "You have no idea how happy you've made me. I don't know if it will all work out, but just the fact that you're willing to try... it means the world to me."

"I'm glad to help," I said, though in the back of my mind I was thinking the arrangement helped me as much as it helped them. As Leo had called it that day in the coffee shop, it was truly a win-win for everyone.

Next thing I knew, Leo was popping the cork on the champagne, and he was making a toast to...new beginnings.

twelve

. . .

leo

TONIGHT WAS ABOUT RAINE. She was prepared to make a huge sacrifice for my wife and me, one that would change her body and her life forever. We hadn't ironed out every single detail yet, but this whole dream had grown from a simple and rather far-fetched idea to something with a semblance of a plan.

Speaking of plans…tonight I planned to worship her body like she was a goddess, and I knew Maggie was on the same page.

"How do you feel about massages?" I asked after we finished our champagne.

Her eyes lit up. "I love getting them. I'm not very good at giving though."

"No need to reciprocate tonight," Maggie said. "Tonight is all about you. And we want to make you feel so good."

"Well, I'm down with that!" She stood up, swaying a bit like she was dizzy.

I reached out an arm to steady her. "Are you okay? Do you need to sit back down?"

"I think it's just a combination of the excitement and champagne," she explained. "I'm fine."

"Okay, well, first stop, the bedroom." I bent down and scooped her into my arms.

"Whoa, don't hurt yourself!" she protested. "I weigh a lot."

"Well, what's the point of having these massive arms if I don't put them to good use?" I joked as I carried her down the hall to the master suite. I set her at the end of the bed, and Maggie swooped in to take over.

"I'm going to undress you while Leo gets the massage stuff together, okay?" she checked.

"Wow, okay." Raine smiled and stood still, letting Maggie unzip her dress, unhook her bra, and even slide her panties down so she was completely nude, standing before us like the goddess she was.

I walked around her in a circle. "So beautiful... You take my breath away, Raine."

She giggled. "Thanks."

Maggie stood in front of her, gently caressing her curves and pressing soft kisses to her shoulder, her breasts, then finally claiming her lips with a passion that could only be described as explosive. It made me hard to watch them making out, fingers tangled in each other's hair, tongues twirling, ragged breaths escaping when they came up for air.

I laid the massage oils out on a tray on the nightstand and waited for them to part. "Raine, why don't you lie down on your stomach, and we'll get started?"

Her lips pursed as her eyes bounced between us. "Um... I'm feeling a little underdressed..." She bit her lower lip as she tapped her chin with one finger. "You know what would make me more comfortable?"

"What's that?" Maggie took the bait.

"If you were both naked too," she expressed wittily as she climbed onto the bed.

My wife and I exchanged looks, smiling, then we dropped trou and joined Raine on the bed, one of us on either side of her. I dripped a few drops of the jojoba oil on her right shoulder blade, then smoothed it out with my fingers. If I wasn't a cop…maybe I'd be a massage therapist. I had strong hands, patience, and I loved making ladies feel good.

"Oh god…" Raine sighed as I made long strokes down the right side of her spine.

"Feel good?" Maggie asked. "Leo is the absolute best."

"I believe it," she mumbled into the pillow as I repeated the motions on her left side. Then I worked my way down to her lower back and her ass, kneading and smoothing her skin, making it shine with a glow from the oil.

As I worked on her ass, Maggie focused on her shoulders and neck. She was a pretty good masseuse in her own right —my muscles were thick and corded, but she did a good job tenderizing them. Her hands wore out pretty fast on me, but she'd have more stamina for Raine's smaller, less developed physique.

Everything about Raine was delicate and feminine, from her flawlessly smooth skin to her dainty hands and feet. As I rubbed every inch of her, I thought about whether this body would carry my future child. And I envisioned how she would look, her stomach swollen with my baby.

The image I painted of her in my mind made me so fucking hard.

"I'm going to turn you over now so we can work on the front," I said after a solid forty minutes of massage.

She was half asleep, lifting her head to utter in a drowsy, suggestible voice, "Whatever you wanna do to me…is just fine…"

Maggie snickered as I reached underneath Raine and carefully flipped her over, letting her get comfortable on the pillows before we began to work again. I concentrated on the lower half of her body while Maggie devoted herself to the top. I worked on one foot, then the other, eliciting tiny gasps and moans, and Maggie used firm strokes down her arms and lighter ones on her breasts.

"You guys have no idea how incredible this is. Pretty sure if there's a heaven, it must be like this," she moaned with her eyes closed. She hadn't opened her eyes since we turned her over, and that was just fine with me. When I lifted her leg to work on her calves and thighs, it felt like dead weight. She had surrendered complete control to my wife and me, and I loved every moment of it.

When I worked on her other leg, I stroked up her inner thighs nearly to her pussy lips, and she surprised me by grabbing my hand and moving it directly over her mound. Maggie was working on her breasts at the time.

"Do you want me to massage here?" My voice was a deep rumble breaking the stillness of the room.

"Uh-huh," she answered, her eyes still closed.

I massaged her inner thighs and then her mound before moving down to her lips. I parted her seam with my index finger, causing a light whimper. She arched into Maggie's touch as my wife's finger and thumb trapped Raine's nipple between them and squeezed gently.

"Please…" was Raine's only verbal response.

Maggie lowered herself to Raine's breasts, cupping them

as she took a nipple into her mouth and suckled. Raine's hands moved to the sheets, clutching them as I slid my finger deep within her. Her pussy clenched tight around my digit before I withdrew it and plunged inside again.

"Yes…" she moaned. "Make me come…"

We went to work, Maggie sucking and licking her nipples while I lowered my mouth to her clit and began to feast. The noises that came out of Raine's mouth as we worked her into a frenzy were wild, primal and nearly unhinged.

All the tension we'd released from the muscles throughout her body seemed to settle in her core, and now she was poised for one hell of an orgasm. I felt it building as she rocked against me, her head thrashing side to side as she got closer and closer. My dick was leaking pre-cum onto the sheets as my fingers fucked her and my mouth worked on pushing her over the edge.

Right before she came, Raine pulled Maggie up to her face, their lips crashing together as her pelvis bucked against my mouth, and the storm of her climax reached its peak. She screamed out, the sounds swallowed by Maggie's hungry kiss, drenching me in her juices as I rode out each wave.

When it was over, she lay in ecstasy, panting and trying to catch her breath.

She wouldn't forget this night for a long time.

maggie

I went to the bathroom while Raine was in recovery mode. When I returned, Leo was cradling her in his arms, whispering soothing words to her. They looked so sweet like that, but as soon as I entered the room, Raine sat up straight.

"Everything okay?" I checked in. I was still naked,

standing there in my five-feet-two glory with my forty-year-old sagging breasts and wide hips, thick thighs, and dimpled ass.

From the look on Leo's face as his gaze raked over my curves, you'd think I was the epitome of beauty. And I was, in his eyes. I loved that about him.

He looked at me with a love that bordered on worship, even as he held another woman in his arms. And that was why polyamory worked for us. Because, no matter how many other partners we had, our love never faded, never wilted—instead, it grew and multiplied. It flourished.

"I want to watch him fuck you," Raine uttered, her hooded eyes piercing into me. Her hair was mussed and wild, her smudged eyeliner giving her a feral look. Her lips were kiss-swollen, and her skin still glowed with the massage oil we'd fervently rubbed into her muscles.

Leo looked down at his cock, which was straining toward his stomach, bobbing up and down as if in agreement with Raine's idea. "I'm pretty sure I'm up for that." He winked.

Raine moved to the other side of the bed and patted the space beside her. "C'mon, Maggie. Right here. I wanna suck your tits while he fucks you."

Well, I wasn't going to argue with getting a turn, even though we'd said tonight was about her. "If you're sure you're not ready to go again?"

"Girl, I need a moment. My limbs feel like jelly—in a damn good way. I really want to watch you fuck. I think it'll be so hot."

Leo stepped off the bed, stroking his cock slowly as I made my way to the middle of the mattress, the warmth from Raine's body soaking into my skin. "Well, do whatever you'd like to me."

Leo chuckled as he climbed in between my legs. "I'm

ready to go now…but I can go down on you first if you'd like."

"Uh…pretty sure I'm ready." I reached down and swiped a finger through my folds. I'd gotten so wet watching Raine come undone under my husband's tongue.

"Mmm…that's my girl, always wet and ready for me." Leo waggled his eyebrows as he pressed the tip of his cock at my entrance and slowly pushed forward, sinking inside me as his weight settled against me.

"Oh, god…" I stretched to accommodate his girth, feeling so fucking full. What a delicious feeling. When I opened my eyes and looked over at Raine, she was biting her lip, intensely focused on where his cock disappeared inside me.

"You want to touch it?" I asked, and she nodded.

She army-crawled over to us, mesmerized by Leo's slow thrusts inside me. "You're stretched so beautifully. Love the way your lips are hugging his shaft." She traced around my entrance with one finger as Leo pushed up on his hands to give her better access.

He groaned as she reached between our bodies and circled his cock with her thumb and index finger. She slowly slid it up to his balls and then down again, making him shudder.

"Fuck her, Leo, show me that beautiful cock sliding in and out." Propping herself up on her elbows, she rested her chin on her hands.

My husband put on a show, stroking in and out of me at an agonizingly slow pace, making we shiver with anticipation before slamming home hard and fast. The sudden changes in rhythm took my breath away, but soon Raine realized I was watching his face to see what was coming next.

"I'm gonna take care of that," she promised Leo, and,

next thing I knew, she rose to her knees and crawled toward me. She swung her leg over my hip, settling herself right on my soft belly so I couldn't see Leo's face as he continued to slowly pump in and out of me.

"Focus on me." Raine leaned forward and nipped at my lips, swallowing my sigh as Leo drove hard into my cunt. "Good girl," she praised me as she caged my breasts with her hands, squeezing them tight as my husband continued to surprise me with slow, shallow strokes and then one hard, deep and fast when I least expected it.

"I want you to come inside her," Raine said over her shoulder, "but let's make her come first. Then I'll turn around and watch you fill her up with your cum."

Damn, this girl had a naughty mind, and I was here for it.

"Play with her clit while I fuck her," Leo suggested. "That will get her off the fastest."

Well, he wasn't wrong. Raine went back to her position on her side, then she became the queen of multi-tasking. She played with my clit with her right hand while she pinched and teased my nipples with her left. Just that alone would have made me come pretty fast, but with Leo stroking deep and steady inside me, it was a recipe for an exquisite orgasm.

Soon I was crying out, my pussy clenching Leo's cock as the spasms rocked through my body from head to toe. Raine looked particularly pleased with herself before she swung her leg back over me, facing the other way this time.

Then she told Leo, "Now it's your turn."

leo

Raine taking charge and playing director was incredibly hot. After we made Maggie come, she climbed on top of her again, this time facing me. "Now it's your turn," she informed me.

I leveled my gaze on her and smirked. "Tell me what to do."

"Kiss me while you fuck her nice and slow," she directed, leaning forward until my arms wrapped around her and our lips collided.

She tasted like Maggie, smelled like her too, as my tongue fucked her mouth in rhythm with my cock in my wife's cunt. Fuck this was hot, feeling the sensations of my wife's dissipating climax, still lightly fluttering around me as Raine's hot, wet mouth devoured mine.

She was playful and passionate, moaning, licking, biting, and just those sensations were almost enough to take me over the edge, but I knew she wanted to watch the moment I reached my peak and drained my balls.

She pulled away, and I gritted my teeth, trying to keep from exploding inside my wife. Her pussy was so wet, and with my balls slapping against her, making an absolutely obscene noise…it was about to push me over the edge. But what did Raine want to see?

"Can you fuck her until you're about to come and then pull out and come all over my tits?" she begged. "I'd like you to paint my tits with your cum."

"Oh, god," Maggie moaned behind her. "I wanna watch that."

"I can try. Lean down and put those tits right here so I can aim for them, and then Maggie will be able to see."

I sat back on my heels, giving the ladies enough time to

rearrange themselves and giving my cock a little breather so I could give this my all. A little edging would help my cum shot be more impressive too.

Maggie propped herself up on the pillows as Raine leaned forward, her voluptuous ass sticking up so high, my wife could barely see over it. Maggie gave it a firm pop with her palm. "Hey, down in front!" she joked.

Raine giggled and wiggled her booty in front of my wife's face. "Hey, can't help it if I've gotta fat ass."

"Mmm...I love that ass." Maggie slapped it again, making it jiggle as a red handprint appeared on her left cheek.

Damn, that was hot.

"Ready, ladies?" I checked before I lined my cock up again with my wife's dripping cunt. Maggie barely nodded before I rammed it up inside her, causing her to cry out in surprise.

"That's it," Raine coached from her new vantage. Her face was close enough she had a great view of my cock slamming into my wife's tight hole. "Fuck her, Leo, nice and deep... Mmm, that's it; how does it feel?"

"Damn good. Wet. Tight," I gritted out between thrusts.

"I wanna see your cum all over me," she continued. "That's it, use that pussy. Faster, baby, pump that cock. Oh, god, you're getting close, aren't you?"

I practically growled, "Almost there..."

Just a few more pumps, and I fisted my cock on its way out, cum rocketing out the tip. The first spurt landed on Raine's outstretched tongue and then dripped down onto her heaving breasts. Then two more big ribbons flew several inches right into her cleavage, and finally one hit her in the belly.

"Oh, god, oh, yes." One of her hands rubbed at her clit as

the other rubbed circles in my cum around her nipple. "Fuck, I'm coming again," she moaned as she rocked against my wife's body.

I pushed her down on top of my wife so her head rested on Maggie's chest, and shoved my still-dripping hard cock into her spasming pussy, letting her contract around it as her orgasm slowly faded.

Holy fucking shit…

Not sure how that could have been any hotter.

thirteen

. . .

raine

"WELL...DID you guys come to an agreement?" Danielle asked when I met her for lunch a couple of days later.

"I think so... Uh, oh god, Danielle, am I completely crazy for agreeing to do this?" I asked the question out loud that I'd been asking myself for several days straight.

"If you'd told me last year that I was going to fall in love with two men and get knocked up by one of them, carry his baby and not know until delivery which one impregnated me, I'd have said, 'Oh, fuck no, I would never do anything so unbelievably insane,' but here I am doing exactly that." She raised her hands, palms out. "I am not here to judge you at all."

"I knew you wouldn't. That's why I'm glad I have you to talk to. But I'm still pretty confused about most of it," I admitted.

"I can do my best to answer your questions, at least about the pregnancy part. But only up to about week fourteen. I think that's where I am now. Morning sickness is finally getting better. For fuck's sake, I thought I was going to be puking my brains out for the rest of my life!" she complained.

"Bring it on," I said, making the correlating gesture with both hands. "I honestly can't even imagine it. I've been trying to picture peeing on the stick and getting the two lines and telling Maggie and Leo, but I…I don't know, I just can't see it yet."

"I know I never saw it coming." She grinned and stirred the ice in her drink before taking a sip. "I never imagined how over the moon Aris and Noah would be either. They are taking this dad thing so seriously. Like they are almost trying to out-dad each other. It's adorable!"

I stared at her, blinking slowly. "What do you mean?"

"Well, Noah is looking for a house right now, and Aris keeps rejecting all of his picks because he doesn't think they're safe enough or that there's the right space for a nursery or whatever. Like he said, 'Oh, that one was built in 1954. It probably has lead paint.' Or 'Look at that staircase. That doesn't look safe. You couldn't put a gate on those stairs.'"

I clasped both hands over my mouth, chuckling. "That's freaking adorable! Leo will probably be like that too. Actually, their house doesn't look that child-friendly, to be honest. It's gorgeous, don't get me wrong, but it's very adult. I guess they're prepared to make changes to it."

"Have you talked much about how involved you'll be in the baby's life?" she changed the subject back to me again.

"No, not really…" I let out a sigh. "I'm just trying to focus on the getting pregnant part now. I've been off the Pill for a week. I know it can take a while to start ovulating again. I think I'm gonna buy some of those predictor kits and see if I can figure out what's going on with my hormones."

"Wow, you're really serious about this, aren't you?" She reached out and patted my hand. "But don't forget about the after-baby time too. You really need to figure that shit out before you get pregnant. What if you guys don't see eye to eye on how involved you're going to be?"

"Honestly, Dani, I don't know if I want to be involved." I scrubbed my hands down my face. "I'm really confused about all of it right now. They're poly—I don't know how involved they would want me to be, but what about my future? My career? I can't live off their surrogate payments forever. After the baby is born, that's probably it, right? I mean, I'll have to move on with my life."

"You still want to get a job designing costumes, don't you?" Danielle asked.

I scoffed. "Well, of course I do! I'm not working my ass off for this MFA for nothing!"

"Have you talked to Molly at all?" she asked. "You met her before, right? She's the one who was part of Cynda and Jason's polycule and then fell in love with that Scottish hunk? She finished the master's program last December and now she's working in Indianapolis. They have a theater scene there, you know. You should see if they're hiring."

"Yeah, maybe I will." I sighed. "You're not bi, right?"

Danielle giggled. "Um…why, you wanna fuck me?"

I rolled my eyes. "I mean, you're pretty and all, but… Seriously, Danielle, I'm just thinking a lot about Leo and Maggie and my relationship with them, what I want out of it, what they want out of it. I just don't know how these poly relationships work. I have zero experience with it. I mean, I have experience with men. I have experience with women, but not a man and woman at the same time who are married to each other. It's a totally different dynamic."

"Well, you should talk to Cynda about that, to be honest. She's our resident polyam guru. Tell you what, why don't I set up a girls' night out for the four of us? Well, five, probably because Molly might want to bring her girlfriend, Poe. Are you interested in that?"

"Yeah, that sounds good, actually. Maybe I'll bring Bonnie too. She has been grilling me about Maggie and Leo, but I don't know how to tell her about the surrogacy thing. Do you think I should?"

"I mean, if you're living with her, and you're pregnant… if you're throwing up anywhere near as much as I am, she's gonna put two and two together," Danielle warned me.

"Yeah, you may be right." I shook my head and huffed out another sigh. "Not to mention all of their questions have brought up some interesting stuff about my own genes, you know?"

She leveled her hazel gaze on me. "They know you're adopted, right?"

I nodded. "I told them I'd try to find out more, but… honestly, it's pretty daunting. I don't even know where to start."

"Didn't you say you did the DNA test last year?" She tilted her head like it would help her memory. "And you thought you found a sibling?"

"Yeah…a half-brother on my birth mom's side contacted me, but I kind of blew him off. Maybe I will try to reconnect. It's so awkward though. 'Hey, I'm thinking about having a baby for this couple I know, and they want to know what kind of genes I'm packing.'"

"Well, maybe don't word it like that!" Danielle laughed. "Oh, Raine, just try to relax. I know there's a lot to think about, but it's all going to take time. Everything will fall into place. I have a good feeling about all of it."

"You do?" It was a role reversal. Usually, I was the optimist, and she was the pessimist—though she would probably call herself a realist. I was the one who didn't usually get myself bogged down in all the minute details of something, just focused on the vibes and the big picture, but this was all forcing me to drill down. I didn't like it. I felt like a fish out of water in more ways than one.

She nodded and patted my hand. "It's weird that I'm the one telling you things will work out, but I feel like you're on the right track. Where you're meant to be." She tucked a piece of her long hair behind her ear. "Oh, hey, what's going on with the case of the missing jewelry?"

"Well, believe it or not, Leo is going to help me out. He knows some university cops. He's going to ask them to look into it. Waiting to hear back from him any day about it, in fact." I didn't know him that well yet, but I trusted him. He seemed like the type of person to never let anyone down. I needed someone like that in my life.

"Nice! Well, I am really hoping they'll figure something, and you'll be off the hook. That way you can put your surrogacy funds to better use." She leaned closer to me as if fishing for the juicy details. "How much are you getting paid, anyway?"

"Maggie is drawing up the contract as we speak," I said. "I should know soon."

Dear Tyler,

Hi, I know when we spoke last year, I said I wasn't

ready to communicate with my biological relatives. A lot has changed since then, and I am now in the position that I need to know some family medical history if at all possible. You wouldn't happen to know any of that on our mother's side, would you? If not, perhaps you could put me in touch with someone who would?

I hope all is going well for you in life. I'm open to further communication if you are.

All the best, your sis,

Raine Rivera

I sent the message before I had a chance to change my mind. Now I'd just have to wait and see if he could help me with my questions. That only helped with one side of the family, but it was something.

leo

Days off during nightshift work always felt weird. No one else is off work, and you don't know whether to sleep during the day or wait until night so you can feel normal. I'd done it both ways, and neither ever felt right. It took a toll on my body.

I decided to split my sleep with a nap in the morning, then trying to sleep with my lovely wife at night. But let me tell you the other caveat of nightshift work—if you attempt to sleep during the day, doesn't matter what time, every single person who has ever wanted to contact you will do it while you're trying to sleep.

Case in point: as soon as I started to drift off, my phone buzzed with a text.

I always checked because I worried it would be Maggie, and she would be in the middle of some sort of crisis.

Another fun thing about being a cop—you could imagine way more and much more colorful (read: bloody) crises than non-cops.

But it was Raine:

> Raine: Hey, hope I'm not bothering you, but
> I wondered if you'd had a chance to talk to
> anyone over at the IU police department
> about the missing jewelry?

Oh, shit. I'd gotten so caught up in discussing our surrogate strategy with Maggie and what all needed to be in the contract that I'd forgotten Raine's predicament that I'd promised to help out with. I wasn't starting off this relationship on the right foot by making promises and not keeping them, was I? Guilt shot through me—especially since I never wanted her to think we were using her for her eggs and uterus.

I mean, her eggs and uterus were quite desirable, but we wanted the whole package.

> Me: I need to get some more info from you.
> Pictures would help. Can we meet up to
> discuss?

> Raine: Sure. I can come there, or you can
> come here. My roommate is in and out
> though.

> Me: Maggie is at work, so I have some free
> time this afternoon if you want to drop by.

And just like that, we had plans for an afternoon date. I texted Maggie to let her know, and she responded:

> The Wifey: I'm gonna fantasize about you
> fucking her all afternoon.

I smiled. I loved that the idea of me fucking another woman turned her on so much. I felt the same way about seeing her with other partners.

> The Wifey: Damn it, now I'm getting horny.

A few minutes later:

> The Wifey: Might have to lock my office
> door and take care of myself. You don't
> think anyone will mind, do you?

> Me: Go for it, babydoll. Send me a pic if
> you do.

Mmm, now that she'd planted the thought in my mind, I hoped I could convince Raine to partake in some afternoon delight. She was probably too young for that reference, though, right?

A few hours later when my doorbell rang, I was freshly showered. I left the stubble on my face, hoping she liked the slightly feral look of an Italian man who misses a day of shaving.

"Hey," she greeted me, lifting up on her tippy-toes to press a kiss to my cheek.

"I think we can do better than that." I took her hand and whirled her into my arms, caging her against the wall beside the door, my face inches from hers. "I'd prefer greeting you with a real kiss."

She audibly gulped. "Okay?"

"Do you have a problem with that?"

"Um…no?" Her wide, innocent eyes raked across my face, then closed when I angled my head and cupped her jaw in my hands to give her a proper greeting. My lips grazed hers tentatively, the softest nibble before parting her lips with my tongue and drawing out a moan that went straight to my crotch.

Fuck…already hard for her, and we hadn't even discussed her dilemma yet. It was going to be a long afternoon at this rate.

"Uh…" Her eyes shot down to my crotch.

I backed away. "Yes?"

She looked about to say something, but then she giggled and covered her mouth with her hand. "Sorry, I know I'm here to discuss the missing jewelry, but I couldn't help but notice…" She trailed off there.

I grabbed her hand and pressed it to the front of my shorts. "You couldn't help but notice how hard I am for you?"

"Well…I mean, yeah. Kind of hard not to notice. Pardon the pun." She was still giggling. "Sorry, I'm like a twelve-year-old boy sometimes."

I pulled her back into my arms. "You are nothing like a twelve-year-old boy, Raine. You are one hundred percent woman, and I know what your pussy feels like when I slide my cock deep inside it."

Her face flushed ever so slightly. "Me too…and it feels amazing."

"So, fuck first and discuss the other stuff after?" I tossed the ball into her court, releasing my arms from around her so she could make a decision.

"What about Maggie?" She stepped toward the kitchen. "I don't want her to feel left out."

I passed her, heading into the kitchen. "Want a drink? I'm

gonna have a beer."

"I'll have one too." She leaned against the countertop. "But you didn't answer my question about Maggie."

"Do you want to know what Maggie thinks?" I handed her the beer I'd just opened for her before opening my own and taking a swig.

"Well, yeah, of course I do." She took more of a sip than a swig of her beer.

I slid my phone out of my pocket and scrolled to the messages my wife and I exchanged before Raine's arrival. Her eyes widened as she perused them, then nearly bulged out of her head when she got to the photos my wife showed of her lush tits pulled out of the lacy cups of her bra, and her businesslike skirt hiked up so her thighs were exposed.

"She masturbated right there at work?" Raine's mouth gaped open.

"Yeah, thinking about you and me fucking," I clarified. "She has her own practice, you know. Well, she has one partner, and they share a secretary. She must have had a clear schedule this afternoon."

"Well, in that case, I wouldn't want to disappoint her." Raine shrugged and gave me a hopeful eyebrow waggle.

I downed the rest of my beer, then I lifted her up on the countertop.

"Whoa!" she protested. "What are you planning to do?"

"You wearing anything under that dress?" I noticed she tended to favor summery dresses now that summer had fully kicked in.

"Panties," she said, squirming under my gaze.

"Not if I have anything to say about it." I hooked my fingers under the waistband, my eyes never leaving hers, and ripped them down her thighs, making her squeal.

"Damn it, Leo, did you—"

But she didn't get a chance to finish her sentence because I'd already buried my face between her thighs, feasting on her pussy and stealing the words right out of her mouth.

She gave up on trying to speak, resorting to soft sighs and raspy moans as I let my tongue and fingers do the talking. It wasn't long before she was coming all over my face, and when I looked up, her entire face and chest was flushed pink from my efforts.

"What about you?" she asked breathlessly.

"Oh, don't you worry about me." I pulled her down from the counter and whipped her around so she faced the other direction. I lifted her skirts to her waist and gave her full booty cheek a firm smack.

"I'm gonna fuck you doggy-style in the living room. There's an ottoman in there that's the perfect height. C'mon."

She didn't argue with me, just allowed herself to be led into the next room. Without a word, I pushed her down onto the ottoman on all fours. "Do you mind if I take a picture to send to Maggie?"

There she was, on her hands and knees, her dress hiked up around her waist, and her thick thighs and full ass cheeks on display, the right one decorated with a vivid pink outline of my hand. She looked over her shoulder at me, her eyes hooded. "Go ahead."

I tapped on my camera app and found the best angle, then snapped a few pics and sent one to Maggie. The rest were going to become part of my spank bank.

Maggie texted back right away, and I immediately showed it to Raine.

> The Wifey: Look at that perfectly round
> *peach emoji*. The only thing that could
> make it look better is if it was decorated
> with your cum.

"Damn!" was Raine's reaction.

I walked around in front of her. She lifted her head and watched me unfasten my shorts and let them fall to my knees. I still held the phone in my other hand.

"You're gonna suck me now, get me nice and hard for you, and I'm gonna send a pic of your throat stuffed full of my cock to my wife," I warned her.

She choked out a "Yes, sir," like a good little girl as I fisted my cock and brought it to her lips.

"Open wide, baby." I didn't give her a chance to take it slowly. I rammed it deep down her throat, making her gag. The picture I shot showed her watery eyes and lips straining around my thickness.

Sent that off to Maggie and got this response:

> The Wifey: Holy shit, look at that mouth—
> made to take your cock. Get him nice and
> hard, baby girl, so he can fuck you.

Raine shuddered at the sensation as I held the phone in one hand and her head in the other, guiding her mouth up and down my shaft a few times before allowing her to pop off.

"You feel so fucking good, but I want to put this load in your pussy." I walked back to the other end of her and nestled my cock in the tiny space formed where her ass, pussy and thighs all converged.

"Do it," she sighed. "I need your cum inside me, sir."

Fuck, the way she was obeying me and being such a

good little fuckdoll was driving me wild. I hoped I could last. I pressed my tip to her entrance and just allowed the first few inches inside her before stopping.

She whined, "Oh, god, don't stop there! Fill me up…please?"

I reached forward, wrapping a hand under her chin and gently squeezing her neck, forcing her to arch back toward me. "You want this cock?"

"Yes, please," she begged in a raspy murmur as my hand tightened around her neck. "Oh, fuck. Leo! Fuck me, my god, what are you waiting for?"

She could barely get the words out through the fingers constricting her airway. Pushing back against me, she attempted to take me deeper, but I controlled myself with expert patience.

"Are you ready for this cock?" I asked her, my voice husky with need. My patience was running out as I pulsed against her entrance. She was dripping wet, and the tip of my dick glistened with her juices. My balls tightened as I thought about filling her up with my seed.

I was going to be doing a lot of this over the coming weeks, and I couldn't fucking wait.

"Fuck me!" she cried out. "Please…I…I need your cock."

My jaw clenched as I tried to fill her inch by inch, but when I got to the halfway point, I grabbed her hips and buried myself with a punishing thrust, making her squeal at the sudden intrusion. "Hold on because I'm going to take you hard and fast. Be a good girl and let me use this pussy."

"Please," she whimpered, "please…"

That was all I needed to hear before my hips exploded in a relentless assault, pounding into her, balls slapping, sweat beading, thighs trembling. I gripped her hips so tight, I was sure I was leaving marks as what felt like a bucketful of cum rocketed up my dick.

"I'm coming, baby, draining my balls deep inside you," I groaned as the spurts kept coming.

She cried out, her own climax surprising her as she bucked against me, squeezing every last drop of cum from me before I collapsed, breathless, on her back.

fourteen

. . .

leo

MY FUN ROMP with Raine did lead to actual information, and after she left, I called up my buddy Beau Garrison at the university police department.

"Hey, Katz, how's it goin'? Haven't seen you on the beat in a while," he answered.

"I've been on nights, feels like forever now," I complained. "Only two weeks, but you know how nights are."

"Fuck, we don't do that bullshit here. It's days or nights, not both. I guess I'm the lucky one—means I have to go to all my kids' sports and shit." His laughter bellowed down the line. "What can I do ya for?" his thick Southern Indiana accent rumbled down the line.

He knew I wouldn't call just to shoot the shit. "Gotta friend who's a grad student in the theater department, studying costume design. The department's trying to bill her for some expensive jewelry set that was with a costume she checked out of the wardrobe department—it's like twelve thousand or something insane. She swears she never saw it. She had it checked out for a few days, and it was in the lab during the time. I wondered if you guys have video surveillance in there? I'm guessing you do, or at least outside the door."

"Costume department…in the theater building? I gotta check and see, man. Hold on." He put me on hold, where I heard a delightful message about calling campus security if you need a ride home from a party if you're drunk, or if you think you're being followed. Then Garrison came back on the phone.

"Yeah, man, there's a camera in the actual lab, one in the costume storage area, and one in the hallway where both of the rooms are. Do you have the dates?"

I rattled off the info Raine gave me. "I can also text you some photos of the costume and the missing jewelry. Does that work for you?"

"Sure, man, let me give you my cell number." He read it off, and I entered it into my phone, then fired off the photos Raine sent me.

"I don't have much time, and I'm getting ready to go off-shift, but I'll look into this as soon as I'm able to," Beau promised. "Anything else I can do for you?"

"No, man, just that. I really appreciate it."

"No problem, brother. Take care."

I hung up. That was one thing crossed off my list. Now I planned to make a tasty dinner for my wife, who would be home shortly.

maggie

The house smelled absolutely divine when I arrived home from work, and my handsome man was there to greet me at the door wearing nothing but his apron. Then I found out he'd grilled salmon for dinner.

"You went out on the deck in nothing but that apron?" My gaze roved up and down his manly body.

"I may or may not have had a pair of shorts on then." He chuckled. "Didn't want to rile the neighbors up too much. I already have my fair share of beautiful ladies to satisfy. Old Mildred over there is just gonna have to find someone else."

"Oh my god, her name is *not* Mildred!" I teased him. "I think it's Joan… Isn't it Joan? And she's not that old!"

"She's every bit of seventy!" Leo fired back.

"Well, when's this dinner happening that I smell because my stomach is growling? I didn't get a chance to eat lunch today." I set my purse on the little desk area in the kitchen where I always kept it and stepped out of my heels.

"Oh, I guess you were too busy playing with yourself in your office to eat lunch?" Leo waggled his brows at me as he went to stir something on the stove.

"Well, maybe… Damn it, those pictures were so fucking hot. I almost had to go do it again after you sent the ones of Raine. Who gave her the right to be so goddamn beautiful?" I began setting the table, plates and silverware clinking as I arranged them on the placemats.

"I don't know about you, but I enjoyed myself immensely." He plated the parmesan potato and veggies he'd roasted in the oven.

"I mean, it would have been more fun to be here in person," I admitted, "but someone has to go to work." I got out two wine glasses and chose a pinot noir I'd been saving for a while. It wasn't exactly a special occasion, but we were getting close to finalizing our agreement with Raine.

And maybe in nine months or so, we'd be popping the champagne to celebrate the birth of our child!

"How's the contract coming along?" Leo seemed to read my mind, as usual. He carried over the platter of potatoes and veggies and followed that with the tray of salmon he'd already grilled.

I took out the loaf of bread he'd popped into the oven after the potatoes and transferred it to a bread basket. I was so hungry, I wanted to cram the entire loaf in my mouth, after smothering it with butter, of course.

"It's almost done. I should have it ready for Raine to look at by the end of the week. I hope she has a lawyer or someone to review it. I don't think any of it will be contentious, except maybe the payment."

Leo gulped down a mouthful of wine. "Is it what we talked about?"

I nodded. "It's slightly less than we would pay if we were going through the agency and had to pay for the IVF out of pocket. So, it's still a great deal for her too."

"I'm trying to help her with the missing jewelry the university is trying to bill her for. I talked to my buddy in their PD today, in fact. He's going to review some security video footage and see if anyone pilfered the jewelry. I just don't want Raine to have to spend our money on that. I want her to use it for herself, you know?"

"Leo, do you think she would still do this for us even if she didn't need the money?" It was a question that had been knocking around inside my head ever since the first time we spoke to her about it.

"Does it matter?" was his profound response. When I just gave him my lawyer's glare, he chuckled. "I'd love to think of her as purely altruistic too, but it's not very realistic. Why would anyone give up their body for nine months if they weren't getting something out of it?"

"You don't think she'll have any issues giving up the

baby…do you?" That was the main fear that'd been keeping me awake at night. "I mean, it will genetically be hers and yours. I won't really have any claim to it."

"That's why we have the contract," he reminded me. He swallowed down the rest of his wine. "And, besides, I do think she's a good person. Did you ask Noah if he knows anything about her? You've known Noah for a long time."

It was true—Noah had been my client ever since he started his practice several years ago. But I hadn't talked to him about Raine. He only knew her through Danielle, his girlfriend, so I wasn't sure how much he could offer, and I didn't want to put him on the spot. It was up to Leo and me to vet her, after all.

I'd like to think that with me being a lawyer and him being a cop, we were both good judges of character. We'd certainly seen enough bad seeds in our day. And Raine didn't strike me that way at all.

"Why don't you set up a date with her?" Leo suggested. "Our date today was impromptu and a bit rushed, but go out and have a girls' night. Enjoy each other's company. I am sure the more time you spend with her, the better you're going to feel about this arrangement."

"You're probably right…" My voice drifted off as I swallowed down the rest of my wine.

"Probably right? Can I get that in writing?" My husband winked.

"I love you so much." I looked across the table at him, his handsome features illuminated by the soft glow of the light fixture hanging above our table. He had that outline of scruff on his jaw that I loved so much. It always made his eyes look extra dark and brooding. He wasn't brooding, not really, but he had that sexy swagger. If you just saw him, before he opened his mouth, you might think he was a bit rough and demanding. The biggest surprise was that, under that muscle and intimidating exterior, he was a cuddly teddy bear.

And I loved that about him so much.

"Why are you looking at me like that?" He leaned forward, elbows on the table, licking his bottom lip.

"I'm thinking about ripping that apron off you and finding out if I can smell Raine's pussy on you…"

He smirked. "I took a shower, but you can go exploring down there anyway if you'd like…"

"Still horny even after your romp this afternoon?"

His lips spread wider. "For you? Always."

raine

Visiting Danielle at her polycule's house always felt like coming home. Since I didn't really have family of my own nearby, and neither did she, we had both been adopted into Cynda and Jason's polyam fam.

Cynda greeted me at the door, slinging her arms around me like she hadn't seen me in years. "Raine! Welcome home, baby girl. I just got dinner on the table. You'll join us right?" She didn't even wait for me to answer before she called out, "Get another chair. Raine's staying for dinner."

Then Danielle ran down the hall and practically bowled me over with her hug. "Hey, lady! Great to see you!"

"Wow, you guys are all in a great mood!" I glanced around at all the smiling faces.

Then Jason and Cynda's boyfriend, Darth, wandered out from their bedroom. "I'm in a bad mood. There, does that balance things out a bit?" He was always a contrarian, so I didn't think much of his statement.

"Hi, Jason. Hi, Noah. Where's Aris?" I looked around for

the handsome nurse with his striking Greek god physique and sexy manbun.

"He's at the gym, but he'll walk in right as we sit down to eat," Noah said. "He times it perfectly."

Danielle grinned. "It's truly a gift. C'mon, let's go get seats next to each other."

"I brought the contract," I shared with her as we sat down at the table. "I wanted you guys to look over it, make sure there's not anything bad in there."

"What contract?" Cynda's ears apparently perked up as soon as she heard the word.

"It's our surrogate contract," I explained as everyone began to take their seats. "I'm not sure if Dani told you, but I've agreed to be a surrogate for Leo and Maggie. You know the Katzes. They were here for Dani's cast-off party a couple months ago."

"Yes, yes, Noah's lawyer and her very handsome husband." Cynda waggled her eyebrows.

"Down, girl." Jason shot her a teasing glare. "Don't you have enough man meat at your disposal?"

"Shut your mouth," Cynda shot back, "ain't no such thing!"

We all laughed. I loved being here so much. I probably wouldn't see these guys too often after Noah, Aris and Danielle found a house.

"Well, anyway, I brought the contract Maggie drew up, and she advised me to have someone with legal and/or medical expertise look it over. I know we at least have medical expertise here."

"I'm happy to take a look at that aspect," Noah offered.

"And I used to be a paralegal," Cynda said. "So I can take a gander too."

"Damn, woman, what haven't you done?" Danielle exclaimed, in awe of the polycule's venerated mother figure.

"I just want to make sure I'm getting a fair deal," I explained, "and that they are too. I want everyone to be happy, to get what they want. If I can help them, and they can help me—it's a win-win as far as I'm concerned."

A couple of hours later, the contract had made the rounds. Noah seemed impressed at how the medical end of it was addressed. "She definitely did her research, but I shouldn't be too surprised. I've known Maggie for a while, and she never takes shortcuts. She always does her due diligence."

"I don't see any issues from a legal standpoint." Cynda lifted her reading glasses to rest on top of her gray-tipped corkscrews. "It seems fair. It's very well laid out. There are reasonable steps if amendments need to be made, and any of you can back out before pregnancy is confirmed."

"So you think I should sign it?" I glanced around the room. Aris had indeed joined us, just exactly when the first bites of Cynda's delicious dinner were about to be consumed. Darth had left our gathering to play video games in his room. So, it was me, Dani, Cynda, Noah, Jason and Aris.

The consensus became apparent as all five heads began to nod.

Dani rushed into the kitchen and ran back to where we were gathered in the living room. "Here's a pen."

I was surprised to see the pregnant lady move so fast. "Oh, you think I should sign it right now?"

"Yes!" She clapped her hands together. "Then we can celebrate with a toast!"

I took a deep breath, held the pen against the line for my signature, and inscribed my full name,

Raine Elizabeth Rivera

Then I dated it.

It was done.

Danielle was already breaking out the champagne and sparkling grape juice for her. I took a sip of my champagne, wondering if maybe I should be drinking the juice as well. After all, I'd been with Leo twice since I went off the Pill, and I hadn't gotten my period yet. I wasn't sure what to expect now that I'd stopped taking the hormones.

My phone buzzed, so I glanced down. I had an incoming email from my brother. My heart leapt as I read it:

Hey, Raine,

Sorry for the delay getting back to you. I've been traveling out of the country and didn't have access to this email account. Your message was a little vague, so I hope you're well and nothing bad is going on for you health-wise. I am sorry to say I don't have a lot of family medical information other than that, as far as I know, we're a pretty healthy bunch.

I know you didn't want her info when we first started, but now maybe you would. I'll give it to you, and then you can decide if you want to reach out.

Our mother's name is Reina Clarke, and her phone number is 517-555-2752. Yeah, I thought it was weird you guys have almost the same name.

Anyway, best of luck to you, and I hope you will keep in touch.

Tyler Clarke

fifteen

. . .

maggie

IT HAD BEEN a few years since Leo had been off work for the Fourth of July. Usually, I stayed home and caught up on reading, but this year, we'd been invited to Cynda and Jason's home for a cookout. Raine was invited too, and it would be one of our first appearances as a throuple.

"Are we a throuple though?" Leo asked as he watched me trying to coordinate red, white and blue outfits for us.

"Well, there's three of us...and we're in a relationship." I laid a red-and-white-striped polo shirt on top of a pair of navy-blue shorts to see if he'd bite.

"I'm not going looking like a candy cane," he said. "Or Where's Waldo. Or the IU basketball team's candy-striped warm-up pants."

"The warm-up pants have vertical stripes," I argued, rolling my eyes. "Fine, how about plain red?"

"I don't like to wear red." He put the striped polo back in the closet and opened up one of his drawers. He pulled out a shirt with a thin blue line flag on it. "How about this instead?"

"Fine." I really didn't care what he wore. I wasn't that kind of wife, so I wasn't sure why I was bothering.

"Back to the throuple thing." He poked his head through the top of the t-shirt. "Right now, we're more of a couple with a surrogate partner."

"In a legal sense, I suppose we are." I nodded in agreement.

"Well, do you think it will change?" He stepped into a pair of shorts, not the ones I had laid out on the bed, but a pair of baggy tan ones he wore all the time and had a bit of paint splattered on one leg. I wasn't going to let that bother me. He was a grown man, and if he wanted to wear paint-splattered shorts, that was his own problem.

"Do you *want* it to change?" I dug in my jewelry box for a pair of flag earrings my sister got me several years ago.

"I just wondered what would happen after the baby is born, that's all." He fastened his shorts and gave himself a once-over in the mirror.

"I can't believe I'm the one saying this since I'm the planner in this relationship, but I think we're gonna have to cross that bridge when we come to it." I poked the earrings through the holes in my earlobes and put the backings on.

He turned to face me. "So you don't have feelings for Raine, then? Like poly feelings?"

"Are you asking if I'm in love with her?" I stared at him across the room. He was standing in the doorway with one arm propped against the frame.

"Well, yeah…you know, do you love her?"

I fastened my gold necklace, giving myself time to think of what I wanted to say, how I wanted to answer. "I think Raine is a lovely young woman, and I really appreciate that she's trying to help us have a baby. Of course I think she's beautiful, and I love having sex with her. But I wouldn't say I'm in love with her."

Then my mind went to the obvious: *why is he asking this?*

"Okay. That's pretty much where I am with it too," he said. "I just wondered how she saw things. If she sees us as a throuple."

"Why don't you ask her?" Speaking of obvious, that seemed like the obvious solution.

"Maybe I will." He grinned as I walked toward the door. I tried to brush past him, but he caught me in his arms. "You gotta pay the toll if you wanna pass."

"The toll, eh? And what's that?"

"A kiss, duh!"

I rose on my tippy-toes as his arms wrapped around me. Mmm, it felt nice to be in his arms. I closed my eyes as our lips made contact, sending a flurry of tingles through me. All these years together, and he still affected me like this. He still made me weak in the knees.

"You ready to go?" he asked when I opened my eyes and caught him staring down at me with an adoring look on his face.

"Ready if you are." I smiled back up at him.

"I can't wait to show off my two lovely ladies." He spun me in a circle, and then escorted me to the garage.

I bent down and gave Blue a pat on the head. "Be a good boy while we're gone."

"Should we take him with us?" Leo asked.

"They have cats, right? We better not."

We waved goodbye to our pup and headed out.

raine

"Hey, how are you feeling?" I put my arm around Danielle's shoulder as she stretched out on the lounger in Cynda and Jason's back yard wearing nothing but a tube top and a pair of boy shorts.

"Like a bloated pig," she huffed. "This heat is killing me, and I'm only five months along! I can't imagine what I'd feel like if I was nine months right now. I'd probably go bathe myself in ice."

We watched the guys set up a volleyball net across the yard. "Well, if you think you're hot now, just wait until they get this volleyball game going. It's going to be like *Top Gun* up in here."

Danielle was too uncomfortable to giggle. She merely let out a snort. "Can you get me some water?"

"Yeah, babe, just a sec." I headed to the cooler, pulled out two icy-cold water bottles and brought them over. She took hers and immediately stuck it between her boobs.

"Ahhh…" She closed her eyes and smiled. "Now that's nice."

"Hey, so I just finished up my first period after going off the Pill," I shared.

"Oh…so I guess you didn't get pregnant last month?" She opened her eyes and stared at me as I took a swig from my water bottle.

"No, despite Leo's best efforts." I sighed as a bead of water dripped off my bottle and landed on my arm. "But I probably didn't ovulate, you know? This month I have a better chance. Maybe I should get one of those kits that tells you when it's best to get knocked up."

"Such an eloquent way of phrasing it!" Dani teased me.

Then she gestured to herself. "I know you're in a big hurry to look and feel like this."

"You're still beautiful, so don't even. You're getting the cutest little tummy!" I moved my hand like I was going to touch her belly, but she glared at me.

"I already had a tummy, so there's nothing *little* about what's going on here now." She looked down at her emerging baby bump. "But it *is* pretty cute, right? Noah and Aris have been rubbing shea butter and coconut oil into my skin every night. They take such good care of me."

"That's amazing. I know Leo and Maggie will take good care of me too," I confidently asserted.

"Hey, so did you ever hear back from your mother?" She took the water bottle out of her cleavage and unscrewed the cap.

"Nope." I sighed. "It was worth a shot, but no. I sent her a text. Maybe she thought it was spam and deleted it?"

Dani rested her head against the lounger and closed her eyes again. "Didn't your brother tell her that you might be reaching out?"

"When we first talked, he told me they aren't close. They don't live in the same state, and they don't talk much. He had her number, but it's possible she's changed it. I don't know."

"Social media?" Dani's eyebrows quirked as she returned the cold bottle to her tube top.

"I mean, I could try. I don't know how common a name Reina Clarke is. The area code suggests she lives in Michigan, but who knows if that's actually the case." I was daunted by the idea of tracking her down, yet I felt compelled to for Leo and Maggie's sake.

"I hope you hear back from her soon," Danielle said.

"Maybe you should tell her she's going to be a grandmother?"

"Yikes, that might scare her away even more!" I laughed.

"Looks like your fam is here." She lifted her sunglasses and pointed toward the house. Leo and Maggie were rounding the corner with Leo carrying a cooler and Maggie carrying what looked to be a pie.

They both simultaneously spotted me and waved. Cynda rushed to greet them and took the pie and cooler, so they headed my way. Leo was wearing a thin blue line flag shirt, and Maggie was wearing a pair of red capri pants with a navy and white shirt.

I didn't look very patriotic in my short, ruffled sundress with daisies on it, but I did have a matching headband in my hair, which was blowing in the breeze as they made it to my side.

"Hey, sexy lady." Maggie wrapped an arm around my waist and pulled me into a soft kiss on the lips. When she released me, Leo took me into his arms and also gave me a kiss.

"You remember Danielle," I reintroduced them, and everyone nodded and smiled.

"I hear congratulations are in order," Maggie said.

Danielle smiled and patted her tummy. "Yup, hoping the sun helps *le bébé* bake a little faster."

Aris and Noah must have been waiting for us to finish our conversation because, as soon as they saw Maggie and Leo arrive, they wandered over. Handshakes and hugs all around as everyone got reacquainted.

I looked around the yard, not only at the six of us standing in our little group, but at Jason, Cynda, Darth, Lachlan, Molly, Poe, and a few other new faces whom I hadn't met yet. It looked like Poe might have a girlfriend, judging by the fact she had her arm around another femme-presenting person. There were fifteen or twenty people celebrating the Fourth of July in this yard, a holiday devoted to life, liberty and the pursuit of happiness. And we were all pursuing our happiness with multiple partners.

We were all polyamorous, and we were all connected either by love, friendship, or at the very least, like-mindedness, and we were so lucky to live in a place where we were free to love anyone we chose.

I wasn't the most patriotic person in the world, but that realization did cause a few tears to sting at the corners of my eyes. Sure, there were people in our country who didn't like us, understand us, or support us—but they couldn't stop us from gathering here today to celebrate Independence Day.

leo

My two ladies were looking especially alluring today in their festive outfits—my wife in her patriotic colors and my girlfriend in her little daisy dress that kept conveniently blowing up so I could see her pale blue panties underneath. The sun was setting, and Jason and Darth were pretty gung-ho on setting off fireworks, but I was more interested in creating a different kind of spark.

Cynda saw me mixing drinks at the makeshift bar and headed over. "Having fun?"

"The best time. Thanks so much for having us. I'm usually out arresting drunks right about now on the Fourth, you know?"

She laughed. "You're welcome here any time, Leo. As a matter of fact, our camper is available if you three want to spend the night. I don't want anyone making extra work for the cops on duty in your stead, you know?"

"Oh, we would never." I grinned. "That's very generous of you to offer." I pointed across the yard toward the driveway. "That camper is yours?"

She nodded. "Yes, feel free to bunk up if you'd like. It's unlocked and should be fully stocked with anything you need."

"Incredible offer, thank you, Cynda. Please express my thanks to Jason too. He looks a little busy strategizing with Darth over the fireworks show right now. Don't want to interrupt him."

She laughed and patted me on the shoulder affectionately. "Good idea."

She went over to talk to Molly and Lachlan as I carried the drinks to where Maggie and Raine were waiting for me. "Hey, Cynda offered the camper to us tonight if you guys want to crash here."

"Oh, that's sweet of her!" Maggie exclaimed. "That means you can drink too if you'd like, babe."

"Oh, right!" I rubbed my hands together. "In that case, I'll be right back." After returning to the bar, I mixed my own drink and then rejoined the ladies. "Bottoms up!"

Maggie held up her red Solo cup like it was a biohazard. "How much fucking alcohol did you put in this thing? Geez!"

Raine took her first taste. "My god, Leo, this could fuel a rocket!"

They both laughed as I took the cup from her and sniffed it. "You want me to make you another one? I'll drink this one."

Maggie scoffed and linked her arm with Raine's. "C'mon, beautiful. I'll make you an actually potable drink." She handed me her cup, rolled her eyes and marched off toward the bar with Raine in tow.

Noah slid up to me, watching them leave. "Hmm, looks like you drove them away. What'd you do?"

I sighed. "I guess the drink I mixed was too strong." I held out Maggie's cup to him. "Wanna try it?"

He held his hands up, palms out. "I have surgery in the morning, so I'm not drinking tonight."

"You have surgery the morning after the Fourth of July?"

"Sinus problems don't take holidays," he said with a wink.

I downed the contents of Maggie's cup, so now I'd had three of the rocket-fuel drinks wreaking havoc on my system. The buzz began to burn through me, making me feel tingly and my brain feel a bit floaty. The ladies wandered back over to me a few minutes later with new cups.

"These are much better," Raine agreed as they each took a sip.

I started to make a smart-ass remark, but my balance seemed to have taken a holiday. "Wow, you're right, those were strong. Maybe too strong."

Raine caught my arm, trying to hold me up. "Leo, do you need to sit down?"

I waved her away. My words weren't slurring yet. I was fine. "Maybe I should have one more just for good measure." I started for the bar again, but Maggie grabbed me by the back shorts pocket.

She tugged me back toward her and Raine. "Oh no you don't, you little lush. You're gonna stay right here and watch the show with us."

As if on cue, the wheeze and pop of a firework exploded several feet above us. I looked up to see tiny gold stars making a pattern in the sky. "Look, it's a golden shower!"

Raine chuckled. "Oh, boy, is this what we have to look forward to all night?"

"Well, at least he's a happy drunk, right, baby?" Maggie elbowed me and damn near toppled me over.

Another whiz through the sky and a crackle. "Purple Rain!" I exclaimed. "Those are the Artist Formerly Known as Prince's favorites."

"Wow," was all Raine could say to my joke.

"Maybe we should get him to the camper before he passes out?" Maggie suggested. Noah heard her and came over to help.

Next thing I knew, Noah was on one side of me, and Aris was on the other, escorting me to the camper and then helping me step up inside while I regaled them with reasons they should let me stay outside. "But I wanna kiss my girls under the fireworks! Isn't that a romantic thing to do?"

"Sure, buddy, but you can't kiss them if you're passed out on the ground," Noah warned.

"You'll feel better if you lie down," Aris agreed.

"But how'm I gonna fuck 'em if they're out there, and I'm in here?" I raved.

"We'll be just fine fucking without you," Raine said as Aris and Noah got me settled on the bed at the back of the camper.

"Do you need the bathroom or anything before we head out?" Noah asked.

"No, man, but thank you for taking care of me. What would a guy like me do without guys like you?" I crooned as they both stood over me, arms crossed over their chests like I wasn't the funniest drunk guy they'd ever seen.

I was definitely the funniest and *funnest* drunk guy.

At least at this party.

sixteen

. . .

maggie

"HOW EMBARRASSING!" I apologized to Raine when we went back to watch the rest of the fireworks show. "He hardly ever gets to drink, and he definitely cannot hold his liquor."

"Well, it doesn't help that he had three of those one-million-proof drinks in about three minutes," Raine said. "It's kinda cute though, don't you think? He's supposed to be all manly and taking care of us, but we ended up taking care of him tonight."

"A role reversal for sure," I agreed. "It's good for him to unwind once in a while. Work has been tough lately."

"Why's that?" Raine asked as she sipped the mild fruity drink I made for her.

I looked up at the sky at what was probably the "finale" of the show Jason and Darth put together. It got very loud with consecutive booms, producing *oohs* and *ahhs* from the small crowd around us. It gave me a chance to consider what I could tell her about Leo's job. He didn't talk about work much, but when he did, it was usually to vent about something that happened with a "client" or something one of his superiors did that, in my estimation, only made him less safe out on the street, not more. I didn't want to overstep and share something with Raine that he would not share with her himself.

I felt a need to protect him—and that surprised me. I didn't spend too much time analyzing why because, when the loud booms finished, Raine was still staring at me, expecting an answer.

"Oh, you know, it's a tough job. There's growing pressure on cops to be one hundred percent perfect all the time. Yeah, there are bad cops out there, but most are just trying to do their jobs the best they can. It's hard to be perfect *all* the time, especially when you have to make split-second life-and-death decisions. I mean, it's hard to be perfect all the time at *any* job."

"Tell me about it." Raine ran her fingers through her hair. "I know my job sounds easy, but the directors at the theater where I'm working this summer just rejected half of my designs for their big finale next month. I had to redo a bunch of them because, though my designs were historically accurate, the directors didn't think the costumes were right for their particular cast. You gotta please the directors, of course."

I smiled. "I get it. I'm always trying to please my clients but still have to adhere to the law, you know?"

"Yeah," she nodded, "I can't imagine doing what you do. Or what Leo does, for that matter. I'm not sure I could work a job where I didn't create something, where I couldn't use my imagination."

"Oh, we have to use our imaginations sometimes, just

not in the way you do." I chuckled as a soft breeze rustled my hair and blew up the hem of her dress.

"Damn it! I've been fighting the wind all night!" She laughed. "So I guess we're gonna camp out with Leo tonight?"

"You don't have to stay if you don't want to," I assured her. "I can handle Drunkie, don't worry."

A sheepish smile spread her lips as she looked back at me. "I don't mind staying. It might be fun to hang out with you some more."

A warmth spread through me as I took her hand in mine and led her toward the camper. We said goodnight and thank you to Cynda and Jason along the way. It was interesting—I felt protective of Leo, but there was something so sweet and vulnerable about Raine that made me feel protective of her too.

I reflected back on that question Leo asked me when we were getting ready for the party earlier today—if I'd fallen in love with Raine. Feeling protective of her was a type of love…wasn't it? Maybe I needed to reevaluate my feelings.

If all went according to plan, she was going to be the mother of our child. But it wasn't that fact that drew me in. She seemed naïve and vulnerable in some ways, but deep down she had an old soul. She had an unwavering kindness and zest for life, an artist's eye, and a passion for beauty and nature. I loved those things about her. She provided a nice contrast to my pragmatic Type A personality.

"Don't have too much fun!" Jason called after us as I shut the camper door.

"If this camper's a-rockin', don't come a-knockin'!" Raine exclaimed once it was just the two of us.

I giggled. "Good one. Hey, you want something else to drink?"

"Just water, if there's some in here?" Her eyes danced with anticipation, like the fireworks had burst inside them instead of in the sky.

I opened the small fridge, and sure enough, it was stocked with water, juice, and sodas. I pulled out two bottles of water and set them on the counter.

"I had such a great time today." She twisted off the cap and took a swig. "I've never been to such a laidback Fourth of July gathering, you know? Where everyone just hung out, and it was so low-key. This introvert really enjoyed it."

I nodded in agreement. "People are so much nicer to be around when they can be who they want to be and can drop all the pretenses, don't you think?"

She set her water bottle on the counter and pushed some strands of my hair behind my ear. "I totally agree."

Before I knew it, her lips were on mine, pressing a tender kiss to my mouth that tasted vaguely of the fruity mixed drink I'd made her earlier. Then her fingers tangled in my hair as our tongues dueled for dominance.

That was one thing I'd noticed—she was usually submissive to me or Leo, but I had a feeling she had her own dominant side. My feeling was confirmed when she pushed me back against the small loveseat and straddled my hips, continuing to kiss me as her hands roamed underneath my shirt to cup my breasts.

"You're so beautiful, Maggie," she whispered in my ear before she nibbled on the lobe, sending shivers throughout my body. "I want to worship your curves. Kiss every inch."

I bit my lip as I stared up at her piercing cat eyes. She'd forgone the heavy black eyeliner today, and she looked so young, so innocent in her frilly daisy dress. I knew she was anything but.

She pulled the dress over her head and yanked it off,

sending it flying across the camper. Then she reached down and tugged on the hem of my shirt. "This has to go. Now."

I obliged, lifting it and tossing it aside. Our bras went next, our bare breasts smushing together as our tongues tangled and fingers threaded through wild, windblown tresses. A need grew in my core as she broke our kiss and lowered her mouth to take my nipple between her teeth. My head fell back as desire flooded through me.

I'd never wanted another woman like I did this goddess writhing over me. I wanted her hands on me, her tongue inside me; I wanted her to come on my face again and again.

Across the camper, Leo let out a long, obnoxious snore, and Raine and I both exploded in laughter. "Damn, he is sure missing out on a lot of hotness," I said, stroking my fingers across the soft skin of her cheek.

"Let him sleep it off," she said with a nonchalant shrug. "Tonight is for girls only."

raine

I woke up sandwiched between two immovable figures. It took me a few seconds to figure out where I was and who the figures belonged to.

Leo and Maggie.

Of course.

It was my first time spending the night with them, and Leo was passed out the entire time. I extracted myself from their limbs and stood up, surprised at how much headroom there was in this camper. But, then again, I was short.

Eh, I'd woken up in stranger places when I was an undergrad.

"Going somewhere?" called a gruff voice as I tiptoed toward the tiny restroom.

I whipped around. "Good morning, Leo. Sleep well?"

He sat up, swinging his legs off the edge of the mattress and rubbing his head. "Pounding headache. Ugh."

"Well, you had like a million beers and then three drinks that were probably the equivalent of moonshine as far as proof is concerned," I teased him. "That is one well-earned headache."

"If you say so," he groaned. "I don't even remember coming inside the camper. How'd you guys get me in here?"

"Aris and Noah helped," I admitted. "Hey, I gotta run. I have a meeting with the dean today about my outstanding bill I still haven't paid."

"Oh no, fuck. I forgot to follow up with Beau about the video. He's supposed to be looking at it to see if someone tampered with the costume while you had it in the lab."

"I appreciate that. I can make a payment toward the money I owe with the allowance you gave me this month. They'll just have to take that until I can pay it all off in a few months." I sighed.

"No, no. That's not right. Let me go ahead and pay it for you. We'll call it an advance," he offered. "Besides, I want to figure out what *really* happened to the jewelry. I don't want IU getting your surrogate money, you know?"

"It's not going to IU." I laughed. "It's going to the owner of the jewelry. Some antiques dealer. I don't remember his name. Or, probably more accurately, IU already paid him, and I'm just paying the school back."

He crossed his arms over his bare chest. "I don't care. It's not your fault that jewelry went missing."

I shrugged. "No, but I was responsible for it."

He stepped toward me, ducking a little even though he didn't need to. "Hey, don't go yet."

"I have to pee, man!"

"Oh, okay, do that, but then I want to tell you something." His eyes held a mysterious gleam.

I hurried to take care of business in the tiny bathroom, then flushed and washed my hands. I wished I had a toothbrush—my mouth felt all kinds of gross, but surely he wouldn't try to kiss me, right?

"What did you want to say?" I stepped back out into the main part of the camper.

"Come here." He reached for my hand, and when I accepted, he pulled me toward him. It wasn't a hard yank, but I still ended up in his lap. "That's more like it."

He stroked a hand down my back, all the way to my ass, making me sigh. Then he stroked two fingers down my face. "Sorry I didn't get to spend more time with you last night."

"It's okay. Maggie and I had fun." I smiled up at him. "There's always next time."

"That's true." He pressed a kiss to my forehead. "I hope next time you spend the night, I'm a little more coherent."

"A *lot* more coherent, I hope." I laughed as I started to rise from his lap, but he pulled me back down.

"I'm going to call Beau and find out what happened with those videos he was supposed to watch. And you let me know how your meeting goes, okay?"

I nodded. "I will."

I stood up this time, and he let me. I headed for the camper door, and when I looked over my shoulder, he was staring at me.

"Is there something else?" My question hung in the space between us for a few moments.

He started to say something, then chuckled and shook his head. "See you soon, Raine."

Instead of having one person yelling at me, I had the fun experience of having three people yell at me. The Costume Czar herself, the chair of the theater department, and the dean of the whole school.

"It's been forty-five days," Dr. Pataski, the chair, informed me with a disappointed scowl on her face.

"I'm aware. Thank you for pointing that out." I put my hands together in a prayer motion and bowed my head slightly. I wasn't a spiritual person, but it was a prayer lifted to the heavens to prevent me from going ballistic in this office. My goal was to weasel out of this meeting and finish up my final time at IU, collect my MFA and then get on with my life.

"When do you expect to make the payment?" Dean Chow asked. "This has made it up the chain to the president's office, and she's putting a lot of pressure on us to recover the money we've paid out to Mr. Wheeler."

"I completely understand, and I'm sorry you're in this situation," I relayed in the calmest voice I could muster. I was a costumer, but right now I was worthy of the Oscar for best actress, I was putting on such a stellar performance. "I am a nearly unemployed broke college student, so I'm doing the best I can. I can make a three-thousand-dollar payment toward the total sum I owe today. But I also know the university police are looking into this matter, and I expect to hear the outcome of their investigation shortly."

"The university police?" The dean's eyebrow quirked. "I don't recall them being involved."

"Well, they are…somebody named…" I scrambled to

remember the name Leo gave me. "Beau Garrison," I name-dropped. Maybe that would help?

"Well, you can pay the three thousand today. See the admin assistant on the way out. But don't forget that we'll be withholding your diploma and transcript until it's paid. Aren't you set to finalize your coursework and hand in your thesis next month?" Dr. Pataski sneered.

I nodded.

"Right. Well, I hope all your hard work toward your MFA isn't going to go to waste," Dr. Wharton, the Costume Czar, said. "I believe I'm on your thesis committee as well. It would behoove you to have this debt paid off before we receive your thesis."

I pinched the bridge of my nose as I channeled my internal calm person. I didn't really know anyone who was as chill as I needed to be right now because I was this close to flying off the handle and giving these three women a piece of my mind.

I stood up and forced myself to shake all of their hands. "Thank you for meeting with me. I'll get you the rest of the money as soon as I can."

So, I'd need to touch base with Leo to find out what Beau Garrison said—if that was even the correct name. And if he couldn't help me, then I would need to talk about that advance he mentioned in more detail.

I just hated the fact that Leo and Maggie were already paying me, and I wasn't even pregnant yet...

seventeen

. . .

maggie

I SHOULDN'T HAVE BEEN nervous to meet Raine for coffee, but I was. And when she arrived, looking adorable in her black gauchos and a bright yellow cropped top, she looked nervous too.

"Thanks for meeting me," I said as she sat down. "You look so cute today."

She rolled her eyes. "Bonnie told me I look like a bumblebee."

I laughed at that. "Well, she must be jealous. I hope you gave her a nice sting."

Raine added some creamer to her coffee. "Good one." She took a sip and then added some more. "What did you need to see me about? Is something wrong?"

"No, no…it's nothing, really. I just wanted to see you before I leave." I smiled and took a sip of my own coffee.

"Leave? Where are you going?" She blinked a few times, her dark brows pulling together.

"I'm going to a conference for a few days. It's no big deal,

I just… Well, we haven't really talked about…um…our agreement since you got your period and—"

"Right. I'm probably going to be fertile soon," she said.

"Yes, exactly, though probably not until I get back. I'm only going to be gone three days. I'm guessing it will be sometime next week, right?"

She shrugged. "I really don't know what to expect. I hope I ovulate this cycle, but from what I read, it may take longer."

I tried to keep the disappointment off my face. Patience was the name of the game. How many cycles had I already waited through? Dozens of my own. I had hoped someone Raine's age, someone who likely didn't have any medical issues, would get pregnant right away.

"Well, surprise! I bought you an ovulation predictor kit," I said softly so no one in the semi-crowded coffee shop overheard. I pulled the discreet paper bag out of my purse and pushed it across the table. "Strangest gift ever, right?"

"Oh, cool. I was gonna get one of these myself. Thanks!" She stuck it in her own purse and grinned. "I'll start testing tomorrow."

"Good. And hopefully it will happen not long after I get back, and you can come spend the night or weekend or whatever. I mean, I'm not gonna chain you to the bed or anything, but I want to give it a proper go, you know?"

She had a hard time containing her laughter. "You wanna chain me to the bed?" She waggled her eyebrows at me.

I couldn't help but giggle too. "I mean, you're not our sex slave…unless that turns you on?"

"I don't know, that kinda sounds hot. Does it come with breakfast in bed?"

I was glad we could joke around about this—that kept it from being awkward. "I think breakfast could be arranged. I thought we'd make a fun weekend of it. You know, like a movie marathon or whatever sounds fun to you."

"What if Leo is working when I'm ovulating?" she asked.

"Oh, good question, and, yes, we've discussed that. He's going to take off work if he needs to. At least two days. Hopefully it will fall during one of his three or four days off, but you know how the universe works. It will happen at the least convenient time possible."

"Of course!" she agreed, grinning. "Well, I'm pretty flexible except for tech week at the theater. That's the week I actually have to be there for final fittings and last-minute adjustments to the costumes."

"And when is that?"

"It's in two weeks. Surely it'll happen before that. My period was a little more than a week ago."

"Right. Well, fingers crossed." I literally crossed my fingers on both hands and held them up as a sign to the universe that I'd take any help it could offer.

raine

"What in the world are you doing?" Bonnie asked as I paced around the kitchen, trying to figure out what to do.

I stopped just long enough to say, "Um…Maggie got me this ovulation predictor kit, and I took the first one this morning. I'm freaking out, that's what I'm doing!"

"So, you guys are really doing this, huh?" Bonnie looked between me and the test I'd put on the counter so I didn't hog the bathroom while she was trying to get ready.

"Uh, yeah, what part of freaking out do you not understand?" The panic in my voice was unmistakable.

She drummed her fingers on the counter as her head quirked to the side. "The why part?"

"It's already positive!" I continued my pacing. "Maggie is away at a conference. We thought it wouldn't be positive until next week. I...I don't know what to do."

"Positive means you need to boink or what?" Bonnie had a way of summing up the issue rather succinctly.

"Uh, yeah. Like ovulation is happening within the next twenty-four hours." I'd read the test pamphlet backward and forward, and I wasn't expecting two dark lines to show up on the first day. I was thinking negative today, and then the second line getting darker over the course of the week. Then boom, positive and bow-chicka-wow-wow time.

"Hmm, guess you better call your stud," Bonnie advised. "Good luck. I'm off to shower!"

I sighed. Maybe I should call Danielle? No, there was only one thing to do. I texted both Maggie and Leo:

> Me: Um...wasn't expecting it so early, but the test was positive.

> Leo: What does that mean?

> Maggie: Girl, get yourself to my house pronto allegro.

> Me: But you're not here?

> Maggie: You don't need me! *laughing emoji*

> Leo: Could one of you please clue me in? What's going on?

> Maggie: Go wash your dick, Hubs, and don't jerk off. You need to save all that baby batter for Raine.

> Leo: Does this mean I need to call out sick?

Maggie: You mean call out horny?

Me: You two are too much. So...um...I guess I'm coming over?

Leo: As soon as you can get here. Mags, you sure you're good with this?

Maggie: I'd rather be there, of course, but I can't exactly leave Denver for a fertility emergency.

Me: Okay, I'll come over, but I have to get some work done too, you know.

Maggie: We're not chaining you to the bed, remember?

Leo: What's this about chains? *raised eyebrow emoji*

Me: I'll be there as soon as I can.

Was this really happening? I thought I'd have a few days to prepare, and I thought Maggie was going to be there too. The fact that this was all different than the expectations I'd set in my head was really throwing me off.

But I didn't have time to second-guess. I needed to get this egg over to meet one of a million Mr. Rights.

leo

Sarge was understanding when I called out for work. She knew what was going on—well, not the surrogate part, just the trying to make a baby part. This was one of many times I found it preferable to have a female boss.

I'd been meaning to get up with Beau Garrison today to

ask him about the surveillance videos from the theater building, but it looked like I was going to be fucking all day
instead. Oh, well. Maybe I could fire off a quick call between
rounds.

While I was debating where to start our little fuckfest, the
doorbell rang. I walked over and swung the door open,
wearing nothing but my boxers, and I was *not* expecting to
see none other than Beau Garrison standing right there on
my porch.

"Oh!" My blood froze in my veins as he shot me a
quizzical look that seemed to be asking, *Where the fuck are
your pants, man?!* "Uh, hi, sorry. I thought you were someone
else."

"I texted you that I was on my way," he said, holding up
his phone. "You didn't get it?"

"Uh, no, sorry." I held the door open and gestured him
inside. "I'll go put on some clothes. Just wait here."

He grumbled something about this being the second-
most awkward call he'd been on for work this week, and
somehow I didn't doubt it. He was standing there in full
uniform, and I was wearing my skivvies.

"Be right back," I assured him as I hightailed it to my
bedroom to find some clothes. I had one foot in the leg of my
pants and the other one about to slide in when the doorbell
rang again.

Oh, fuck. Of course Raine would show up when Beau
was here. Oh well, better they meet now. I just hoped she
didn't show up half-dressed.

I stubbed my toe on the corner of the chest at the end of
my bed as I rushed out of the room. Muttering curses under
my breath, I half limped, half ran to the foyer, where a very
surprised-looking Beau was greeting and even more
surprised-looking Raine. At least she was fully clothed in a

floral sundress and sandals with crisscrossing straps that tied around her ankles.

How the fuck am I going to get out of this one?

"Um, am I interrupting something?" Raine stood on the porch, with Beau holding the door open.

I limped into the room. "Come on in, Raine. I didn't know Beau was stopping by, but it's fine…"

"Where's Maggie?" Beau's eyes trailed up and down Raine's body as if his head was filling with ideas about why she might be there. And I figured most of his ideas were probably correct. "I guess I should ask if *I'm* the one interrupting something."

"Raine, this is Officer Garrison from the IUPD. Beau, this is Raine Rivera. She's the grad student who was billed for the missing jewelry," I explained as diplomatically as possible.

"Oh, gotcha." He shot me a knowing look. "Well, it just so happens I'm here about the jewelry."

Raine flashed me a panicked look, and I tried to return a reassuring look. I'd wrap this up quickly, and then she and I could get down to business. Yep, that kind of business.

"Have a seat." I gestured for both of them to follow me to the living room, where Raine took the armchair, and Beau took one end of the sofa. I sat down on the loveseat and turned my attention to Beau.

"Sorry for taking so long to get back with you. There was a lot of footage to be reviewed, so I enlisted some help from interns. It took a while for them to get through all of those dates, but they found something on April twenty-first at about ten p.m. Someone came into the costume lab and was rummaging around. We have them on camera touching the costume in question and removing a small pouch from a black case that was with the costume."

Raine gasped, her hands flying up to cover her mouth. "Oh my god, really?"

"Yes, and I just wanted you to know we're waiting on someone from the theater department to review the footage to help us ID the perp."

Raine looked down at her hands for a moment, counting on her fingers like she was trying to remember something. "April twenty-first was the night *Pygmalion* ended, so there were a lot of people in the building. Ten o'clock was probably right around the time of curtain. There was a cast party in the green room afterwards. There would have been a lot of people around: faculty, undergrads, grad students, some costume and stage crew folks. There were probably at least fifty people who had access to the costume lab that night."

"Well, hopefully Dr. Pataski can make a positive ID," Beau continued. "I'll follow up with her later this week, but I just wanted to stop by and let Leo know where the investigation stood."

Raine stood up and rushed to Beau's side, holding her hand out, which he took reluctantly. "Thank you so much, Officer Garrison. You have no idea how hard it's been to focus on my thesis and my future plans when I didn't even know if I'd be able to graduate. I really hope I can be cleared of any wrongdoing here. They billed me for twelve thousand dollars, and I have been trying to make payments, but that's a lot of money for a graduate student!"

He stood up too, still shaking her hand. "You're quite welcome, Ms. Rivera. I hope you'll be exonerated soon. And get whatever you've paid back."

I walked Beau to the door, giving him an appreciative pat on the back. "You have no idea how glad I am you were able to help Raine out. I owe you big-time. Just let me know if there's anything I can do to return the favor."

He looked right at me and pursed his lips for a moment like he was choosing his words carefully. Finally, he said, "Well, sounds like you owe me *two* favors—the second being keeping your secret for you." He flashed me a wink and waggled his eyebrows.

My nostrils flared as I considered my response. "It's not what you think."

"It's not? Maybe I should stay and join in? What are you doing, playing Monopoly or something?" He chuckled.

"Beau, you've always been a good friend to me, so I'm not going to say anything rude." I straightened my spine. I had an inch or two on him. "Maggie is aware that Raine is here, so there's no secret to keep."

"Oh, it's like that, then?" He clapped me on the shoulder. "What a lucky man, Katz. Lucky, lucky man. If I had a hot young grad student over to my house when my wife was gone, she would flip the fuck out."

I shrugged. "Well, sorry not all wives can be as cool as Maggie."

With that, I opened the door and practically shoved him out onto the porch. After all, I had things to do.

Well, I had *someone* to do.

eighteen

. . .

raine

AS LEO WALKED the kind IU police officer out, I made an important realization. I was no longer in desperate need of money.

Panic sank its claws right through my skin, freezing me in place as thoughts raced through my head. Was I really doing the right thing? Was this too weird? What would happen if I got pregnant and decided I wanted this baby for myself?

Could I actually give my baby, a tiny human I grew in my own body, to someone else to raise?

Would I be a part of their life? What if I took a job thousands of miles away?

My mom gave me away when I was born, and now I was going to do the exact same thing to my child?

Leo arrived in the room after shutting the door, and the clicking sound the lock made almost felt like a prison cell door slamming shut. But he appeared with a beaming smile, rubbing his hands together with obvious excitement.

"Well, ready to get started? Where do you want to be fucked, my dear?"

I slowly backed away, palms raised toward him, shaking my head. I didn't know what to do. Didn't know what to say.

Maggie. If Maggie were here, she'd talk me down. She'd have all the right words. Her silver tongue would validate my concerns, and then, one by one, they'd melt away.

But Leo was standing here with a predatory gleam in his eye, and all I could think about was his breeding fetish, and I felt like prey, a deer in his shiny headlights.

"Raine?" He stepped closer to me still, holding a hand out to me. "What's wrong?"

"I...I don't know if I can do this," I barely gritted the words out.

"What? Why?" His formerly excited expression transformed into pure confusion as he rushed toward me, his arms open wide. He gathered me into his embrace, holding me close to his chest as my entire body was racked with sobs.

"I'm so, so sorry," I kept blubbering as I spread tears and snot all over his chest.

He let go of me and took a step back, but my eyes were on the floor. He reached for me, tucking his finger under my chin and lifting my eyes to his. "Let's go talk about this, okay? Do you want some breakfast? Did you eat at home already?"

I shook my head as another tear dripped down my cheek. "No, I came as soon as I saw the test was positive. I mean, after I texted with you and Maggie. I didn't even have coffee."

"No coffee? Well, we can't have that. Come on, let me make you something to eat." He reached for my hand, and I let him take it. He guided me into the kitchen and gestured toward one of the barstools. "Here, have a seat. What sounds good?"

I shrugged. "I don't know. Nothing really."

"That sounds like omelets to me. That's what I heard." First he put a new pod in the Keurig and placed a mug under it before turning it on. Then he grinned as he began to take things out of the refrigerator: eggs, cheese, milk, some sausage, green peppers and an onion." He started slicing and dicing and cracking eggs, and before I knew it, the whole kitchen was filled with a savory aroma.

And I was sitting there sipping my coffee that I couldn't even remember him handing to me, but he must have, in the expertly choreographed breakfast ballet he was performing before my very eyes.

There was something about watching him move that calmed me down. He'd taken off the button-down shirt he was wearing when I arrived, and was now simply clad in a white t-shirt. The bands of the short sleeves hugged his biceps as he wielded the knife and spatula, and I was mesmerized.

"Maggie would probably never admit this," he leaned on the counter in front of me, "but I'm a much better cook than she is."

"Well, I'll believe it when I taste it." I crossed my arms over my chest and nodded. Though he did grill a mouthwatering steak when I came for dinner after our hike at McCormick's Creek.

"My dad was Jewish, and my mom's family is Italian," he explained. "Trust me, that's a formidable combination when it comes to feeding people."

Clearly, my panic attack was subsiding because I found myself answering, "Feed people what, exactly?!"

He plated the omelets and turned back to me, smiling. "Ready to talk about what just happened in there?" He carried the plates over to the small glass table in the breakfast nook. "Go ahead and get started. I'm just gonna make some coffee for myself really quick. You need a refill?"

I shook my head and picked up a fork. "This smells really good."

"Bet it tastes good too." He gave me a cocky grin as he pressed the button on the Keurig to make another mug of coffee. A few minutes later, he was carrying that and some buttered toast over to the table.

I sighed as I chewed my first bite of the tasty omelet. The cheese and sausage were kicked up a notch by the green peppers, onions and whatever seasoning he added. It melted on my tongue. I grabbed a piece of toast. "This is amazing, actually."

"You doubted me, didn't you?" He took a bite, chewed and dabbed at his mouth with a napkin. "Hot damn, I really outdid myself!"

We both ate in silence for a few more minutes before he set his fork down and cleared his throat, drawing my gaze. "Did you have a change of heart after Beau's news?"

I collected my thoughts. Everything that had swirled in my head in such a jumble of nerves and regret had stabilized, and I only felt silly at this point.

"I think I had a panic attack," I admitted. "I'm feeling… well, nervous. I feel a lot of pressure to make this happen for you guys. I know I don't really have control over whether or not it works, but it's like I want to do my best. Like an exam I want to ace. I don't want to disappoint either of you, and… I also have questions about what's going to happen after. You know, like if I have a kid in the world."

Leo smiled and covered my hand with his own much

larger, warmer one. "I'd think you were crazy if you didn't have reservations and second thoughts, Raine. This is a huge commitment. After this is all over, if we're successful, you'll still be a mom, even if Maggie and I are raising the baby. Is that what you're worried about? Changing your mind about the baby? Or are you thinking, if you don't owe the money for the jewelry, maybe you shouldn't have agreed to this in the first place?"

I shouldn't have been surprised that he was so good at reading me, considering his job. But I didn't know how to tell him he was right, while also being wrong about me changing my mind. I hadn't changed it. I signed a contract, and I wasn't one to go back on my word.

He was right, though, about it being normal to have second thoughts.

To be anxious.

To feel this much pressure, so much pressure, I had a panic attack.

This was a lot to ask of a person. And he knew that, acknowledged it.

"Well, first I thought about the money. And, well, even if I don't have to give some of it to IU…it's not like I have a full-time job yet. I need to start looking, of course, though that's going to be difficult if I'm pregnant, you know? But you're compensating me for my time and efforts. In some ways, it's ideal because it buys me time to find the perfect job. I figure I have a year, really. Not that many graduate students can be so relaxed during their job searches."

"Right." He patted my hand and smiled. "Well, I hope that makes the time commitment easier for you. What about the other stuff, the after the birth part?"

"I'm worried about that too," I admitted as I took another

bite of the delicious omelet, even though I was already getting full.

"Tell me what you're worried about," he offered, "and I'll see if I can alleviate your fears."

"Well," I began as I swallowed my food, "what if I want to be part of the baby's life after he or she is born?"

"That's an easy one." He grinned. "You wanna be part of it? You will be. Simple as that. Done."

"Do you mean like…how?" I blinked, confused about how he could be so sure.

"I know it might be hard to believe this," he began, "but Maggie and I have discussed this a lot, and we don't intend to raise our child or children as a monogamous married couple. We're polyamorous, and we plan for our child to know from the beginning."

"I see." It wasn't that I didn't believe him, just that I wasn't sure how I fit into their plans.

"Do you?" He reached over and grabbed my hand. "We want you to be part of the baby's life, Raine. We don't expect you to pop out the baby and then hand it over, sight unseen, and then we dump you like you were just a baby factory to us."

I chuckled because it reminded me of Maggie's chained-to-the-bed sex slave comment.

"Unless you *don't* want anything to do with the baby," he continued. "We won't force you to be part of their life either."

"But the contract," I argued. "It stated clearly that you and Maggie would be the legal guardians."

"Yes. Maggie wasn't sure the best way to word that in the contract, but the way the law is written…you can't have more than two parents, at least not in Indiana. It's not the most progressive state, as you know. Now, in California, you *can* have more than two parents. Some other states are starting to recognize more complex families, such as polyamorous ones or children conceived with donor eggs or sperm."

"I see. So I couldn't have any legal rights as a parent?" I clarified.

"Is that what this is about?" He leaned toward me. "Or is there something else?"

I sighed. It wasn't about that. It was about feelings and attachment and…ownership of sorts. But not about the baby.

I didn't know how to tell Leo that I was afraid of falling in love with him.

Of falling in love with Maggie.

Because then what?

Before I could say anything else, or Leo could try to allay any more fears, our phones both buzzed at the same time.

> Maggie: So, Round 1 is done, yes? Please confirm.

We both stared at our phones, reading the message, before our eyes locked.

Leo smiled and stroked a finger down my cheek, closing his eyes as he relished the feel of my skin against his. "If you don't want to do this, or you're unsure, I'm not going to pressure you."

"You're not pressuring me." I glanced at the text again. "Maggie might be…but she doesn't mean to."

"Maggie will understand if you want to back out," he told me. "We still have our appointment with the agency in November. That's only a few months away. We can do this that way, and go back to just being friends with you. We don't want you to do anything you don't want to."

His smile was sincere. His words were soothing. But what did he mean about going back to just being friends?

What if "just being friends" wasn't enough for me?

I fell back on my initial assessment of this entire thing: how could I not want to help such an amazing couple bring a child into this world? They wanted to be parents so badly. I had it in my power to make that dream come true—well, I had a pretty good shot at it, as far as I knew. And I'd be benefitting as well, financially speaking.

What were the risks? That was what I kept trying to figure out.

Were there any risks at all? Or just benefits?

Maybe the biggest risk was falling in love with Leo and Maggie…or with my own child.

leo

"Well, what do you think I should tell her?" I held my phone up. "If I don't answer her soon, she'll start calling."

"Well, we don't want that," Raine joked.

I took a good look at her in her feminine floral dress, her legs crossed primly with her napkin in her lap. She'd eaten most of the omelet and a whole piece of toast. She was fueled with food and caffeine now, and I was sure her head was much clearer.

But what of her heart?

I knew that was what really mattered when it came to this decision.

"Tell her to give us a minute, geez!"

The brightest smile spread across my face as I typed out a message to my wife. She sent back a stopwatch emoji and teeth-clenched-with-anxiety face.

I stood up and offered Raine my hand. "Let's just go lie

down and cuddle, okay? And we can go from there. No need for pressure, just two people who find each other attractive going for a cuddle. Does that sound acceptable?"

She nodded, a small smile on her face as she scooted her chair away from the table and allowed me to guide her down the hall to the master bedroom.

"Naked cuddle?" I asked, hoping she would agree.

Trying to conceal a sheepish grin, she reached around to unzip the dress, letting it fall to the floor. Her beautiful curves were on full display under pink satin and lace. Her bra molded to her perfect breasts like it was made especially for her, and the matching panties hugged her hips. I could barely breathe as I watched her unhook the bra, tossing it onto a nearby chair, and step out of the panties, leaving her wearing nothing but a smirk.

I tugged off my white t-shirt and pants—yep, I'd chosen to go commando when I had the unexpected company earlier—and pulled back the comforter and top sheet. She slid under the blankets on her side, gasping when the cool bottom sheet met her bare skin. I joined her, rolling to my side to face her as I pulled the covers over us.

"Well, are you gonna cuddle me or what?" Raine snarked. She tried to be completely serious but then burst into giggles when I looked surprised.

I slid my arm around her and pulled her flush with me. This close, I could smell her cherries and vanilla scent, and her hair looked so smooth and silky, all I could think about was running my fingers through it and then yanking it in my fist as I pounded into her. That thought alone sent a rush of blood to my cock, making it twitch to life, then swell. But I was gonna try to stay in cuddling mode as long as I could.

"Raine, I'm so glad you came into our lives. No matter what happens from here on out, I just want you to know how lucky I am to know you," I told her. "You are so giving. The fact that you would even consider what was, by all reason and logic, an absolutely crazy proposition on my part just shows how open your mind and heart are."

She seemed to melt into me, pressing her lips to mine for a sweet, lingering kiss that stole my breath. My fingers slid through her silky raven tresses, tilting her head so I could access the tender skin on her neck. Soon she was sighing, arching her pelvis toward where my cock strained for her warmth. She lifted her thigh, wrapping her leg around my hip and dragging herself closer to me, close enough to feel my hardness press into her.

"Fuck, Leo," she let out a soft sigh, "I can't help but want you... even if it is crazy and I'm still confused about everything."

"We can do other things," I assured her. "We don't have to, you know... I want you to be sure. But I wanna make you come either way."

She groaned as my cock throbbed against her, then she rolled onto her back, trying to pull me on top of her. She couldn't quite get the leverage to move my heavy frame, but I swung my leg over her hip and hovered over her, leaking precum onto her thigh as I captured her lips in a kiss that left her panting.

"Please, Leo..."

"Tell me you want my cock inside you."

"I want your cock inside me."

"I don't believe you," I growled near her ear as I rubbed myself against her mound. "Convince me." There was no way I was going to fuck her and come inside her pretty pussy unless she really, truly wanted me to.

She reached down and wrapped her fingers around my cock, notching it at her entrance. "I need your cock inside me, Leo. I want you to come in me. I want you to get me pregnant."

Fuuuck, she was so wet. My cock throbbed at her entrance, waiting for me to be certain this was what she wanted. She lifted her hips, trying to swallow me as I held my breath, forcing myself to hold back when all I wanted to do was push deep inside her.

"Fuck me, Leo. Breed me. Drain your balls inside me, baby. I need your cum," she whimpered, grinding up against me. Her pussy lips wrapped around the head of my cock, giving them a tight, wet kiss, and I didn't know how much longer I could resist.

"God, I'm gonna come just from grinding against you, fuuuuck," she moaned. "Leo…I'm ready. I want to do this for you and Maggie. It's not just lust talking, though I need to come too… I just had a panic attack, but I'm over it now. I need you." She let go of my cock, and her gaze locked onto mine.

I searched her face for any signs of deception, but all I saw was a young woman who had struggled with some anxiety but had figured out a way to soothe her nerves. She closed her eyes and sucked in a breath. "God, I really do want you," she said as she breathed out.

This time, I fisted my cock and notched it at her entrance, the heat engulfing me, sending a desperate shock of need throughout my body. My balls tightened as I clenched my jaw, hoping I would be able to make her cum before emptying inside her.

"Let me get you off first." I hesitated over her, pulling back slightly till my cock wasn't touching her lips any longer.

"No, I'm gonna come as soon as you slide into me," she vowed. "You're driving me absolutely mad."

"You're sure?" I met her dark, lusty gaze again.

She wrapped her legs around my hips and arched up into me. "What do I have to do to prove it? Fuck, Leo, take me. Have your way with me!"

That was it. I couldn't hold back any longer. I guided myself to her entrance again and plunged inside her, feeling her walls tighten around me and suck me deeper. "Oh, god…why do you have to feel so fucking good?"

"Breed me," she growled in my ear as she began to writhe against me, hands on my ass as she tried to take me deeper.

"Grrrr…." I slid part of the way out and then slammed back into her again, reaching her depths as she cried out, convulsing in my arms as her pussy rhythmically milked me.

"Now, Leo! Now," she cried out as she thrashed, her orgasm making her a feral creature, desperate for my cum.

I pumped as hard and fast as I could, getting off on my goal of spurting as much seed into her as I could. My orgasm hit me like a bolt of lightning, an exquisite shock that rolled through my body from my dick to the tips of my fingers and toes, resounding in spine-tingling pleasure again and again and again until it slowly subsided.

And when I tried to move, she gripped me tight, not wanting to let me go. "No, stay. Make sure every drop gets inside me."

"Oh, god…" My dick pulsed at the idea. It wouldn't be long before I was hard again, and I could go another round.

But for now, I held her, kissing her neck and breasts and telling her over and over what a good girl she was, praising her for how well she took my cock.

nineteen

. . .

maggie

IT WAS VERY hard to concentrate on the presentations at the conference when my mind and heart were back in Bloomington, Indiana, with Leo and Raine. I texted them to ask if they'd at least gotten round one done. An eternity later —*okay, it was five minutes*—Leo texted back that they were about to go for round one.

Now it had been an hour after that, and no response. *Should I text again? Should I call?*

Never mind that I was sitting in a riveting presentation about emerging issues in healthcare law.

It was hard for me not to be there for this momentous occasion. With any luck, I was missing the conception of my child. The fulfillment of all my dreams.

I was jealous.

It had nothing to do with trust. I trusted Leo and Raine. It had to do with missing out. I was jealous that they were getting to have this experience together, and I was missing it.

That was normal, right?

I didn't want to feel like a bad person. This was Leo's idea. I didn't know if I would have ever come up with it, to be honest. And bypassing the whole medical establishment to conceive this baby the old-fashioned way was going to save time and money. It made all the sense.

It was natural.

And so were my feelings, which were all over the place. I could barely sit still.

Finally, my phone buzzed, and I grabbed it as fast as a lizard's tongue darting out to catch a fly.

Leo: Round 1 is in the books. Fingers crossed!

Me: Whew. Glad to hear it. Try to get at least two more rounds in today, please?

Leo: We'll do our best.

I had to keep reminding myself that the real issue I had with all of this was the lack of control. I was used to being in control of everything, and for this, I had to completely surrender it. I had to defer to Leo and Raine and…whatever higher power could ensure egg met sperm, and a baby was the ultimate result. I had to have faith that could happen without me.

And for a woman used to making things happen through sheer will and tenacity, that was hard.

leo

"I'm so sore…" Raine groaned as she propped her feet up on the ottoman and shook the popcorn in the bowl.

"Um, sorry?" I sat down beside her, grabbing the bowl

and stuffing some popcorn in my mouth. "If it makes you feel any better, my balls are so empty, they hurt too."

"Well, aren't we a pair?" She leaned against my arm and took a handful of popcorn. "Look at us, all fucked out."

I sighed. "Surely Maggie will let us have the rest of the night off. That's, what, four rounds?"

"At least." She rolled her eyes. "You talked to her on the phone, right? While I was in the shower?"

I nodded. "She seemed pleased with our efforts."

"She's such a task-master. Can you imagine if she was here? Cracking the whip over us?" She made a whip-cracking sound and gesture before erupting in giggles.

"Might be kinda sexy," I argued. "We could have dressed her up in some latex and let her have at it."

"Oh, hey, I did get an email from the theater department chair this afternoon. I think your buddy turned over the evidence, and they want to see me in their office tomorrow morning. So, if we're gonna fuck again tomorrow, it's gonna have to be early."

I chewed and swallowed my popcorn, pausing the movie that was about to begin. We'd been talking all the way through the opening credits. "You're gonna make me get up early on my day off? No fair!"

"I'm gonna make you get up alright," she joked. "Thank you, by the way, for having your friend look into the jewelry theft. It's truly amazing to be exonerated!"

"You're welcome. Now, do you want to watch this movie or what? You picked it out!" I reminded her.

"Of course I do!" she assured me. "The costumes are to die for!"

I put my arm around her. "Didn't this movie come out before you were born?"

"Well, yes, but who cares? Glenn Close is magnificent! They somehow made John Malkovich sexy. I can't believe you've never seen this before. It's basically like an FMF gone wrong. Someone should have told these folks about polyamory."

"Well they didn't call it a 'dangerous' liaison for nothing," I quipped.

"Touché!"

We were both cracking up as the movie finally began. Then she shushed me like an overbearing librarian and snuggled up to my warm body as she munched on popcorn. My beautiful girl was radiating that freshly fucked glow, and I was the one who gave it to her.

I was pretty content right now, despite my achingly empty balls. Hopefully they were hard at work manufacturing more baby batter for our next escapade.

My phone buzzed with a text from Maggie, but I didn't want to interrupt the movie. I'd text her back before bed.

raine

I felt like a naughty, naughty girl on my drive to campus. I…ahem…aroused Leo at six o'clock this morning by perching between his legs and waking his cock up with gentle licks. He rose to the occasion beautifully, and I rode his cock until he came deep inside me. Then he made me flip over onto my back so his jizz didn't seep out. He even made me put my legs in the air.

He didn't want me to shower before I left for my meeting, lest I wash out some of his seed, but I vetoed that idea. I decided to park in the garage on the former Jordan Avenue, which was now called Eagleson Avenue—I could never seem to remember the new name. It was just across the street from the theater complex on campus. Before I got out of the car, my phone buzzed with a text.

> Maggie: Hey, how did it go last night and this morning? Did you stay over?

Hmm. I thought she would already know the answer to that, but maybe Leo fell back asleep after our romp this morning?

> Me: Sure did. I think we are at five rounds now. We'll try to squeeze in one more this afternoon.

> Maggie: Afternoon delight, I like it!

> Me: I'm on campus now—about to meet with the theater chair about the jewelry heist. Leo was able to hook me up with an IU officer who reviewed the video footage. I just hope they admit they were wrong and I get my money back.

> Maggie: Excellent! Well, if you need any legal advice, let me know. Pro bono, of course.

> Me: *kiss emoji*

> Maggie: *heart emoji*

I smiled as I locked my door and headed through the thick humidity to my meeting. It was going to be a super-hot July day, and it already felt like a furnace out here. Maybe we'd catch a break, and some storms would roll in this afternoon to cool everything off.

"Come in, come in," Dr. Pataski greeted me, all plastic smiles as she gestured to one of the chairs across from her desk. Sitting in the other was the Costume Czar we all loved to hate. "Dean Chow couldn't make it today, but she sends her best."

I settled in the chair and gave Dr. Pataski a professional smile. I did not look at Dr. Wharton at all. I really did not like that woman.

"Thank you for coming in on such short notice," Dr. Pataski said. "It has come to our attention that someone did indeed enter the costume lab during the time period you were responsible for the vintage jewelry, and, through investigative means, we have identified the person who stole the items in question."

This is the Best. Day. Ever. Vindication is sweet!

I leaned forward in my chair. "So I'm off the hook?"

"Yes, Ms. Rivera. You've been cleared, and the university will be pressing charges against the person who stole the jewelry." She laced her fingers together and placed her hands on the desk in front of her.

My heart, which had been racing since I entered the building, was finally starting to calm down. "May I ask who this person is?"

"We are not at liberty to say, though, once the arrest is made, I assume it will be public record," Dr. Pataski shared. "So…as they say, 'stay tuned'!"

I looked over at the Costume Czar to see if an apology was on her lips. She just offered me a cold, hard stare and then said, "Your thesis is still due next month. Hope you've been working on it."

"This distraction hasn't helped," I admitted. "But it will be done. Don't worry."

"We're sorry for the inconvenience." Dr. Pataski stood up and extended her hand to shake mine. "Here is a check for the amount you had paid toward the replacement cost of the jewelry. Again, we're very sorry to have put you through this."

So that was all I got: a half-ass apology, a handshake, and my own money back. Whatever, I'd happily take it if it meant this ordeal was behind me. They probably would have done more ass-kissing if they knew my girlfriend was a lawyer.

I stepped back out into the oppressive sunshine and texted Danielle.

> Me: What are you doing? I need to celebrate!

> Danielle: What are we celebrating? Never mind, don't care. I'm starving. Lunch?

> Me: It's ten o'clock.

> Danielle: Brunch?

> Me: OK. Uptown Café in fifteen?

> Danielle: We'll be there.

> Me: We?

> Danielle: Me and le bébé!

> Me: Duh!

I was back at my car by the time I was finished with the text conversation, so I climbed in and drove to the other side of campus, parking a street over from Kirkwood, and sweating my ass off to get to Uptown Café. I'd taken that shower against Leo's will, but by the time I returned, I was gonna need another one.

Danielle was already there when I arrived. She threw her arms around me. "You're glowing, my friend! Are you already knocked up?"

She said it loud enough that two older ladies dining nearby whipped around to look at us. I gritted my teeth and whispered, "Keep it down," to my exuberant friend.

We were seated far away from those two ladies, which was a relief. After we settled in at our table, my friend tried again: "So, are you knocked up or what? Is that what we're celebrating?"

"For fuck's sake, Dani, it's almost like you, a pregnant individual, do not know how the whole gestation process works. I am just now ovulating, well, sometime in the past twenty-four hours or so. I'm not gonna know for a while if it worked," I explained.

"Oh, right." She shook her head. "I'm gonna blame that on preggo brain. So what *are* we celebrating then?"

"Leo helped me get out of that bill I owed the university for the missing jewelry." I could barely get the words out without a giddy squeal.

"That's fantastic news!" She reached across the table, grabbed one of my hands and squeezed it tight. "So how did he manage that?"

"Well, you know he's a cop..."

Danielle nodded.

"He contacted a buddy at IUPD, and he went through all the hours of video from when I had the costume and accessories checked out, and they caught someone stealing it red-handed!"

"Oh my god!" Danielle's hands flew to her mouth. "That's so cool! Like something that would happen in a movie. So who was it? Someone you know? Were you framed?"

"Now hold on there, Agatha Christie. They wouldn't tell me who actually did it. But they did call me in for a meeting today to tell me my debt has been cleared. And to return the three grand I'd already paid." I swiped a hand over my forehead in a gesture of relief. "Now I can finish up my thesis, get it turned in, and get the hell out of here."

Danielle stared at me, blinking a few times. "Well, not literally though…"

It took me a moment to realize what she meant. And before I could answer, the server came by and took our orders. So I had plenty of time to decide how to respond.

"Well, no, not literally. I won't be leaving right away. I will have to wait to see how this plays out." I gestured to my lower abdomen.

"Speaking of which," Dani leaned in like she was going to whisper a secret, "did you ever hear back from your mom?"

It had been a couple of weeks now since I texted her, and I had heard nothing. I fingered the R pendant hanging around my neck. "No…I'm beginning to think the number Tyler gave me isn't hers anymore."

"Have you tried to find her on social media?" Dani queried.

"No…but I should, right? If nothing else, just to see what she looks like."

"Your brother gave you her full name, right?"

I nodded.

"Look her up on Facebook!" Danielle urged. "C'mon. I bet you anything she didn't get your text."

I grabbed my phone and searched for "Reina Clarke" on my Facebook app. I hardly ever logged on there, but my mom and brother used Facebook, so staying friends with them made it seem like we were a half-ass family.

"Oh, I found her. Damn, that didn't take long!" I only glanced at the profile long enough to conclude it was her: same name, and she had tagged Tyler Clarke, my half-brother, in one of the photos I could see. It was from a few years ago.

I handed it over to Danielle. "Here she is. Just like that. Wow."

"Oh my god, you really look like her! She's so pretty!" Danielle gushed.

Her hair was gray at the temples and cut in a bob that accentuated her delicate features. She appeared to be much thinner than me, but I could see where I'd gotten the shape of my eyes, nose, mouth and cheekbones. My features looked like hers with a bit of a twist.

"It says she's an art teacher," Dani read in her About Me section. "You must have gotten your artistic eye from her."

I scoffed. "Maybe."

"So…do you think your dad was…white or…?" Danielle looked up at me. "Are you going to ask her who he was?"

"I don't even know if I can get her to talk to me, Dani." This conversation was making me feel triggered. I was feeling the same panic I felt yesterday after Leo's cop buddy left. "For all I know, she got my text and just decided she doesn't want to talk to me."

"She looks so nice, though," Dani argued. "And she's an art teacher. Wouldn't she want to know the little girl she gave up all those years ago is getting a Master of Fine Arts?"

I heaved a sigh, but before I could face any more pressure from her, our food arrived. I knew better than to try to replicate the amazing omelet Leo cooked for me yesterday morning, so I played it safe and got a Belgian waffle with strawberries and blueberries on top. It smelled absolutely divine.

"Just say something simple," Danielle was still rambling on about this as she buttered her toast and stabbed a sausage link with her fork. "Like, 'Hey, I think you're my mom! I'm about to start my own family, and I've been wanting to know more about my roots.'"

"Yeah, okay, whatever," I mumbled after stuffing a bite of waffle in my mouth. It was incredible, the fruit bursting on my tongue with flavor, perfectly balanced with the sweetness of the waffle and maple syrup. I wanted to dive into this and forget this conversation ever happened.

Danielle grabbed my phone, and her thumbs went flying. "Done!" she cheered before she shoveled a bite of sausage and eggs into her mouth.

I put my phone back in my purse. I didn't expect Reina Clarke to answer anytime soon. I didn't even want to think about it—the idea made my stomach feel queasy.

I spent the rest of breakfast trying to get Dani to tell me what names she and the guys were discussing for their little bundle of joy. When she wouldn't come clean, I started making up my own names like Odysseus—a nod to Aris's Greek heritage, or Guy—a nod to Danielle's French heritage.

I couldn't think of a funny one for Noah, so I suggested "Moses," another Biblical name.

"I think I prefer it when we talk about you," she said, cramming her mouth full of her last sausage.

"Speaking of sausage," I eyed her now empty plate, "I better get back to Leo…"

When I made it back to my car, I pulled out my phone to see if Leo or Maggie had texted me. Nope, nothing from them, but I did have a Facebook message. My heart started to pound as soon as I realized it might be from my birth mom. I pressed the notification, and the message from Reina Clarke popped up.

My heart stopped as I read it.

Please stop contacting me. I did not want to be involved with you when I carried you, when you were born, or at any time after. My parents refused to pay for me to get an abortion, and I had no way to pay for it myself. They said it was my own fault I got drunk at a party and got preg-nant, and I should suffer the consequences.

Have a nice life and all, just don't contact me again.

Then my heart plummeted, shattering into a million pieces as I dropped my phone in the passenger seat, a painful wail shuddering through my body.

twenty

. . .

leo

I TEXTED Raine but didn't hear back. It had been a couple of hours now since her appointment with the theater folks. I assumed she'd come back here afterward so we could get another round or two in before her egg expired. Maggie was adamant that it only lived for twenty-four hours, so we had limited time to shoot as many swimmers up there as possible.

Maybe she didn't get as good of news at the appointment as we thought she would?

Blue and I curled up on the sofa watching an afternoon baseball game, and I must have drifted off because the ringing phone made me jolt awake. It was Maggie.

"Hello?" I managed in my groggy half-asleep voice.

"Sleeping on the job?" accused my wife.

"Hey, baby. How's the conference today?"

"It's fine. Wrapping up this afternoon, and then the final session is tomorrow morning until noon. Then I'm on the plane and will be back in Indy by six o'clock," she reminded me as if I wasn't counting down the hours till she was back home.

"Good. Wow, the time's gone fast, hasn't it?" I yawned and stretched, trying to get my brain and body back into daytime mode.

"Maybe for you," she scoffed. "You got to spend all your time fucking, right?"

"Well, I think we made it five rounds," I reported.

"Didn't you get another one in this afternoon?" Her voice had gone from teasing to serious in a heartbeat.

I blinked a few times. "What time is it?" It was still bright outside, but it was that golden late afternoon light.

"It's almost five o'clock there. It's three o'clock here in Denver," she said.

"Oh, right. Um…Raine had a meeting on campus this morning, and she hasn't come back yet."

"What do you mean she hasn't come back?" Now there was panic in her voice as well.

Blue hopped off the sofa and looked up at me forlornly, his *take me out now, or I'm gonna shit on your floor* look. "Well, I texted her around noon, but I didn't hear back."

There was silence, and that was bad. Very bad. I braced myself for the impact as I walked over to get Blue's leash. He trotted behind me, right on my heels.

"Leo, what do you mean you didn't hear back?" Her voice sounded beyond panicked now.

"Exactly what I said. She didn't text me back." I clipped the leash to Blue's collar and opened the back door.

"But you guys were supposed to fuck again this afternoon," she said as if I'd forgotten her rigorous—and rather vigorous, for that matter—fucking schedule.

"I know that, but she didn't come back here after her meeting, and she didn't return my text." I led Blue down the steps and to the tree line, his preferred pooping location.

"Did you call her?"

"Well, no, but—"

"What were you doing all afternoon?" she demanded.

"Well, Blue and I watched some baseball, and then—"

"Then you fell asleep, right?" It was most certainly an accusation.

Oh no, now the lawyer is coming out.

"Do you have her address?" Maggie asked next, but it still sounded vaguely accusatory.

"Um…no?"

"I'll text it to you," she said. "Go over to her apartment and check on her, for fuck's sake."

"Well, maybe she's sick, or something bad happened at the meeting." Wow, she was really freaking out about this, wasn't she? What was she going to do when Raine actually got pregnant? Expect an hourly check-in?

"Go find out. And call me back later," she instructed.

I sighed. "Fine."

I couldn't afford to have two women upset with me, though I had no idea why Raine would be upset. Maybe Maggie was right. I should go make sure she was okay.

raine

I had been curled up in a ball for so long, my joints ached when I finally moved. Climbing down from my bed, I noted it was almost six o'clock. The sun was starting to sink in the sky, but it was still bright. Maybe the humidity had eased up. I didn't plan to find out.

Bonnie was going to be gone all evening, and for that I was grateful. I only wanted to be alone right now. I'd ignored texts and calls from Leo and Maggie. What was I supposed to say?

My day had been a total roller coaster, and now I was at the very bottom.

Food? I asked myself. *No.*

My stomach was still full of that Belgian waffle and plenty of self-loathing. I wasn't even supposed to be here.

My mother wanted to abort me. I was conceived through…rape? I guess? She said she was drunk. That meant she couldn't give consent. She likely didn't even know who my father was. And I would never find out any more than that.

She didn't want me then. She didn't want me now.

I was just some random person who wasn't wanted and shouldn't even be here.

As I contemplated a shower, I realized I had been sitting on the edge of my bed for at least twenty minutes. Then there was a knock at the front door.

"Go away!" I shouted in the general direction of said door.

I should be working on my costumes for the Brown County theater.

I should be working on my thesis project.

I should be drowning my sorrows in liquor.

I should just be drowning.

"Raine?! Are you in there? C'mon, open up!" came a deep, gruff voice through the door.

Leo.

Fuck. If I didn't answer him, he'd probably call his cop buddies over here. And if I told him what I was thinking… he'd probably have me committed.

My entire body throbbed with pain, from my head to my

feet, as I staggered toward the door. Makeup was likely smeared all over my face. My hair was a wreck. I'd taken off the dress I'd worn to my meeting today, and all I had on was a ratty Taylor Swift concert tee and my panties.

The persistent knocking came again, louder this time. "Raine, please open up. I need to know you're okay."

I groaned before swinging the door open.

Leo was standing there in basketball shorts and a loose-fitting t-shirt, something about a police charity 5K. Concern was etched on his face, and as soon as he assessed my condition, he opened his arms wide.

Second breakdown he'd witnessed in the last two days. Fuck, what kind of baby could I give him?

A mentally unstable one.

He deserved better. Maggie deserved better.

"Just let me hold you," he pleaded, spreading his arms even wider. The concern in his voice gutted me, and my body just gravitated to those open arms like there were magnets in them, and I was made of iron. And maybe I was.

He wrapped those arms around me and squeezed me to his chest. "I guess you don't want to talk about it since you didn't answer my calls or texts."

I silently sobbed into his broad chest, his warmth drawing tears out of me somehow when I thought they'd long since dried up. How could I tell him? How...could I even go on with myself?

He reached down and swept me off my feet, lifting my bulky frame into his massive arms, and then he carried me to my bed. Just like yesterday morning, he laid me down on the mattress and climbed in next to me, pulling me back into his embrace as I said absolutely nothing.

He just held me there, whispering to me in deep, dulcet tones, "It's okay, baby, I'm here. I've got you. Whatever it is, we can figure it out. I'll take care of you. Let me take care of you, baby."

maggie

By five o'clock Colorado time, I still had not heard back from Leo. I tried to call and got his voicemail. I didn't even bother trying Raine. Something was going on, and being this far away was sending bolts of anxiety through me like lightning strikes. I was at dinner with one of my lawyer friends, and she noticed I was visibly trembling.

"Maggie? What's up?" Lorelei's concerned gaze roved my face. "You haven't touched your dinner. Is there something wrong with it?"

"No, it's not that." I stared at my phone helplessly.

"You still haven't heard back from your husband?"

Lorelei and I had known each other for a long time—we met in law school. She now practiced law in Maryland, so I didn't see her often, only at conferences. But we stayed in contact. She didn't know everything going on in my life, but she did know Leo and I were looking into surrogates.

I shook my head. "No...he isn't answering his phone either."

"He's not at work, right?" she asked, and I shook my head. "You're sure he wasn't called out for work?"

She knew about his work with the crisis management team. I shrugged. "Maybe. It's possible. But I can't shake the feeling something bad happened."

I couldn't explain that there was an issue with our girlfriend/surrogate, and I felt completely out of control right now. The lack of communication was only magnifying my panic.

She grabbed my hand and squeezed it. "What can you do

to make yourself feel better right now? Do you want to order a drink? Would that relax you?"

"No, no. I'll be okay." I forced a smile as I met her concerned gaze. She smiled back, and I returned to pushing the vegetable medley around on my plate. My stomach was churning—there was no way I was going to keep any food down like this. It all sounded so unappetizing.

"You know, the thing tomorrow morning isn't that important. You could see if you could switch your flight…?" she suggested. She knew how rare it was for me to be this out of sorts.

I sighed. She had a point. Maybe I could change my flight.

"I can take notes for you tomorrow. I hate to think of you being miserable all night," she continued.

"Okay. Let me check." I pulled out my phone and brought up the airline's app. After doing a quick search, I saw it was possible to switch my flight to one at eight o'clock tonight. I'd land in Indianapolis well after midnight, but my car was parked there. I could just drive home early and surprise Leo. We'd get this mess figured out.

"Thank you, Lorelei. You've always been a great friend to me." This time when I smiled at her, it was genuine.

"Hey, I'm just trying to get you to follow your heart. I know all this fertility stuff has been really hard on you, my friend. I am really praying that everything works out for you guys. I know you're going to make incredible parents." She grabbed my hand across the table and squeezed it tenderly.

"Thank you. Here, I'll leave some cash for my part of the check. Then I better go get packed up and hustle to the airport." Just making this decision was already lifting some of the panic.

When I stood up, Lorelei gathered me into her arms and

whispered in my ear, "Best of luck, sweetie. I know every-thing's going to work out for you guys."

But as I headed back to my room, a shudder racked my body as I imagined horrifying reasons for Leo and Raine to go incommunicado.

twenty-one

. . .

leo

LATE IN THE NIGHT, I awoke to Raine trailing fingers down my arms, down my hip, my thigh. I sighed and rolled over onto my back, bringing her with me. Her head rested on my chest, rising and falling with my deep breaths. Her fingers roamed between my pecs, making trails in the thick mat of my chest hair, and then down my hairy stomach to my stiffening cock.

"We don't have to…" I kissed the top of her hair, inhaling her sweet scent. "Go back to sleep, baby. It's the middle of the night."

I couldn't remember what time I arrived. Raine answered the door a blubbering mess. I didn't know what triggered her, but I assumed something bad happened at her meeting with the theater department. I'd find out from Beau if there was an issue after the department reviewed the video surveillance footage.

Maggie was going to be home tonight, so I'd get Raine through this rough patch, and we'd figure it all out together.

Everything would be rainbows and unicorns again by the time Maggie arrived. She didn't need to come home to find I'd messed things up.

Raine's fingers wrapped around my dick, yanking all rational thought from my grasp. "Will you make love to me?" came her small voice.

She had never used that terminology before, and when I heard the L word, it tugged at my heart. But she didn't wait for an answer. She rolled onto her back and tried her damnedest to pull me on top of her.

Of course, she couldn't move me, being approximately half my size. But I found myself straddling her, guiding my cock into the tight embrace of her pussy and her wrapping her legs around me. When I heard the front door open and flinched, she said, "It's just Bonnie coming home. Don't stop. Please don't stop."

We moved slowly, my hips grinding my cock in and out of her with deep but leisurely strokes. Her fingers trailed up and down my back with soft caresses as she sighed with pleasure.

"Do I feel good?" she wanted to know as her hips rocked in time with mine.

"Yes, baby, so good…so tight."

"Are you gonna come inside me?"

"If you want me to." Thinking about filling her was bringing me to the edge, but I wanted her to come first. "Come around my cock, Raine. Let me feel you squeeze me, milk my cum from me."

"Okay…" She sighed softly as she buried her face in my chest and tightened her hold around me. Her legs hooked around mine as she took my cock deeper and faster.

"That's it, baby…give me that orgasm," I urged her on,

nibbling on her earlobe and then down her neck until she cried out in ecstasy.

Her pussy fluttered around me as tears spilled out of her eyes. I couldn't stop. I was already falling over the cliff when she began to shatter around me.

It took a long moment for me to catch my breath and be able to come to her aid. She sobbed against me, squeezing me tightly as she drew in shuddering, gasping breaths.

"Raine, what's wrong? Did I hurt you?"

"No…no, you've been absolutely amazing to me. You and Maggie both," she managed between sobs. "I just don't know if I can do what you're asking me to do. I—"

I pulled out of her, leaving a trail of sticky cum on her thigh. "I'll be right back, baby. Hold on." I went to the bathroom to get a warm washcloth and ran right smack dab into…

My wife?

maggie

I had been waiting patiently for Leo and Raine to finish fucking. When Bonnie let me in, she said she wasn't sure when he got here but, as far as she knew, they'd been asleep for a while. But when I crept to the door, I heard him moan. I'd know that sound anywhere. So I went back to the living room to stew.

The longer I sat there, the more uncomfortable I got. Not because he was fucking her. Hell, they were trying to make a baby. And I wanted them to. I drew up and signed a contract. And I'd been bugging them for two days about getting in as much sex as possible.

So why was I upset? Uncomfortable? Because I thought she was going to be at my house, not him at hers? That was ridiculous. What difference did it make whose bed they were in? Did it make it more my baby if it was conceived in my bed?

No, of course not.

But before I could psychoanalyze myself any further, the bedroom door creaked open, and I sprang into action. I didn't mean to march down the hall with such determination, but it happened anyway. And I certainly didn't expect to collide with a huge solid wall of a man. I practically bounced off him.

"Maggie?" he gasped.

My eyes had adjusted to the dark—I'd told Bonnie to go ahead and turn off the lights before she went to bed—so I could just make out the contours of his face and body in the pitch-black hallway. He was naked. That, I expected.

"I thought you were getting back tomorrow?" He wrapped his arms around me and drew me into his chest. He smelled like sex and Raine.

"It is tomorrow," I choked out, my arms still stiff at my sides. I didn't want to hug him right now. I didn't know why, but I didn't.

I was suddenly irrationally angry.

Angry that I was standing here in the dark surprising my husband who had just fucked another woman.

Angry that I didn't know if I should be jealous of him or of her.

Angry at my body because I couldn't conceive and carry my own baby.

It just hit me all at once, and I was sure my utter exhaustion from traveling and running scenario after scenario through my head about what might be going on for hours on end didn't help.

"You didn't answer your phone," was all I said.

"You told me to come check on Raine," he whispered. "So I did. She was upset."

The door creaked again, and I looked up to find Raine standing in the doorway with a towel wrapped around her. "Raine, are you okay?" I asked, but she ignored me. She went straight into the bathroom and shut the door.

Before I could say anything else, the lock engaged, and the shower began to run. I turned back to my husband. "What the fuck is going on?"

He grabbed my hand and guided me to the living room. After fumbling around for a minute or two, he found one of the light switches. The entire space was flooded with brightness, burning my eyes and inflicting me with an immediate headache.

"Raine wasn't answering my texts or calls," he said, "so you told me to come over here. You gave me her address." He sounded defensive for some reason.

"I know that much." I sounded just as snarky.

"I came over and knocked on her door, but she didn't answer at first. Then I pounded and yelled that I needed to know she was okay. She finally came and opened it, then collapsed in my arms in tears. She never told me what was wrong. I carried her to bed and just held her while she cried. Then we must have fallen asleep."

"Well, you must have woken up at some point," I argued, "because you were clearly fucking when I got here."

"We thought that was Bonnie getting home," I admitted. "I'm sorry. I left my phone right here." He reached over to the end table next to the sofa and picked it up, scanning his missed calls and texts, probably all from me.

"So…you just fucked her without bothering to find out why she was crying?" I didn't mean to sound so accusatory, but…well, was that what he'd done?

"She woke me up and asked me to," he defended himself. "So I did. I was half asleep, so I'm sorry if I wasn't thinking extra clearly. I've basically been used as a stud service the past two days, and I'm just doing the fucking best I can to get you a baby."

"Get me a baby?" I shot to my feet. "That's what you're doing?"

He said nothing, just stared at me, his nostrils flaring.

There was silence for a moment until our heads both turned toward a tiny squeak in the hallway. Raine.

She stood, shivering, in a towel, her skin ghostly white. My heart ached for her. I turned toward my husband. "Fine. You're done. We don't need your services any longer. Just get the fuck out of here."

I rushed toward Raine and pulled her into my arms, trying to soothe her as Leo stood, assessing the situation. The scowl on his face disappeared, and he simply picked up his phone and keys and headed out the door, letting it quietly click shut behind him.

"Where's he going?" Raine asked, those three words filled with nothing but pain and longing.

I was jetlagged, exhausted, angry and hurt, but I knew Raine needed to be taken care of. First, I took her to her room, guiding her to the bed to sit while I rifled through her drawers for some comfy clothes. Then, while she got dressed, I went to her bathroom and got her brush. I sat on the bed, combing the tangles from her wet hair while she stared stoically at the wall.

"Oh, Raine…sweetheart, I hate seeing you like this. I'm sure you're exhausted, but will you tell me what's going on? You know Leo and I care about you, and we want to make sure you're okay. You're clearly not right now. I want to understand what happened so I can help you if I can."

She still said nothing, just reached for her phone, which was on one of the nightstands next to her bed. She pressed an icon, scrolled, pressed again and handed it to me.

I skimmed the text, emotions slamming into me as I tried to figure out who it was from. I looked up at her with questioning eyes.

She mouthed, "My mother," before bursting into tears once again.

I held her to me, rocking her back and forth, and I tried—and failed—to soothe her.

After what felt like hours, she pulled back and looked at me out of red-rimmed eyes, her cheeks streaked with tears. "I can't do this anymore. I'm sorry. You both deserve better than me."

"Oh, Raine," I pressed her to me again, but she immediately pulled back.

"Please go," she said. "Please. I don't want to talk anymore."

My heart welling with the wounds of defeat, I stood up from the bed and quietly made my exit, same as my husband had done mere moments ago.

twenty-two

. . .

raine

ONCE LEO and Maggie both left, Bonnie stumbled out of her bedroom and into mine. "What the fuck is going on?" She was wearing her Care Bears nightgown that had seen better days, and her strawberry blonde hair was plaited in a long braid down her back.

"Sorry for all the noise." I sniffled and reached over to grab a tissue from my nightstand.

"Do you want to talk about it?" She sat across from me on my bed. "I'm wide awake now. You want coffee?"

I looked around my room, my gaze finally landing on the clock on my dresser. "Three a.m. Nice. I don't want to keep you up. Don't you have to go to work in the morning?"

"I haven't decided yet." She sighed and pulled my comforter over her. "Did you get into a fight with Maggie and Leo?"

I folded my arms across my chest. "Not really. But I think we broke up."

She blinked a few times, trying to make sense of my words. "Wow. Don't you have a contract or something?"

I already felt pretty shitty about myself, but the fact that I was breaking our contract made me feel even worse. What were they going to do about it though? There was a clause that we could back out if I wasn't pregnant yet. And if I turned out to be…what would they do, sue me? It wasn't like I had any money. The contract was more to protect me than them…except for when it came to who got the baby.

"Well, if I got pregnant, then I guess I'll just give them the baby and that will be the end of things." I scrubbed my hands down my tear-streaked face.

"Wasn't that your plan anyway?" Bonnie leaned forward. "I thought you were doing this to finance a gap year so you could look for a job. Even if your intimate relationship is over with them, they'll still have to pay you the money if you don't break that part of the agreement, the growing their baby part."

"Yes, that's true." I closed my eyes as the circumstances closed in around me like prison walls. "I guess there's nothing I can really do now except wait and see if I'm pregnant."

"And that takes what, like two weeks?"

"Some tests you can use a few days early. So maybe ten days?" I had done a little reading on this. "I don't have time to worry about that right now anyway. I have to get my thesis done. It's due next week, and the Costume Czar, who is on my committee, already hates me, especially since she found out I wasn't responsible for the antique jewelry that went missing. I have to really wow the committee so everyone else passes me because she probably won't."

Bonnie's nostrils flared. "Well, that doesn't sound fair."

"To quote my mom, 'life's not fair.'" My adoptive mother

had told me that so many times, I might as well have gotten it tattooed on me I was finding out how right she was the hard way this summer.

My phone rang before I could say anything else. I figured it was Leo or Maggie, hoping to work things out, but I could see Danielle's face illuminated on the screen from across the room. I dove for it, getting to it just in time before it went to voicemail.

"Hello?"

"Hey, it's Aris," said a smooth male voice.

My heart immediately began to race. "Where's Dani? Why are you calling me at three in the morning?"

"We're at the ER with Dani," he explained, more calmly than what seemed reasonable for three o'clock in the morning. "She started having contractions around midnight, and we thought we better get her checked out."

"Oh my god! Is she okay? Is the baby okay?" I practically screamed into the phone. Bonnie leaped up and rushed over to where I was pacing across the rug, her features wide with panic.

"They're monitoring her and the baby, and they've given her some medication to stop the contractions. They're admitting her. She wanted me to let you know what's going on. She hoped you'd be able to stop by in the morning."

"What's wrong? Is Dani okay? Is the baby?" Bonnie was trying to ask questions and play charades with me while I was trying to digest Aris's words. I started to rip my dresser drawers apart searching for some real clothes.

"I'm going to come now," I told him. "I'm already awake, and I can't sleep anyway. I need to make sure she's okay."

"I'm sure she'll appreciate the company. Noah had to go back to bed because he has surgery in the morning. If you come, maybe I can get a few hours of sleep before work. I don't really want her to be here all day tomorrow by herself, but we're short-staffed this week at my office because one of the other nurses is on vacation."

"Sure, of course, no problem. Bonnie and I will come now." I turned toward her, and she nodded.

"Thanks, Raine," he sounded relieved. "You're the best."

I didn't feel like the best. I still felt pretty much like the worst, but I was worried about my friend and about her baby.

I filled Bonnie in, and her face filled with determination. "Yeah, I'm in. Let me get some clothes on, and we'll get out of here."

maggie

I sat in my car in the dark silence for a few minutes. The crickets were so loud, the silence made them seem deafening. I shouldn't have gone to the conference—that was the main thought that started a cascade of other inadequacies and mistakes I needed to contend with. Atone for.

My hand hurt after a hard pound to the steering wheel, which did absolutely nothing for my sanity or stress levels. I started up my car and backed out of my parking space, weaving my way out of Raine's apartment complex.

What the hell were we doing? We met this twenty-something-year-old woman and expected her to have the maturity and poise to handle not only a poly relationship with an almost forty-something couple but to somehow also be their surrogate?

Were we absolutely insane?

I pointed the car toward our home on the other side of town, dipping down side streets aglow in streetlights until I reached the back country roads that would take me to our address. What would it be like to escape for a while? Pretend to be someone else, someone with different problems, and one of them wasn't a broken reproductive system?

But I had nowhere else to go. I couldn't rely on my family. Leo wasn't close to his family either. Maybe that was why we desperately wanted a baby—we wanted to create a family because ours had continually let us down.

The garage door opened, and I walked into a dark house. Blue greeted me, tail wagging as he licked my hand and welcomed me home after my trip. *Oh, yeah, my suitcase.* Well, I'd get it in the morning. Later in the morning. It was already three o'clock, but I was still sort of on Mountain Time.

The bedroom was dark, but my eyes had adjusted enough to make out the broad-shouldered lump on the far side of the bed that was my husband. I stripped down to nothing, not wanting to rummage through the drawers for pajamas, and slid in behind him, the big spoon to his smaller —*well, he could never be considered small, but you get the picture.*

I listened to his steady breathing—he was already asleep. I knew without a doubt that Leo had done the best he could with Raine. I wasn't thrilled they had sex when she was so upset—I hoped she didn't feel like she was obligated to because of the contract. But Leo had insisted it was her idea.

He wasn't able to pull out of Raine what the issue was, but I did. Was it because it was easier for her to talk to me, a woman, or had we attained a closeness she hadn't with Leo?

My head hurt, my heart hurt, and the future was one jumbled, convoluted tangle of mangled hopes and dreams.

I didn't think things would look any better in the light of dawn, which was only a couple of hours from now.

But we would see.

leo

I felt my wife slide in behind me, wrap her arm around me and snuggle up to my back, but I didn't move. My breathing stayed deep and steady as I pretended to sleep. *Fake it till you make it, right?* I did want to get a few hours of sleep, and I knew Maggie needed it too after the conference and travel. We would be able to discuss this with clearer minds if we both got some rest.

I was reminded of all the domestic situations I had ever responded to. Not that she and I were having a domestic situation. Yes, we'd said some snarky and hurtful things to each other, but it was nothing like the fights that escalated to the point where the police needed to intervene.

I had responded to a fair number of domestics, and they could be scary as fuck. Especially when one or both of the couple had access to weapons: almost always knives and often guns. Police nearly always separated the two warring partners. Especially if it was nighttime. We would find a place for one of them to stay, usually with relatives. If there was violence or threats of violence, that other place would be jail.

But the point was they needed to be separated, to cool off, to get some time apart. Clearer heads would prevail once time passed. Once sleep washed over volatile emotions.

That was what all three of us had encountered tonight: volatile emotions. And they'd clashed. There was no way three people could always be on the same page, but one thing I felt when I left Raine's apartment earlier tonight was loss.

I was afraid I was losing her, that I had already lost her. And I wasn't just sad about that. I was sad for Maggie too, that Maggie may be losing her as well.

It had nothing to do with the surrogacy or a baby who didn't exist yet—probably—and everything to do with what Raine had come to mean to me and to Maggie over the past couple of months.

Maggie's soft snores fell on my bare back, and I smiled at the blessing of sleep, of the peace it would bring her. I rolled over to face her, pulling her into my embrace, and she barely budged. I leaned in close, smelling her unique scent and thinking about how much I loved her.

As if she'd heard my internal thoughts, she whispered, "I love you, Leo. So much. We'll figure this out in the morning."

That's my girl, I thought as she drifted back into the realm of dreams. But then I saw the empty space on the other side of us and wished our beautiful Raine was there with us too.

twenty-three

. . .

raine

I WAS ARGUING with the nurse at the desk about it not being visiting hours until eight o'clock when Aris saved me. Because the nurse apparently needed to save face, she snapped at us, "Only two at a time." Bonnie volunteered to wait her turn.

Aris guided me down the hall, which was so quiet, I could hear the whooshes and beeps of machines in patient rooms. He gently pushed open a wide door, and I got my first glimpse of my beautiful friend, her usually gold skin looking sallow against the bright white sheets. A gown covered her baby bump, but there were wires extending from it to monitors nearby.

"You came!" she cheered. "What's wrong with you? You look like hell."

"Um, thanks, so do you," I fired back as I approached her bed. She reached out for a hug as I sat on the edge, careful not to disturb any of the tubes or wires she was hooked to.

"What the fuck happened?" I started. "You were fine

when I saw you yesterday morning." Ironically, the same could be said for me, but I didn't want to burden her with my drama when she had much more pressing bad shit going down.

"I don't even know! We were just eating dinner, and I started to feel weird. My stomach felt like it was clenching like a fist. Well, not my stomach…my…you know." She pointed to her medium-sized bump. "And then my back started to hurt, and when I went to the bathroom there was a tiny bit of blood."

"Oh my god, Dani! Well, I know it wasn't Cynda's cooking. It wasn't Aris or Noah being a little too aggressive, if you get my drift?"

She smacked me on the arm. "No! We didn't even have sex today!" She said it like it was an anomaly. "And I'm sure it had nothing to do with Cynda's chicken marsala, which was absolutely chef's kiss." She made the gesture with her fingers.

"So, you came here, and they checked you out, and now what?" I cut to the chase.

Aris stepped over, slipping on his professional nurse demeanor like a mask. "She was having contractions but wasn't in labor yet, thankfully. It's much, much too early for this little one to come, so they stopped the contractions, and now she's gotta be extra careful for the next few months till he or she is big enough to have a fighting chance."

"Bed rest," Dani huffed, clearly not thrilled with the idea.

She reached out and grabbed my hand. "I was so fucking scared, Raine. I thought for sure I was gonna lose the baby. I don't know what I would have done without Aris and Noah. Thank god they were both there. It took both of them to calm me down and get me here."

"So, they're keeping you for a while?" I gestured at the

monitor, which seemed to be measuring a couple of different things, but I had no clue what exactly.

"One is measuring her contractions, and the other, the baby's heartbeat. Both are looking much, much better than when she arrived," Aris explained. "They're going to keep an eye on things for at least twenty-four hours, then they'll probably send her home with restrictions. It's going to suck, but better safe than sorry, right, love?"

Danielle sighed and blew a kiss to her gorgeous Greek man-bunned lover. Then she turned back to me. "It's so weird. When I first found out I was pregnant, I was shocked. Having a baby wasn't on my radar at all—it was something I considered so far out of reach, I hadn't even thought about it in years. I was scared and even a little hesitant to go through with it. But now that I've felt this little guy—or gal—kick and seen them moving around on the ultrasound, I've fallen in love. I'd do anything for them, and I've never even met them yet."

Her words floated around my ears as I struggled to absorb them. *I could be pregnant right now*, my brain finally woke up and screamed in my general direction.

"How did your babymaking fest go?" Danielle asked as though she could read my mind.

"Oh, that…well…" I didn't want to share any of the drama, remember?

"Did you guys fuck lots?" Her eyes widened, sparkling for the first time since I entered the room. Aris, who was busy reading her chart on the computer, snickered.

"Well, yeah, a few times," I admitted.

"Don't be bashful, geez!" She smacked my arm. "So when will you know?"

"I guess I can test in like ten days. But—"

"But what?" Her eyebrows arched.

"Nothing, don't worry about it." I squeezed her hand. "I'm so glad you and the baby are going to be okay."

"Well, hopefully we will be." She sighed, and then a slight smile curled her lips. "The doctor said if I'm a good girl and don't do too much, everything should be absolutely perfect from here on out."

My eyes narrowed in disbelief. "He said that? If you're a good girl?"

"Actually, it was a beautiful woman doctor." Aris walked back over to us.

"Huh, think she'll be around to check on you soon?" I waggled my brows at them both, and they laughed.

I was glad I could provide some levity to this serious situation. And I was glad I was able to keep my mouth buttoned about the shitty message I got from my mom.

By some act of a higher power, Danielle didn't ask if she messaged me back, even though she sent the message. Thinking about it again was making tears sting in the corners of my eyes.

"What's wrong, girly?" Danielle reached up to tuck a strand of my hair behind my ear. "Did something happen between you, Leo and Maggie?"

I shrugged and bit my lip, willing the tears to stand down. I was doing so good, and now I was about to be a blubbering idiot again.

Aris came over and put his arm around me. "Poly relationships can be tough. You know, if you need someone to talk to…Cynda might as well be a certified polyam therapist. She's been practicing ENM in one form or another for a long time."

I swallowed down the tears and nodded. "Thanks, I'll keep that in mind. I just gotta work out some stuff for myself."

"Talking through it really helps," Danielle said. "I can't tell you what a godsend Cynda was to me when I was laid up at her house after my injury. Fuck, it's so weird to think, if you hadn't hit me with your bike, we probably wouldn't be here right now." She gazed up at Aris with adoring eyes.

She really was lovesick. For one thing, she just romanticized him hitting her with a bike. And for another, "here right now" was in the hospital. I restrained myself from rolling my eyes, but the sentiment was there when I said, "Well, we're not really in a poly relationship so…"

"You're not?" Danielle's eyes quirked.

"I mean, not officially. Not that anyone's ever said."

"So just the surrogate thing then?" Aris asked. I guess he knew all about it too. That was one drawback of a polycule —it was hard to keep secrets when all they pushed was communication, communication, communication.

If I talked to Cynda, I was absolutely certain that would be her advice.

I just need to communicate my needs. My boundaries. My desires.

"That's cool," Aris said. "Talking about it would still help though."

"He's right," Danielle ganged up on me. "Cynda is the best. And surrogacy has its own challenges. There are a lot of feelings coming from every direction. It's gotta be hard to navigate all that plus the hormones and all the sex dredging up emotions too. It's like a minefield, really."

One I was a victim of, apparently.

"Well, I need to get going. Bonnie is here too, and they would only let one of us back to see you." I squeezed her hand. "I've gotta do some work on my thesis today—after a nap—but I'll come back and check on you, whether you're here or back at Cynda and Jason's."

"Sounds good, sweetie." She squeezed my hand. "Thanks again for stopping by."

I leaned down and pressed a kiss to her cheek. Then I gave Aris a hug before walking down the sterile hallway, wondering if they had any open beds in the psych unit.

maggie

I awoke to my husband hovering over me. "I'm sorry about what I said last night, about being a stud service to try to get you a baby."

I sighed, looking up into his deep brown eyes. "I know you were just tired and concerned about Raine. I know you want a baby as badly as I do."

"Can I hold you?" His voice cracked with emotion, delivering a punch to my gut. This man—he may have looked like a brute on the outside, but he was soft and tender on the inside. I always worried his job would make him jaded and gristled, but it hadn't happened...at least not yet.

In lieu of answering him, I turned onto my side and allowed him to snake his arm under me. In a heartbeat, I was snuggled up to him, my head resting in that spot where we fit together like puzzle pieces.

"What happened after I left?"

The question hung in the air while I soaked in his warmth and thought about what to say.

"I asked her to tell me what had upset her so much." I ran my fingers through his thick mat of chest hair. I always found it so soothing. "It was bad, Leo..." I exhaled sharply before admitting, "She reached out to her birth mother—for us. To find out medical history stuff."

"Oh." Leo's muscles tensed as he processed my statement. "Yeah, she said she was going to try to find out some stuff for us."

"Right. I remember her saying she found her half-brother through some DNA test, so first she asked him about the medical history stuff. I think he gave her their mom's phone number." I recalled having a conversation with her about it a few weeks ago.

"So I guess her mom finally responded, and it wasn't what Raine wanted to hear?" Leo guessed.

"Worse. It was just a horrible message." I spared him the details. "Very upsetting."

He closed his eyes, and I could feel his heartache for her in his heavy sigh. "Upsetting enough for her to back out of our contract?"

I pulled back a little so I could clearly see his face. "You and I both know that contract didn't mean shit. It was easily broken by either party. There's no legal teeth to this kind of thing." I sighed. "I wanted to try, though, make it look official. At least the financial part of it."

"We've already paid her like five thousand bucks," Leo said. "Guess we're not getting that back."

"No…of course not. But she could be pregnant." I didn't know whether to hope she was or not since things were so strained.

"That might make things even more complicated," Leo spoke the words that were tumbling around in my mind.

"That's true. I guess we'll just have to wait and see." That didn't seem to matter as much as her, though. "She's hurting. That's the worst part of this. I wish…I wish if her birth mother didn't want contact with her, she would have just blocked her number and moved on with her life without messaging her back. It was just so unnecessarily cruel…"

"I can't imagine. I hate that Raine is dealing with this." He stroked a finger down my arm. "Do you think she would even tell us?" his words were laced with fear. "If she was pregnant?"

"To be honest? I don't know. We sort of jumped into this and…" My heart felt so heavy, like I'd wrapped it in iron chains. "I feel like we took advantage of her. She probably feels that way too."

"At the time, it seemed like such a win-win for everyone. She needed the money, and we needed someone to carry our baby. We all got along, and the attraction was clearly there, so why not?"

"We jumped in too fast…" I agreed.

"Gotta strike while the iron is hot," he played devil's advocate.

"So now what?" My voice was nothing more than a whisper when I thought about losing Raine. And it wasn't about the baby. I wanted her. It was hard to imagine not having her in our lives.

"I don't know." He was quiet for a moment, running his finger down my chest and over my breast to the soft rolls of my stomach.

"Maybe she'll come back to us?" I let a tiny glimmer of hope shine through.

"I miss her already."

"Me too…"

leo

Today was the last day I'd scheduled off for babymaking, and the potential baby mama was MIA. My phone was silently mocking me, no notifications waiting when I went to do my morning doom scrolling. After our chat about Raine, Maggie disappeared into the kitchen, and the aroma of coffee wafted back to the bathroom, where I was taking care of business.

I stumbled upon an article in the online version of the local paper, my eyes bugging out as I read it. I finished up and rushed out to the kitchen so I could show Maggie what I'd just learned.

I handed my wife the phone. "Here, check this out."

"IU Theater Professor Arrested for Jewelry Theft," she read aloud. "What does that have to do with anything?"

"That was the jewelry Raine was supposed to pay for!" I clued her in.

"Oh!" She read the article, her eyes growing wider. "So, it was an inside job. Her accuser knew all along she didn't do it. She was framed!"

I was in shock. "Yeah, Raine said this person in charge of the costume department hated her, and she is on her thesis committee."

"Well, not anymore," my wife pointed out. "It said the university has released a statement saying that she no longer works at the university."

"Wow. I'm so glad I had Beau look into it. That jewelry shouldn't have been checked out with the costume anyway. From what I understand, it was an antique and a one-of-a-kind set. Even if the university paid the owner the twelve grand, it's not like he can replace it."

"But what did the costume lady do with it?" She glanced back down at the article.

"Good question. She might have sold it on the black market or something. Who knows? But she really thought she'd saddle Raine with the bill, huh? She would have gotten away with it, too, if I hadn't intervened."

"You're feeling pretty puffed up about that, aren't you?"

Maggie chuckled, patting me on the shoulder before taking another sip of her coffee.

"I assume Raine knows what happened. I thought maybe her meeting with the theater department went badly, and that was why she was so upset last night. But I guess it was the mom thing."

"I'm going to try to text her." Maggie pulled her own phone out of her robe pocket. "Maybe she'll have lunch with me so we can sort this out. I don't have to go into the office today since I was supposed to still be in Denver till tonight."

"I hope she'll talk to you." I took a sip of my coffee. "I know she's upset about what her mother said, but she has to know it doesn't reflect on her as a person. She grew up in a family that wanted her. She had a good childhood, right?"

"She hasn't told me much about when she was growing up, just that her parents divorced and she stayed with her mom. Her dad was in the military, so they moved around a lot." Maggie sighed, and I knew she was hurting for our girl as much as I was.

"I hope she'll be okay… I will give her a few days to cool down before I contact her," I decided.

Maybe we could salvage our relationship, even if surrogacy was off the table.

The more I thought about it, the more I realized I didn't want to lose her as a friend, as a partner. I had grown to care about her…deeply. The surrogacy thing would have been amazing but…maybe it wasn't meant to be. I still wanted her in my life regardless.

Then her soft voice urging me to make love to her filled my mind. She said those words. And I believed I'd done just that. I'd made love to her. And I wanted to…again and again.

twenty-four

. . .

two weeks later

raine

PAIN GRIPPED ME, making me double over as it stole my breath. It radiated from my lower abdomen around my sides to my back, where it blared like a sledgehammer pounding against my spine. Then it crept back around front, pulsing with a deep ache that brought tears to my eyes.

I crawled out of bed, where I'd been spending most of my time in the last week, and staggered to the bathroom. I emptied my bladder, then grabbed some toilet paper. Pulling it away from my body, I glanced down to see a bright red streak across the white fiber.

Fuck.

I closed my eyes as the pain gripped me so tightly, I couldn't move. I should have anticipated this. I'd been on the Pill for years, and it had prevented the horrible menstrual cramps I always got for the first few days of my period. This was my second cycle since I'd stopped taking it, and the cramps had returned with a vengeance.

Grabbing a tampon from the little basket on the sink, I blinked back tears as I realized I definitely wasn't pregnant. I had taken a test a few days ago, when it was ten days past my ovulation. It was negative, but I still knew there was a tiny chance it was too early.

Did I feel relief or sadness?

The jury was out.

Bonnie knocked on the bathroom door, jolting me out of my little pity party. "You about done in there? I need to take a shower."

"Hold on," I grumbled as I finished up and washed my hands.

I opened the door to find her standing there with her hands on her hips. "Are you coming with me to see Dani? I know she'd really like to see you."

I let out the longest sigh ever. Like probably world record qualifying.

"Raine, you haven't been to see her once since she was discharged from the hospital. She thinks you're mad at her or something. I tried to tell her you've just been busy finishing your thesis, but you turned that shit in three days ago, didn't you?"

I nodded, fingering a piece of hair that had fallen into my face. I'd twisted it so many times, I was surprised it didn't just snap off. "I'm sorry, Bonnie. I'm an awful friend."

"You're not an awful friend," she fired back.

"An awful friend, an awful girlfriend, an awful daughter, an awful surrogate mother...the list goes on." I marched out of the bathroom, down the hall to return to my room.

I expected Bonnie to huff and ignore me. I expected to hear the shower start. But what I heard instead were heavy footfalls down the hall until she appeared in my doorway with a look of fury on her face.

"Would you snap the fuck out of it?" It was not a question. More of a demand. "You're being completely intolerable. Summer is almost over, and you've just finished your master's degree. You should be celebrating right now, for fuck's sake!"

"I don't feel like celebrating," I snapped back.

"Is this because Danielle is pregnant, and you're not?" Bonnie was there when I got the negative test a few days ago. She was the only person I told.

"No," I answered that with no hesitation.

I wasn't jealous that Danielle was pregnant. I was happy for her—truly, I was.

"Then what the hell is going on with you?" Bonnie's voice softened as she reached out to touch my arm. "Please come with me today. It would mean a lot to Dani. She's been so bored, even though there are always fresh faces over at Cynda and Jason's. And Noah and Aris have been gone a lot, working and looking at houses, and Dani can't even go with them. She's on super-strict bed rest. She can only be out of bed for like an hour total all day."

Ugh. That sucks.

Now on top of all the other terrible feelings I had, not to mention worrying that my uterus was staging a coup and wanted to completely incapacitate me, I had guilt stabbing its ugly sword into me. "When are you leaving?"

"I'm flexible," Bonnie said. "I know we'd both have to shower and get ready."

"Blurgh." I needed ibuprofen and a heating pad before I did anything. "Give me an hour."

Her face lit up like I'd just told her she won the lottery. *This girl must be desperate for friends*, I told myself.

I had been selfish the past two weeks. I was trying to take care of myself, which meant applying for jobs, finishing my thesis project, and coming to terms with the fact that this chapter of my life was over. My time in Bloomington, the summer job at Brown County theater, my master's classes, and my relationship with Leo and Maggie.

Getting my period today just confirmed it.

It was time to take all that I'd done and learned here, pack up my stuff, and move on to the next chapter.

leo

Maggie and I had barely seen each other in the last two weeks. The last night I remembered sleeping together was the night after we last saw Raine. I'd been on night shift for work, then called out two nights in a row when I went back to day shift.

I felt like I'd been averaging about three hours of sleep a day, and Maggie wasn't doing much better. She was going to court for a malpractice case, and she'd been practically living out of her office as she prepared.

But tonight...we would actually have tonight. I was making lasagna—my mother's recipe, which meant it was damn good—and I had already chilled some wine. The garlic and cheese aroma was already beginning to permeate the entire house when the garage door opened and Blue notified the entire neighborhood that Mommy was home.

I stood in the doorway between the mudroom and the kitchen with Blue in my arms, trying to get him to settle down instead of jumping all over Maggie as she made her way inside. I expected her to look tired, haggard from all the overtime she'd been working, but when her face appeared in the glass panes of the door, she was wearing a bright smile.

Her hair was pulled back into a slick, professional-looking bun, and she looked sharp in her navy-blue suit and crisp white blouse. She wore a chunky gold necklace and matching earrings that swung as she walked toward me. "Hey, I vaguely remember you from somewhere?" she joked.

Blue wiggled right out of my arms and onto the floor, where he greeted her with exuberant affection. "Hey, dog, it's my turn, okay? Back off!" I tugged him away and swept in to greet my wife, taking her into my arms and dipping her backwards as my lips captured hers.

"Well, damn, to what do I owe that greeting?" she asked as I gently raised her back to standing. There was a sparkle in her eyes that I hadn't seen since before she left for her conference in Denver.

That was weeks ago now.

That was…the last time I saw Raine.

"I have some good news," she said, beaming.

"Oh, me too! You first."

"No, I'll share mine with you over dinner. It smells amazing in here. Is that lasagna?" She appeared to sniff the air just like Blue did any time we were cooking meat.

"That's a great schnoz you have there, love." I took her purse and briefcase and put them up on the built-in storage rack next to the door. "Come on. I'll pour you a glass of wine."

"Who could resist that offer?" She followed me into the kitchen, where I got to work uncorking the wine and pouring some for both of us.

"Mmm, this is a good vintage." I smacked my lips and smiled. It was nice to be like this, together, the whole evening stretched between us. It had been a while.

Still, I'd been thinking about Raine a lot, and… I couldn't help but think it would be even better if she were here too. I hated the way things ended between us. And all of our attempts to contact her had gone unanswered. She clearly didn't want to have anything to do with us.

And we'd never heard if any of our efforts from a couple of weeks ago paid off.

The oven dinged to let me know the lasagna was ready before I could go down the rabbit hole that was my feelings about Raine. I pulled the pan out, letting its steamy goodness tease my wife's palate as she slowly sipped her wine. "I'm gonna pop this garlic bread in, and then we should be ready to go in about ten minutes."

She nodded and casually scrolled her phone while I finished up in the kitchen. In no time, we were both seated at the table, ready to dig into the Italian feast I'd prepared.

"This looks and smells absolutely divine," she sighed as she placed her napkin in her lap. "I feel like I haven't had a decent meal in ages. I went from eating nasty conference food to bland takeout. I might never want to eat Chinese again after this week. Ugh."

"Well, we're going to be eating this lasagna for a few days—it's a huge pan," I warned her.

"You seem to be underestimating how much of this I plan to put away tonight." She rubbed her hands together with glee as I served up the first piece and set it gently on her plate.

I served myself, and then she lifted her wine glass. "I'd like to propose a toast."

"Go for it." I lifted mine too.

"To us—to our never-ending love and our never-ending ability to roll with the punches, rise to the occasion, and believe in our happily ever after."

"That's sweet, honey. I'll drink to that!" We clinked glasses, and I drained the rest of my wine. I refilled both of our glasses as she took her first bite of lasagna.

"Holy Mother of God, this is amazing!" she exclaimed as she chewed a bite.

"That's a high compliment." I dove into my first bite too, and I had to agree, it was pretty fucking delicious.

"Okay," she set down her fork and swallowed, "I want to share my good news."

"Can't wait to hear."

"First share yours. We didn't quite get to it there in the mudroom when I got completely distracted by the tantalizing aroma of lasagna."

I laughed. "No, actually, the fact that I cooked this meal was my good news."

"Oh!" She joined me in laughing. "Okay, well, that was *very* good news. But I think I can top it."

"Well, don't hold me in suspense."

"The surrogate agency called today," she said. "They had a cancellation. They can get us in Wednesday for our first consultation!"

I nearly choked on my next bite of lasagna. I expected her to say she settled her case and wasn't going to trial, and that she and her client got everything they wanted. I wasn't expecting her to bring up surrogacy at all. We'd barely talked about it since everything fell apart with Raine, but then again, we'd barely seen each other either.

"Well?" She held her fork suspended in the air with the tines embedded in layers of cheese, meat, tomato sauce and pasta.

"Well, that is good news," I choked out.

She didn't eat the bite. She only lowered it to the plate.

"You're not happy? It means we don't have to wait three more months."

"Of course I'm happy. I just wasn't expecting to have the appointment moved up, that's all."

She sucked in a breath, her chest visibly rising. "Is this about Raine?"

Now I set my fork down too. Here we had this beautiful lasagna just waiting to be eaten, and neither of us seemed interested now. What had been a happy, light atmosphere had suddenly turned strained and tense.

I bit my lip, searching for the words to convey what had been spinning around in my head for days now. For weeks. I couldn't find them, so I simply asked, "How do we know Raine isn't pregnant?"

Maggie scoffed.

She fucking scoffed. *What the fuck?*

"Well, if she is, I'm the father of that baby," I said. "And I deserve to know."

She closed her eyes, and I knew what was coming. Sure enough, her eyes fluttered open, and a tear dripped down her cheek. She pushed her chair away from the table.

"Where are you going? Please eat your dinner…please?"

She dabbed at her eyes with her napkin. "You're in love with her, aren't you?"

Her words landed like tiny bombs right on my heart. My lungs squeezed in my chest as all the words, all the feelings I had been trying to suppress converged into one over-whelming sentiment that refused to be denied any longer. I'd pushed. I'd rationalized. I'd distracted myself.

But the truth was staring me in the face.

I reached out and took my wife's hand. "I am. I'm in love with Raine, and I wanted her to have our baby."

I thought she'd burst into tears. I thought she'd run away, trying to escape the truth I'd just detonated right here, right now.

But she didn't. She just gave a small twist of a heartbroken smile and said, "Me too."

twenty-five

. . .

raine

BONNIE WASN'T EXACTLY DRAGGING me over to see Danielle, but she had certainly guilted me into it. I put on my period panties, groaning when the cramps just didn't want to die down, even after ibuprofen and a heating pad. My one solace was that Cynda probably had some sort of magical remedy I'd never even heard of that would fix me up in a heartbeat.

The drive over to the house was quiet. Bonnie knew better than to force me to talk, plus she probably realized I needed to save my words for Danielle. But she was a good friend, forcing me to get out.

In the quiet time, my mind swirled with emotions I didn't want to claim as my own. Regret, yes, but it wasn't regret for getting involved with Leo and Maggie.

Oh, no. It was very clearly regret that I wasn't pregnant.

There was this tiny part of me… I was pretty sure I never allowed myself to fantasize about it because I knew it could never become true. But an eensy weensy tiny part of me couldn't help wondering what it might be like for us all to be together. For me to have with Leo and Maggie what they had with each other, which was, from everything I'd witnessed, serious relationship goals. They supported each other, were exceedingly loyal, always thought of the other before thinking of themselves, and they just knew how to have fun and be themselves around each other. Their relationship was so easy, so effortless.

How could I not aspire to that someday?

But it wasn't just that I wanted a relationship *like* theirs.

I wanted *their* relationship. Big difference.

I wanted to be part of it. To be one of them. And that tiny voice in my head I'd been trying to ignore was singing a beautiful song about how having their baby might give me access to their world in ways just being their girlfriend might not.

But that was crazy, right?

Because I was so much younger, and I had my own life to live. I had a career ahead of me that would take me away from Bloomington, Indiana—sooner rather than later.

And I didn't deserve that kind of love anyway. My own *mother* couldn't even stand the thought of me! She gave me away and wanted nothing to do with me. I was a mistake.

A drunken mistake.

"We're here," Bonnie broke me out of my weird alternate reality where I oscillated back and forth between dreams and nightmares. "You coming?"

I sighed. "Yeah, sorry. In my own little world again."

"It's understandable," Bonnie said. "I know this is going to be hard for you, but I wanted you to know I think you're brave for coming over here and supporting Danielle when you're hurting."

Wow. It was like she saw right through me.

"Thanks, Bonnie. You're a good friend." I gave her a watery-eyed smile, and she rolled her eyes.

"Don't get all sappy on me just because you're perioding over there."

We both laughed as we climbed out of the car and headed up to the porch. Bonnie knocked on the door, and Cynda answered seconds later, a beaming smile on her face.

"Welcome, welcome! Dani will be so excited to see you. Come on in!" She ushered us inside to the aroma of cinnamon and apples.

"What is that delicious smell?" Bonnie gushed as we made our way inside. We both waved to Dani, who was laid up on the couch with her feet propped on an ottoman.

"I made apple turnovers," Cynda said with a sly smile. "Would you like some coffee and a turnover? They're just cooling for a few more minutes."

"I'm pretty sure if there's a heaven, it will smell like this," Bonnie said. "Yes to coffee and turnovers for me. Raine?"

I nodded. "I mean, you had me at coffee, but turnovers are a nice bonus."

While Cynda went into the kitchen, we both joined Danielle in the living room. I took a seat next to her on the sofa, and Bonnie sat across from her in the armchair.

"Well, look who it is!" Danielle exclaimed, her gaze landing squarely on me. "I thought you were mad at me for some reason."

"No, not at all. I was just busy finishing up my thesis project, and then I had vicious PMS." I sighed and rubbed my lower abdomen, which was just now starting to feel a little bit better.

Her face scrunched up with an unreadable expression. "I don't know how to respond to that. I mean, the finishing up your thesis is amazing, congratulations! I'm sorry about the

PMS though. You're sure it's not just early pregnancy hormones, right? I thought I just had PMS at first too."

"Nope, started bleeding this morning. And cramping. Damn, I miss being on the Pill," I admitted. "Guess I could go back on it now if I wanted to."

"Wait, what?" Danielle looked shocked. "I thought you were Leo and Maggie's surrogate?"

I huffed out a big sigh. "I pretty much told them I couldn't do it." While I waited for her to process my statement, I promptly changed the subject: "So, how are you feeling? How's the baby? Where are Aris and Noah?"

"I see what you're trying to do, and I'm going to answer your questions, but then we're going straight back to you." She wagged her finger at me, and Bonnie gave a little chirpy laugh as I crossed my arms over my chest.

"I'm doing fine, just bored and restless. I did go to the doctor this week for an ultrasound, and everything looks great. The baby is very active and seems pretty happy. No, we did not find out the gender, so don't ask. It's not important to us, and we're not doing a gender reveal or anything."

I raised my hands, palms out, sensing this had been a sensitive topic. "That's all good news. And your men—are they working today?"

"They're actually out looking at some houses." She held up her phone. "They've been texting me photos."

"It sucks that you're not able to go with them," Bonnie said.

"I trust them to pick out the best house for us. They both have exceptional taste." She winked, and we all laughed.

Cynda walked in carrying a large bamboo tray filled with adorable teacups and small plates with tiny rainbows on them. "Like my new Pride dishes? Darth and Jason got them for me for my birthday."

"Those are so cute!" I gushed as she set them down on the coffee table.

"I overheard you say you started your period, and you're having cramps." Cynda lifted one teacup off the tray and handed it to me. "So I made you my special tea. If you want some coffee after, I brought you that too."

Bonnie shot me an "I told you so" look from across the room.

"Thank you, Cynda. You're the absolute best, and these turnovers look amazing." I sipped the tea. "Wow, this is really good too. I mean, it's not coffee, but really damn good."

She beamed. "I'm glad you like it. Now dig in, everyone. Eat as many as you like because, once all the guys get home, you know these are gonna disappear like that." She snapped her fingers to indicate how quickly it would happen. "It's kinda nice to have a girls' day."

"It definitely is," Danielle agreed, but then her head whipped toward me. "Now, we were discussing Raine and her surrogacy agreement with Leo and Maggie."

Cynda sipped her own tea, daintily holding the cup by its delicate handle. "Are you sure it's just a surrogacy agreement? You all looked rather cozy in the camper during the Fourth of July party."

"We were…" I wasn't expecting this whole conversation to center around me, and I felt like I was in the spotlight. The spotlight was more Danielle's thing, being an actress and all. As a costume designer, I only strived for the spotlight for my designs. Not me.

Bonnie ganged up against me too. "Just tell them what happened, Raine. C'mon. You know Cynda will have the perfect advice anyway."

I sighed. "Fine. But I know you're all going to judge me,

and probably make this out to be a simple misunderstanding. It's not. There are some fundamental issues, and I don't think we can get around them."

"Well, you've got to lay all your cards on the table," Cynda said. "I can't make sense of it if I'm only getting bits and pieces. So first, tell me this: was this just a casual sexual relationship, or was it a surrogacy agreement?"

She had a way of distilling things down to their simplest components. But, like I said, this wasn't that simple.

"It started off as me dating Maggie," I explained. "We danced at The Barn, and then we went on a date. And we were making out, but then Leo came home and watched. And he seemed interested in me too, and then he came to me with a proposal."

"What kind of proposal?" Cynda interrupted. "To be their surrogate?"

I nodded. "Yes. He and Maggie have some fertility issues—well, the issues are with her. She can't conceive or carry a baby due to some genetic and physiological issues. They found out it was going to take six months to get an appointment with the surrogacy agency. So…maybe I would like to do it for them? And they'd pay me, of course."

"So, after that, your relationship became strictly professional?" Cynda asked.

"Well…no…not exactly." I thought back to what happened after I agreed to be their surrogate. "Nothing really changed as far as our dating was concerned. But I did sign a contract, and they did start to pay me a monthly stipend."

"And…you were okay with that? Taking money from them in exchange for getting pregnant and carrying their baby?" She didn't ask it in a judgmental way, just in a curious way.

I folded my hands in my lap, trying to figure out the best way to answer her question. "I was more than okay with it because I thought I had a huge debt to pay the university—long story. And because I don't have a job lined up after graduation. I figured it would help me make ends meet until I find a job."

She leaned forward, absorbing every word I said with the utmost attention. "I see. So, what was the plan for after the baby was born?"

"Um…well, I figured I'd have a job by then, probably someplace far away from here: New York, LA—Chicago would probably be the closest place for me to work as a costume designer."

"So, the plan was for you to have their baby, leave the baby with them, collect the rest of your surrogate fee, and then ride off into the sunset?" Again, not a shred of judgment in her tone.

Well, shit. When she put it like that, it did sound pretty unrealistic, didn't it?

I just stared at her, blinking back tears. It was truly naïve of me to think it could actually work like that. But that was why I backed out. Because I knew it was a shitty plan. For everyone involved, but mostly for me. They would still get everything they wanted. I'd just have the money and a broken heart.

"Well, I'm not doing it now anyway." I looked down at my laced fingers, down to the silver filigree ring with a garnet stone I wore on my right hand. My adoptive parents gave it to me on my sixteenth birthday, and I still wore it.

"So, you figured out you're not a robot, then?" Cynda smiled as she asked me the question. "You figured out that expecting yourself to behave as though you're in a relationship with a man and a woman, bear their child, and then turn around and leave the family unit you'd just created behind, while having zero emotions about it, was a bit of an unrealistic plan?"

"Well, not exactly…"

"Why did you back out of the agreement?"

I noticed Dani and Bonnie had remained completely quiet during this little therapy session. They were both mindlessly munching on popcorn, completely absorbed by the little show playing out—except, instead of popcorn, it was apple turnovers.

All the emotion hit me at once. It was like a sledge-hammer striking the back of my head, and all the feelings I'd been trying to manage for the last couple of months just exploded out of me. Tears welled in my eyes as my throat clogged with despair. I dropped my head into my hands as a sob shook my body.

Dani was right there, pulling me into her embrace, hugging me firmly to her body as I wept. Bonnie came over and got on her knees in front of me, and Cynda came next to me on my other side. These three women wrapped me in their warmth and love as I fell apart in front of them, tears and snot pouring out of my face as I rocked back and forth in a helpless, hopeless state.

When I finally came up, gasping for air, my eyes met Cynda's wise, perceptive gaze. She took my hands into hers and squeezed. "Tell us what's happening in your heart right now, love."

"I wanted to be pregnant," I choked out, scarcely believing the admission was coming out of my mouth.

But it was the truth.

"I think a part of me…" I tried to catch my breath as another sob racked my body. "A part of me pushed them away because I thought I was unworthy of their love."

Bonnie handed me a tissue, and I blew huge blobs of snot out as I tried to formulate my thoughts into coherent words. Dani kept her arm around me, and Cynda continued to hold my hands.

I gestured between the three of them. "Like this…this love…unconditional love and acceptance," I finally articulated, "I've never had it before. My birth mother abandoned me and now wants nothing to do with me. My adoptive parents split—my adoptive dad didn't want a relationship with me. He provided financial support, but he never cared about *me*. And my mom—it was like every word out of her mouth was a lecture on what not to do so I wouldn't end up like her, jaded and alone. She had me so convinced that being myself would repel people, that I never thought I deserved to be loved for who I am."

Spitting out those words caused another wave of tears to erupt, to have their way with me as they attempted to flush my emotional pipes clear of this heartache, this misery.

Because life without Leo and Maggie was just that: heartache and misery.

"Everything was so easy with Leo and Maggie because they just let me be who I am. They didn't expect me to be anything or anyone I wasn't. And they were willing to take whatever I would give them. Leo went to the trouble of calling in a favor from a friend to try to get me out of the money I owed the university. Maggie was always there for me, showing me what being a strong woman looks like. Right before she met me, she had her dreams obliterated when the doctors told her she'd never have her own baby. But she picked herself up, started researching the next step in how she could become a mother, and then they met me."

"Do you think you still have a chance to work things out

with them?" Cynda asked. "It sounds like you regret walking away and breaking the contract."

I pulled my phone out of my pocket. "They both texted me every day for a week straight…telling me that we could forget the surrogate thing. That they missed me. That they wanted me just for me."

I slowly rose from the couch cushion, my legs trembling and knees wobbly, as I realized how badly I'd fucked up. I walked toward the kitchen before turning back around. "I kept telling myself they were only in it for the baby."

"But what if they meant it?" Cynda's eyes followed me as I paced back and forth between the kitchen and the living room.

I shook my head. "I pushed them away. They probably think I'm too flaky and immature at this point."

"You're making excuses again," Danielle pointed out, and Cynda nodded. "You're belittling yourself, selling your-self short."

"Maybe you could talk to them?" Cynda suggested. "Maybe you can talk about what the future might look like and how you might be able to navigate it with a baby and your career?"

I shook my head again, stray tears flying off my cheeks. "I just don't see how it could work for me to stay here with them. Not if I want to work in costume design—"

The doorbell rang, effectively cutting off my rambling excuses. "I'll get it. I'm the one up."

Cynda nodded. "Thank you."

I wiped my face with the tissue Cynda had given me, then rose on my tiptoes to look through the peephole. The pink hair was immediately recognizable. It was Molly, who used to live here with Jason and Cynda. I'd met her at a couple of events, and she was at the Fourth of July party as well. She'd just gone through the MFA program too, though we didn't have any classes together. Her specialty was play-writing.

I opened the door, and she burst inside. "Oh my god, you're all here!" she exclaimed, glancing around from Danielle, to Bonnie and back to me.

"Hi, Molly. Can I get you coffee and an apple turnover?" Cynda rose from the sofa and made her way back toward the kitchen.

"That would be amazing, Cynda, thank you." She ran her hands through her hair. "I was hoping to chat with Dani," she continued, "but I'm super lucky to find you all together."

"What's going on?" Danielle questioned.

"Did you hear what happened in the theater department?" Molly glanced around at all of us again.

"No, what?" Bonnie questioned.

"They fired Dr. Wharton! There was a huge scandal, and I just got the inside scoop from Dr. Pataski. They've tried to keep it on the downlow since fall classes haven't started yet, but it made the local news!" She made her way into the living room and plopped down on the ottoman.

Feeling numb and more than a little shaken up, I took my former spot next to Danielle again as Cynda returned with refreshments for Molly. "Some hot gossip from the university?" Cynda asked, sitting down on the other side of me.

Molly tore off a tiny bit of turnover and popped it in her mouth. That immediately led to an orgasmic moan. "Oh my god, Cynda, I've missed living here so much. This is freaking amazing!"

"So, I wanna hear about this scandal," I said as it finally sank in. Did that mean she wasn't on my thesis committee any longer? They were reviewing my thesis right now. "It's no secret I hated that bitch."

"Right! Well, the chair told me that a student checked out a costume from the wardrobe department that accidentally had an antique jewelry set in its accessory pack."

As soon as she said it, my heart kicked up a thunderous beat. Dani looked over at me, and I flashed her a look that said, *Let's just hear her out.*

Molly continued, "Apparently, when the owner wanted his priceless, one-of-a-kind art deco jewelry set back, Dr. Wharton accused the grad student who checked out the costume of never returning it. The university charged the student the entire value of the set—twelve thousand dollars—even though she had nothing to do with its disappearance. And the student was going to have to pay it because she couldn't prove she didn't steal it or lose it."

Molly took a sip of coffee, then continued, "But then the police reviewed some video footage from the lab where the costume was being stored, and it showed a costume crewmember came in and took the case the jewelry was in. After further investigation, the costume crewmember was able to produce a text that incriminated Dr. Wharton, who paid the crewmember to steal it. So much drama!"

I gasped, my hands immediately flying to my mouth, I was so shocked at this revelation. *That fucking bitch! She set me up!*

"When they confronted Dr. Wharton, she said she had been planning to return the set to the owner, but she never did. It had been months since she orchestrated its theft. And they just fucking fired her. A full tenured professor!"

Dani finally burst into laughter. "Oh my god, Raine, you got her fired!"

Molly's eyes whipped toward me. "What? What do you mean?"

"It was me," I confessed. "I was the student who was charged for the missing jewelry."

Now Molly was the one who was shocked. "Oh my god! I knew there weren't that many costume design MFA students, but I didn't even think about it being you. I forgot you were a costumer. I didn't put two and two together." Then her eyes widened, and a smile curled her lips.

"What is it?" I asked, my curiosity piqued. She looked like she had another secret she was dying to share.

Molly didn't hold me in suspense. "Dr. Pataski told me they were promoting the university's head costume designer to Dr. Wharton's Costume Czar position. So, you know what that means?"

"Um…no?"

Molly shook her head. "Don't be obtuse, Raine! The reason Dr. Pataski was telling me all this was because she wondered if we have a costumer on staff up at my theater in Indy. IU desperately needs to hire someone really fast for the fall season. Classes start in just a couple of weeks, and right now they have no one. They don't have time to orchestrate a national search. I mean, it would probably be an interim position for the first year, but—"

Dani clapped me on the back. "Raine, you have to apply! That would solve all your problems!"

Molly's brows furrowed. "What problems?"

I waved my hand to brush off Dani's comment. "It wouldn't solve *all* my problems, but it would be a start."

Cynda smiled. "Well, you know what the next step is, don't you?"

I nodded. "Yes. Yes I do."

twenty-six

. . .

maggie

MY HUSBAND BALANCED himself over me, driving his cock into me with his jaw clenched in concentration. "Fuck, Mags, you feel so good. You're gonna make me blow my load before I'm ready."

My nails dug into his back as I arched up to meet his thrusts. "Give it to me, give me all your cum, baby."

"Damn it," he moaned, his cock turning to steel as he pumped a few more times and then stilled. "Oh, god, oh fuck...here it comes..."

I held my breath as he spasmed inside me, coating my pussy with his seed. He collapsed on top of me, panting, his whole body shuddering with pleasure.

Wrapping my arms around him, I kissed the top of his head as he completely emptied his balls, every last drop collecting in my channel. He liked to stay just like this for several moments, soaking up every last bit of his climax. I'd already come several times, so I just held him as he reveled in his bliss.

Finally, his head lifted. "That was fucking amazing." He pressed his lips to my mouth, hungrily chewing on the bottom one as he lifted some of his weight off me.

I pulled him back down, enjoying the feel of him squeezing the air from my lungs. "So you still like the breeding kink…even though you can't get me pregnant?"

"It's not really about that," he admitted. "Though…with Raine, there was that chance. That wasn't why I was into her though. I really did—"

I cut him off, "Let's not talk about her. We're trying to move on, right? Once we figure out a path forward with this surrogacy thing, we can go back to dating. I checked my messages on Fet yesterday. Have you looked at your account lately?"

He shook his head. "No…I'm not ready yet. Still missing her."

He climbed off me and lay on his back for a few minutes, staring at the ceiling. "You ready for our appointment?"

"Yeah." I rolled to my side and pressed my hand to his chest, absentmindedly playing with his chest hair. "I don't have a good feel for the process or how long it will take, but I'm anxious to get it underway."

"Oh, you know, it will be like anything else—it'll take longer than we're told and cost twice as much money." He sighed.

I nodded, frowning. "You're probably right about that. Did you stop transferring money to Raine?"

He was quiet for a moment.

I gave him a little smack on the chest. "Leo…we need that money for our actual surrogate."

"I know…but I feel bad it didn't work out, and I know she still needs the money, even if she doesn't have to pay that bogus bill for the stolen jewelry."

I sighed. I understood where he was coming from. My thoughts kept lingering on her as well, on what her future would look like. I wondered if she would ever find the happiness she deserved. I just wished it would have been with us. For a couple of months, she was such a fixture in our home, our bed, our lives…I could imagine her being here all the time, being a permanent part of this crazy life we were building together.

And I had thought about how perfect it would be for us to raise the baby together, the three of us. How much easier it would be, how the baby would have three loving parents, always someone there for him or her.

I'd definitely put the cart before the horse, and I was chastising myself every time an image of her flashed into my mind. I hoped, after our appointment today, I'd have a new focus. A distraction. And with any luck, in a year or so, I'd be holding our baby. It wouldn't exactly be the same, and it would just be me and Leo finding our way through the crazy maze of parenthood, but we could do it. I knew we could.

"I better go take a shower." Leo sat up and swung his legs onto the floor. "What time did you say the appointment is?"

"It's at ten, but we have to drive clear up to the north side of Indy. Traffic might be crazy."

"Right. Well," he leaned back down to kiss my cheek, "let's get the show on the road."

It was basically a theater reference.

Which naturally made me think of Raine.

Maybe expecting to stop thinking of her all the time was a lost cause.

leo

Maggie and I said goodbye to Blue, climbed into the SUV, and I pressed the button to open the garage door. I was just getting ready to pull out when I noticed a car had pulled in behind us, blocking our exit. *What the fuck?*

"What's wrong?" Maggie was in her maps app, entering the address for the clinic on the north side of Indy.

"Someone's parked behind us."

"What do you mean?" She opened the door and leaned out, twisting her body to look behind the vehicle. Her whole body jolted, and she slammed the door shut.

"What's going on?"

"I think it's Raine," was all she said.

What on earth? I climbed down from the driver's seat and headed toward the driveway, where, sure enough, Raine was sliding out of her car. I heard Maggie's door slam shut again as she joined me.

"What are you doing here?" I demanded as I closed the distance between us.

"I need to talk to you guys." Her voice sounded nervous, warbly.

Maggie was the first to respond. "Great timing. We're on our way to the surrogate clinic for our appointment."

"What?" A look of panic flashed across her face. "I thought that wasn't until November?"

"We got an earlier appointment due to a cancellation," Maggie explained. "What do you want?"

Wow, she's not handling this very well, is she? I stepped closer to Raine. "We're trying to move on, Raine. You walking out of our lives and refusing to answer our calls and texts was very hurtful."

She looked down at her hands, twisting her fingers together as she considered her response. "Can I just talk to you for five minutes? Then I'll leave and never talk to you again if that's what you want."

Maggie huffed and shot me a questioning look. I nodded. "Five minutes. Come on up on the porch."

The early morning sun was bathing our porch in soft gold light, making our wicker furniture look especially inviting. We climbed the steps and chose our seats, Maggie and myself on the loveseat, while Raine took the single chair.

"The clock is ticking," Maggie reminded her. I reached over and took my wife's hand, squeezing it gently. Hopefully, she would tone down the attitude. I didn't know what Raine planned to say, but I was sure it took a lot of courage for her to come over here after two weeks of silence.

"First of all, I wanted to say I'm sorry." She wrung her hands as her eyes bounced between mine and Maggie's. "I never meant to hurt either of you. I just couldn't work out why you both liked me. Why you were so caring and loving toward me, and I figured it must just be because I could give you a baby. Then I got my period a couple days ago, and I realized I couldn't even do that!" She gave a dark, humorless chuckle as she waited to see how we would react.

"It was only the first month of trying," Maggie said, her tone softer. "And your body was still getting used to being off the Pill. We knew it would probably take some time. But, even so, after you said you couldn't do it, we told you it was okay. We still wanted you. We wanted you in our lives as a friend…as a lover…"

"I know," she choked out, her eyes glistening with tears. "And I threw it all away because of my own issues with my past and family, my fear of rejection and abandonment."

"It didn't have to be that way," I said softly, my eyes boring into hers.

A tear slid down her cheek. "I...I still want to have your baby," she said. "I didn't realize how badly I wanted it until I got my period and those dreams were officially dashed. But that's not all I want."

Maggie squeezed my hand, and when I looked at her, I saw her eyes were full of unshed tears, her lower lip quivering as she waited for Raine to express her thoughts. We both waited on the edges of our seats to hear her deepest desires.

She swallowed hard and scooted her chair closer to us, so her knees moved into the space between both pairs of our knees. Maggie smoothed down the wrinkles in her floral skirt, and Raine caught her hand, then reached for my hand with her other one. She looked around the circle we'd made, our hands clasped together, and a teary smile curled her lips.

"See this? How we are all connected? This is what I want. And hopefully a little one in the middle, looking to us for care, guidance and love." She cleared her throat and let go of our hands. "But I understand if it's too late. Or if you'd rather go through the agency. I totally get it.

"I know you might have a hard time trusting me after ghosting you guys for two weeks...but I've had a lot of time to think about this and get my shit straightened out, and I'm coming to you today with a totally open heart, communicating exactly what I want.

"So I'm offering myself to you because..." she swallowed hard and gave a tentative smile, "because I've fallen in love with you, and I missed you guys so much. I just haven't been myself. I miss the Raine I was when I was with you. You've both been so loving, so accepting of me, and I... I've never had that before. I pushed you away because I was scared of getting my heart stomped on. But it's worth it…it's so worth it. You are both so worth it."

Maggie was the first to reach for her hand again, practically yanking her across the small space separating us. Next thing I knew, they were both on their feet, and my wife's arms were flying around Raine's figure, squeezing her within an inch of her life. "Oh, darling, we hoped you'd come back. We've fallen in love with you too, sweet girl."

A tear came to my own eye when I saw the beaming grin on my wife's face as she pulled back to look at Raine. "It's not too late. We can still have all that. But what about your career? We know you didn't plan to stay here forever—that your job would take you far away from us."

Raine's face brightened as she turned to me. "Hey, remember when you helped exonerate me at the theater department?"

I grinned. "Yes! And that bitchy Costume Czar you hated ended up getting canned, right?"

"She sure did," Raine continued, "and they promoted the head costume designer into her position. So, guess who urgently needs a costume designer before the fall season starts?"

"Oh my god!" Maggie exclaimed. "You've got to be kidding me?"

She shook her head, tears flying off her cheeks, but I was pretty sure they were happy tears now. "I don't have the position yet, but, considering what happened—I think the department is kinda worried I might sue them since they didn't investigate properly before charging me. Danielle and Molly think I'm a shoe-in, and Molly wrote a really nice recommendation for me. I have an interview next week."

"That's fucking amazing!" I exclaimed. "Almost like it was meant to be." I threw my arms around her, and then the three of us all ended up in one big happy hug.

"Not almost," Maggie said. "It *was* meant to be. *We* were meant to be."

twenty-seven

. . .

two months later

raine

WE'D HAD three cycles now with no luck, but I felt like this was the one. We'd read up on some tricks to help with Leo's swimmers and conception in general, and Maggie and I had a plan.

We were going to torture him until he begged to shoot all those beautiful sperm deep inside me. It started a few days before, when Maggie trapped his manhood in a cock cage. He wouldn't be allowed to touch his dick in the days leading up to my ovulation. We even washed it for him so he couldn't sneak in a wank.

I'd gotten good at pinpointing when my egg was ripe and fertile by using the predictor kit but also other signs like my temperature. My pattern was emerging, and every month we got more data to use. *Science for the win!*

So this was it. My body was ready, and Leo was about to

come unglued. Maggie tied him to the bed, where we planned to spend a few hours edging him until we finally let him come.

He tugged at the cuffs, which held him firmly in place. "You know, this wasn't exactly the domination I was envisioning when it comes to breeding you, Raine. I thought I would be the one topping you."

"Well, we've done that a few times, and it hasn't worked, so it's our turn to be in charge," Maggie piped up, a devilish cackle spilling out of her mouth as Leo struggled against his restraints.

"Tying a cop up is super satisfying, isn't it?" I joined in laughing as we circled our prey, cracking our knuckles in anticipation.

"Well, shall I release the kraken?" Maggie grinned as we stood on either side of the bed.

"Oh, can I do it?" I rubbed my hands together. I couldn't wait to see what happened when we finally exposed his cock to air again. The cage was clear, and I could see his skin turning a mottled red and purple in anticipation.

"Be my guest!" Maggie made a grand flourish and gestured toward her husband.

I crawled onto the bed and made a dramatic show of producing the key to the cage, which I'd been wearing around my neck on a red satin ribbon. Leo winced as I inserted the key, twisted it and loosened the sides of the cage.

When his cock was freed, it sprang to life, waving like a proud flag as its owner squirmed on the mattress. Maggie joined me on the bed, holding something in her hand.

As soon as Leo saw it, his eyes nearly bugged out. Then I realized why: it was a butt plug.

Oh, I had never had as much fun as this in a bedroom.

"Get the lube for me, sweet girl," she said with a devilish grin. She completely ignored her husband's throbbing, waving cock and pushed his legs back with both hands, bringing his ass slightly off the bed. "Will you get him ready for this?"

"Gladly!" I put a few drops of lube on my finger and reached down to rub it under his balls and between his ass cheeks, pressing deeper and harder until I hit his puckered hole.

"Don't let him fool you," Maggie said, "he's been pegged before, both by me and a beautiful Domme. He can take it." She winked and picked the butt plug up from where she'd laid it on his stomach right above his cock.

"I'm gonna suck his cock while you put that in," I announced, spinning around to line my pussy up with Leo's face. His tongue parted my folds as my own tongue gingerly swiped up his shaft, making him bow off the bed.

"Lie still if you want me to take my time and not shove this thing up here in one go," Maggie warned, and I snickered as Leo's groan traveled straight through my clit.

With my lips wrapped around the head of his cock, my tongue lightly flicking against his slit, I watched Maggie insert the plug.

A garbled, "Fuuuuck," slid out of Leo's throat before I ground against him, stuffing his mouth full of pussy. Then Maggie lowered her head to the mattress, pausing to kiss me before we licked up Leo's cock in tandem.

We took turns teasing and licking, sucking and playing with his balls, all while he writhed beneath us. But as soon as he started pumping up into our mouths, trying to control the rhythm, we would stop and move away. He groaned in agony, desperately spearing the air with his glistening cock, his balls growing heavier with cum by the minute.

Cum that would soon be in my pussy. But not too soon…

leo

It seemed like this had been going on for hours, them bringing me right to the brink and then denying me my release. My balls ached. I longed to slide this rock-hard cock deep into Raine's pussy and explode, filling her with all my seed.

"Once I get ahold of you, you're going to regret making me wait so long," I growled.

"Bring it!" was all Raine said.

"Do you think it's time?" Maggie's eyes flitted to where Leo's hands were strapped to the headboard.

"Let me do one more thing first." Raine crawled across the mattress until she reached me, then swung her legs over my hips. She dipped her pussy down to my cock, very lightly rubbing her lips against my oozing tip.

It was not nearly enough, but I could almost come from that if she did it long enough. I needed my hands. I wanted to grip her hips so hard I left bruises as I shoved my cock up into her. But I was still tied up.

She kissed my lips. "How bad do you want this pussy?" she whispered in my ear.

I couldn't form words at this point. It was more like incoherent sounds gurgling up from deep in my throat as I tried to push my hips up into hers.

"Uh-uh-uh!" She wagged her finger in my face. "It's not quite time yet."

I growled, "Grrrrr!" like a primal beast.

"Do you promise to give me every single drop of your cum? Shoot it nice and deep, right into my cervix? I'm so ripe, Leo, waiting for your seed. Do you know how bad I want it?"

"Let me give it to you then," I rasped, my voice hoarse with need.

"Okay," she nodded at Maggie, "untie him."

My wife straddled my face, giving me the opportunity to lick her dripping cunt as she untied me. A few times, I distracted her from her task, and she tossed her head back, eyes closed and mouth open as she enjoyed my tongue lashing her clit. Then she sucked in a deep breath and focused on untying me.

My wrists burned from straining against the cuffs, but they were free. I wasted absolutely no time attacking Raine, throwing her onto her back and driving my throbbing, desperate cock into her.

"Fuck, Leo!" she screamed as I pushed her legs back and forcefully pounded into her pussy. The ache in my balls only grew as I raced toward my release.

"Get ready, baby...I'm gonna fill this tight wet pussy up..."

maggie

This was the moment we'd all been waiting for. Leo had gone feral on Raine as soon as I untied him. He had her right where he wanted her, his cock driving in and out of her like a piston. I lay on the bed with my head inches away from where his thighs and ass were clenching in anticipation of his climax.

I cupped his balls in my hand and gently rubbed. "Give it to her, baby. Come in her pussy."

"Oh, fuck!" he shouted as his body stilled. Then his limbs

shook as he slowly pumped his seed into Raine's already dripping pussy.

"God, there's so much!" she moaned, keeping her legs in the air.

His climax seemed to go on forever, and when he finally pulled away, he said, "I'm still fucking hard! What the fuck?"

"Give it a second," I coached as I reversed my position so I could check on Raine. "You okay, sweetheart?"

Her thighs were trembling as she held them up. "I didn't climax."

"That's okay, baby." I stroked my fingers through her hair.

"No, I want to. It helps the sperm get where they need to go," she said.

"Alright, let me help you." I leaned in to kiss her, giving her lips a little nibble as she sighed. "You took his cock like such a good girl. Now we're gonna make that pretty pussy come."

Leo finally recovered enough to slide up on Raine's other side. "My cock is still hard," he rasped, pressing it against her. "I might have to go another round."

"We're gonna make her come first," I announced, reaching down to squeeze her nipple. She arched her back and moaned, and then Leo took the other one into his mouth.

I reversed course again once Leo took over playing with her tits. This time I flicked my tongue against her clit, and her hand flew to my hair, tangling in my tresses as she thrust her hips up to meet my mouth.

"Yes, suck my clit," she said, "I'm so close."

Some of Leo's cum seeped onto my tongue, the tangy taste surprising me. I need to keep that inside her while I focused on her clit. I sucked it into my mouth, rhythmically swirling my tongue around the swollen bud as her fingers tightened in my hair.

"That's it, fuck," she gritted out as she bucked against me.

It didn't take long before she cried out, "Oh, god, yes! Fuck! Oh my god, yes!"

I didn't feel Leo move off the bed, I was so enthralled by watching Raine come in my mouth, but then his warm body pressed against me from behind. "Lift your hips, baby."

I rose onto my knees, and he guided his still-hard cock into me, sinking deep as his hands gripped my hips hard. "I've gotta come again," he warned me.

"Get close, and then pull out and come in Raine," I instructed.

Her eyes flashed open, and she nodded. "God, it's so hot watching you fuck your wife's hot, wet pussy."

"You like that?" Leo pushed out between clenched teeth. "You like me taking care of both of your pussies?"

"Yes, such a good boy. You wore your cock cage and let us tease you, and now look at how much cum you've made for us. So fucking hot, Leo. That's it, pump that cock and get ready to give me another load."

I wished I could see his face for myself, but I could almost tell what his expressions were from watching Raine. It was so fucking hot to see them like this, their sexy banter while he pounded in and out of me, chasing his next release.

It didn't take long before he said, "I'm getting close, babe."

"Save it all for Raine," I said, bucking back against me. "Oh, god, you're gonna make me come too."

"Go ride Raine's face," was all he said as he pulled out and moved to between Raine's still lifted, spread open legs.

Raine reached down and tugged my arm. "Sit on my face now," she commanded.

I positioned myself, lowering my pussy to her waiting tongue as she gripped my thighs and moaned. Meanwhile, Leo had pushed his cock inside her and was marveling at how sloppy and wet her pussy was.

"Give me more!" Raine murmured before going back to tongue-fucking me.

I nearly fell over as my climax started to consume me, but Leo caught me just as his rocked through his body. Our mouths met as he emptied his seed inside our girlfriend, the future mother of our child.

He pulled away, his whole body shaking. "Fuck…that was fucking incredible, both of you." He was still inside her as I gingerly lifted myself off her face and snuggled into her side.

"I love you guys," she murmured as she pulled me close to her body.

"I love you too." I pressed a kiss to her lips.

"I think we did it," Leo said, still poised on top of Raine. "I think, in nine months, we're going to be welcoming our baby into the world."

"Together," Raine said.

"Together," we both echoed.

twenty-eight

. . .

ten days later

raine

I WAS JOLTED awake by my phone buzzing, and since I was in the middle of my lovers, I had to climb over Maggie to answer. In a husky, half-asleep voice, I managed, "Hello?"

I was worried it was someone from the IU theater's costume department with a costume emergency. I was in charge of such things now, you know. It didn't even register that it was Noah calling.

"Hey, Danielle's in labor," he rushed out.

"What? Again?"

"Yeah, but they're not stopping it this time. She's thirty-six weeks, and they've given the baby steroids to develop the lungs." He slipped out of professional mode and back into anxious expectant father mode, "So can you come?"

"Yeah, of course." I swung my legs off the bed, hitting the fluffy rug on the hardwood floor with a soft thud.

"What's going on?" Leo bolted upright in the bed. "Where's my gun?"

"Hold it there, cowboy!" Maggie said, groggily stretching. "Did you say Danielle is in labor?"

"I didn't, but Noah did." How did she figure out what was going on so fast?

"I'm going to the hospital," I announced to both my lovers and Noah, who was still waiting to wrap up this conversation so he could get back to the mommy-to-be.

"We're in room 115," he announced. "See you soon."

As I pulled on some jeans and a cute top that might make it look like I was more than half-awake when I made my wardrobe choices, I remembered that I had planned to take my first pregnancy test today. It had been ten days since our monthly fuckfest began. But I had already peed, and I was in a rush. I tucked a test in my purse.

I'd take it at the hospital. I probably had a lot of waiting around to look forward to.

Danielle's room was practically a party, with music and dancing and plenty of guests. I was surprised to find my former roommate in good spirits, with a smile on her face.

"Epidural," she explained when she saw my questioning look.

I greeted Cynda and Jason. Apparently, Darth wasn't interested in getting up in the middle of the night to witness the joyous event. Bonnie was there too. I rushed over to give her a hug.

"Well, the gang's all here," Aris said, rubbing his hands together. "Now we just need a baby."

Noah was pacing back and forth, slaying his role as nervous expectant father. He kept glancing over at her monitors. "Oh, you're having a big contraction. Look at that peak! They're coming faster, babe." He went over and took the mommy-to-be's hand. "I'm so glad you're not feeling this."

"Me too!" She crunched on some ice chips and glanced around the room. "I really appreciate you guys being here, but once it's time to push, y'all are moving your fine asses to the waiting room, got it?"

We all laughed and nodded. And it wasn't too long after that statement that the obstetrician and a nurse arrived to check Danielle's progress. We were also sent out of the room for that, but just to the hallway, where we tried to be quiet since it was only four in the morning and patients were either sleeping or trying to expel watermelons through a hole the size of a grapefruit.

Ouch! I cringed just thinking of it.

And you wanna do this too, ya dumb ass, my inner monologue was running. Bonnie squeezed my hand as if she knew what I was thinking. I held my purse to my side. I'd go take the test that might change my life as soon as Danielle started to push.

It was only a few minutes later that Aris poked his head out the door and grinned. "This is it! To the waiting room with you!"

We shuffled down the hall, but I grabbed Bonnie's arm and whispered, "I'm gonna go pee first."

"Okay. When you get back, we're gonna see if the cafeteria is open yet." She waggled her eyebrows.

Coffee. Coffee was what was missing in my life.

I found the ladies' room at the end of the hall and pushed the door open. My fingers trembled as I took the test out of its packaging and held it in place.

Well, this is it!

maggie

"Hey, I want to stop by the hospital with some flowers and a gift for Danielle," I told Leo when he got out of the shower.

"Okay…have fun." He gave me a kiss on the cheek and then moved toward his closet to grab some clothes.

"You're not working this morning, right?"

He turned around to face me, bare-chested, only a towel wrapped around his waist and a polo shirt in each hand. "No, I'm going to the range this evening for a night shoot, remember?"

"You wanna come with me? Maybe Raine would like to get breakfast. She probably hasn't had anything except cafeteria food."

"Hey, the hospital cafeteria isn't actually that bad," Leo corrected me. "Been stuck in the hospital many a time with…um…clients, you know."

"Fine, well, do you want to come with me? I can drop you back at home before I go to work," I offered.

"I guess so. Since I won't see you guys at dinner. Speaking of which, we still haven't had a chance to go out and celebrate Raine's new job as IU theater's costume designer. We've been so busy fucking and all." He held up two polo shirts.

"We'll get to it soon, maybe this weekend. The black shirt," I said. "And leave the scruff. You don't have to shave for your shoot, do you?"

He shrugged. "I guess not. What kind of gift did you get? They don't know if it's going to be a boy or girl, do they?"

I shook my head. "It's not for the baby. It's for Danielle.

It's like a new mom spa basket. So she can enjoy some self-care while the daddies spend time with the little one."

"You are so thoughtful." My husband wrapped his arms around me, still a little damp from his shower, and nuzzled my neck. "You are gonna make such a great mom."

I grinned. "C'mon. I want to leave in twenty minutes."

He made a whip-cracking sound. "Yes, ma'am. You're sure gonna keep our kid in line too, aren't you?"

"Hell yes I am!" I tapped my foot in feigned impatience and pretended to look at my watch. "Let's get a move on."

I really hoped I'd get a chance to keep our kid in line. And either way, I'd be keeping him and Raine in line for sure. After all, our "law and order" household needed plenty of the "order" part.

Raine was in charge of making us all look good, of course.

leo

When we arrived at the hospital, there was a buzz of activity in the waiting room as Aris made an appearance. "She's here!" He grinned, and we joined in the applause already started by Raine, Cynda, Jason and Bonnie.

"Oh my god, it's a girl, I knew it!" Bonnie shrieked. "When can we see her?"

"Give us a few minutes, then you can come back. They're just getting the baby cleaned up." He was beaming ear to ear.

"Does she have a name yet?" Maggie asked.

"Hannah Grace," Aris announced. "Hannah after Noah's mother."

"Aww, that's so sweet!" Bonnie cooed.

"Hannah is a healthy five pounds, twelve ounces," the

proud daddy continued. "She's tiny but strong! You shoulda heard her exercising her lungs for the first time. She's gonna have her momma's pipes!"

"Oh, I can't wait to see her!" Maggie cheered. "Go be with her. Just text us when we can come back. I have some gifts for her."

Raine walked over to us. "I didn't know if you guys would want to stop by now or wait until she was home."

"I don't know if I could wait," Maggie admitted. "This is so exciting. I'm so happy for them. You haven't seen Noah yet, have you?"

"No, not yet. But I'm sure he's over the moon. He was pacing the room, so nervous, when we were back there with her before. Obsessed with the monitor and asking the doctor all kinds of questions that were way over my head." I laughed at the memory of him in expectant dad mode.

It wasn't long before Noah texted Maggie to say our entourage could come visit the new mom and baby. We walked down the hall, me in the middle of Raine and Maggie, holding both of their hands.

When we entered the room, which had soft classical music playing, Raine dropped her purse on a chair and ran over to give her friend a hug. The purse didn't quite land squarely, however, and the contents dumped out all over the floor.

"Ooops, sorry!" she called over her shoulder as she admired the little pink bundle in Danielle's arms.

"We got it." Maggie and I crouched down, scooping the items back into the purse.

Then Maggie froze, holding a plastic stick up. As soon as I saw it, I froze too.

Raine moved away so Bonnie could have a look at the baby and immediately caught our dropped-open jaws.

"Is this what I think it is?" Maggie barely choked the words out as she waved the test stick in the air.

Raine's face exploded with color as her hands shot to cover her embarrassment. "Oh my god! I was going to wait to tell you. I didn't want to steal the show." She gestured back to Danielle and the baby.

"Steal what show?" Danielle was quick to question as Bonnie moved back to the line of well-wishers. Cynda was next to see the baby.

"I'm pregnant!" Raine announced, but before she could get the words out, we were already right there, embracing her in our three-way hug as tears streamed down our faces.

"Oh my god, I knew it!" Maggie cried, pressing a kiss to Raine's lips.

Then it was my turn. I grasped her face between my hands and claimed her lips with my own. "I'm so goddamn happy right now, I can't stand it!"

Raine smiled through her tears. "I love you both so much."

"I love you," Maggie said, squeezing my hand, "and I love you." She pressed another kiss to Raine's cheek. Then she laid a hand on her stomach. "And I love this little one, whoever you are."

"And I love you and you." I kissed one beautiful lady's cheek and then the other. Then I dropped to my knees in front of Raine and pressed a kiss to her lower abdomen. "And I love you too."

epilogue

. . .

several months later

raine

PREGNANCY IS NOT for the faint of heart, but I did find it to have a few good points. People were so nice to me, opening doors, asking if they could carry things for me. Though I could have done without the unnecessary requests to grope my baby bump.

Delivery day was upon us. We had planned a home water birth. Leo and Maggie had everything set up, but, as seemed to be par for the course for me, things did not go according to plan. This little Nugget, as we'd taken to calling him or her, refused to come out.

That meant I was lying in a hospital bed, hooked up to a bunch of tubes and wires, and the eviction process was well underway.

"Baby looks great," Noah assured me as he joined the

cast of characters encircling my hospital bed. "When was the last time the doctor checked you?"

"When she broke my water," I explained, "about two hours ago. She said that would speed things up."

Aris laid a hand on my shoulder. "It could still be a long time, though."

It was strange to see my second-favorite throuple without their new addition, but they'd left their sweet baby girl with Cynda so they could have a bit of a break. Apparently, watching me in labor was their idea of a date? Weirdos.

"You're doing great." Leo patted my arm and wrapped his massive paw around my hand, completely engulfing it as he squeezed gently.

"We're so proud of you," Maggie agreed, bending down to press a kiss to my cheek.

I'd gotten an epidural shortly after the water breaking, so I was sort of coasting through at this point. Laughing and joking with my found family made the time go faster.

"Knock-knock!" came a deep voice from the door.

"More visitors? Aren't you Miss Popularity!" Danielle grinned. She walked over to the door and swung it open, revealing a familiar figure.

My brother, Tyler.

In addition to my found family from the polycule, I'd developed a relationship with my biological half-brother. We met in person for the first time around the holidays, but he wanted to come back and visit when his niece or nephew was born. We thought the baby would already be here by the time he arrived, but, as previously mentioned, the Nugget had their own timetable.

"Hey, Raine!" He walked to my bedside and glanced at the monitors. "How's it going?"

"Oh, you know, I love being center stage, putting on a show for everyone. Like my costume?" I tugged at the sleeve of my blue hospital gown.

"For now," Danielle warned, "but the Nugget's gonna steal the show as soon as they get here. Just wait. You're about to lose your Raine identity and become Nugget's Mom."

"Hey, since they'll have two moms," Leo pointed out, "maybe she'll get to retain some of her Raine persona? I happen to be rather fond of that persona, you know."

Maggie laughed. "We'll be able to give each other lots of breaks, since there are three of us to care for our little Nugget."

"Having three parents is definitely the way to go," Aris agreed. "So much easier to divide and conquer."

"You make it sound like we're going to war," Noah pointed out.

"Well…you know what they say," Aris grinned, "all's fair in love and dirty diapers."

"You're all making me think twice about just marrying one woman," Tyler interjected. "Maybe I need to be on the hunt for two!"

Leo wrapped his arm around Tyler and stage-whispered, "Just so you know—two are a lot of work." Then he turned toward me and Maggie. "Not *my* lovely ladies, of course. You two are always easy!"

We all laughed, but I started to feel an ache in my back and a tightness around my midsection that quickly made my smile disappear. When I looked at the contraction monitor, I noticed they were coming faster and peaking higher. I must have grimaced because Leo immediately noticed.

"Hey, do you think you're getting close?" He brought my

hand to his lips and pressed a kiss to the back of it. "I can get the nurse if you want."

"I think it's about time to kick everyone out who's not a parent to this Nugget," I said between peaks.

"Consider it done." Leo puffed out his chest, and, going into cop mode, ushered everyone out the door amidst a chorus of well wishes.

"Good luck!"

"You can do it!"

"Can't wait to meet the Nugget!"

A few minutes later, I had an overwhelming urge to push.

This is it…finally!

maggie

I took the washcloth and wiped the sweat off Raine's brow. "C'mon, baby, you can do this. Not much longer now."

"But I've been pushing for an hour!" she whined. "And it fucking hurts!"

"Your epidural is worn off now," Dr. Cameron said. "So your pushes are becoming more productive. Just one or two more good ones, and we'll deliver the head."

"'We'll'?" Raine grumbled. "I don't know where you're getting this 'we' business. It feels like I'm the only one doing any of the work!"

I bit my lip to suppress a smile. God, she was gorgeous like this, her dark hair clinging to her sweat-soaked brow, eyes glistening, and cheeks flushed with her exertion. She was gorgeous as she worked hard to bring our baby into the world, a baby who was already so loved, so cherished, and we didn't even know their name yet.

"You can do it," Leo cheered her on. "The Nugget has a ton of black hair. I can see it!"

Raine gritted her teeth and looked at the monitor. Her knuckles went white as she gripped the bedrails. "Okay, I'm trying."

We all counted while her face turned bright red, her jaw clenched, and she gave it everything she had.

"Whoa, stop right there! Relax and breathe," Dr. Cameron coached her. "Head is out!" She suctioned the baby's nose and mouth. "Okay, on the next contraction, we're going to deliver the body."

"Here we go with this 'we' shit again!" Raine's nostrils flared as she bore down again for another push.

"Oh my god, you're doing it!" Leo rushed over to where I was standing on the other side of Raine's bed and put his arm around me. "I can't believe it. It's finally happening."

As the sound of our son's first cries filled the room, my husband's gaze met mine. "We have a little boy!" I cheered.

As soon as our Nugget was placed on Raine's chest, Leo moved back to the other side of Raine. Tears streaked down her cheeks as we pressed kisses to them and got our first look at the brand-new life we had created together.

leo

I backed away from the bed, letting my son's two beautiful mothers have a moment to bond over the baby while I took photos. Looking at their happy tears, I thought about all the miracles that had to happen to bring us this joy, this moment, which was a miracle in and of itself. The nurse took the baby away to clean him up, and I joined the circle, our perfect family circle which had now grown by one member.

"I don't know what to say…" I flicked away a tear stinging at the corner of my eye, trying to keep any from falling, but it was too late. Two streaked down, getting caught in my beard. "This is the most amazing day of my life."

"Congratulations, Daddy," Raine said, her flushed face radiating with joy and a sense of accomplishment.

"You were amazing." I bent down to press a kiss to her lips, then Maggie did the same.

"I can't wait to show Max off to all our friends!" Maggie said. "He's absolutely gorgeous."

"So, we're definitely going with Max?" I glanced from one mom to the other.

"Leonard Maximillian Katz," Raine declared. "It sounds so distinguished. It's got my vote."

Maggie grinned. "Mine too. And Max for short."

"Leo, Max, Maggie, and Raine—sounds like a perfect family to me," I agreed.

The nurse brought the baby back to Raine, and she cradled the freshly wrapped bundle in her arms. His little scrunched face was pink, his cheeks adorably chubby, and his tiny little nose and lips were perfectly sculpted. As we stared at him in wonder, his little eyes popped open. He looked at the adoring faces staring at him and promptly went back to sleep.

I hoped we'd always be able to make him feel this safe and loved. I had a good feeling about it, and from the looks on his moms' beautiful faces, it was pretty clear they did too.

THE END

See all the books in the PolyAm Fam series here:

Https://Books2read.com/PolyAmFam2

Join Phoebe's newsletter here: bit.ly/PhoebeAlexanderNews

about the author

USA Today Bestselling Author Phoebe Alexander writes romance about characters like her: with extra curves and life experience. Her stories often include themes of ethical nonmonogamy, such as polyamory. She believes love is love, and everyone deserves a happily ever after, no matter your size, shape, age, or color.

Phoebe lives near the beach on the East Coast with her husband and multiple fur babies. When she's not writing, she works as an editor and consultant for indie authors. She also volunteers to run a 6000-member indie author support group.

Phoebe enjoys hanging out with her three adult sons, as well as travel, Broadway musicals, dark chocolate, swimming, hiking, college basketball, and making Seinfeld references whenever possible, especially in her books. Her single greatest fantasy is just having some free time. Join her newsletter for bodypositive memes and plenty of dog pics!

facebook.com/phoebealexanderauthor

instagram.com/authorphoebealexander

bookbub.com/authors/phoebe-alexander

tiktok.com/@authorphoebealexander

also by phoebe alexander

Mountains Series

Mountains Wanted

Mountains Climbed

Mountains Loved

Christmas in the Mountains

The Navigator

The Explorer

The Adventurer

Mountains Transcended

Eastern Shore Swingers Series

Fisher of Men

The Catch

Siren Call

Sailors Knot

Turning the Tide

Spicetopia Series

Penny & Pryce

Sugar & Spice

Virtue & Vice

Fire & Ice

Naughty & Nice

Dares & Dice

Loyalty & Lies